CATS' EYES

A CRAZY CAT LADY MYSTERY

BY MOLLIE HUNT

Cats' Eyes, the 1st Crazy Cat Lady Mystery
by Mollie Hunt

Copyright 2014, 2020 © Mollie Hunt
ISBN: 9781500999148

Editing and Design by Rosalyn Newhouse

Published in the United States of America

Cover Art: "Mine" by Leslie Cobb
© *2014 Leslie Cobb*
www.lesliecobb.com

E6-PB

Other Books by Mollie Hunt

Crazy Cat Lady Mysteries
Cats' Eyes (2013)
Copy Cats (2015)
Cat's Paw (2016)
Cat Call (2017)
Cat Café (2018)
Cosmic Cat (2019)
Cat Noel (2019)
Cat Conundrum (2020)

Short Stories
Cat's Cradle
The Dream Spinner

Other Mysteries
Placid River Runs Deep (2016)

The Cat Seasons Sci-Fantasy Tetralogy
Cat Summer (Book 1 - 2019)
Cat Winter (Book 2- 2020)

Other
Cat Poems: For the Love of Cats (2018)

Praise for Mollie Hunt, Cat Writer

"I know Mollie as a true, dyed-in-the-wool cat person, as a cat guardian and a foster parent and, most importantly, as a human being. One thing I can spot a mile away is true passion... and Mollie Hunt has it. People like Mollie are rare in this world because they infuse their own curiosity... with true empathy... the recipe for not only a quality person, but, in the end, a great artist as well."
— *Jackson Galaxy | Cat Behavior Consultant*

Praise for the Crazy Cat Lady cozy mysteries

...an outstanding amateur sleuth mystery that will delight cat lovers and mystery lovers alike. Cats' Eyes has so many exciting twists and turns; it keeps the reader fascinated until the final thrilling scene. I liked the addition of "cat facts" at the heading of each chapter. I learned a few fascinating tidbits that I didn't know. —*Readers Favorite 5-Star Review*

"I knew this novel was about cats but it's theme is cats! Cats are as much the main characters as the main character is! — *Sharon from Goodreads*

"I've now read the first three Crazy Cat Lady mysteries and am in about the middle of Cat Call. Each book drew me right into the story and kept me intrigued and guessing all the way. They're as cozy as can be for cat enthusiast, but there are also some real scares..." —*Catwoods Porch Party*

About the Cover Art
The story of "Mine" by Leslie Cobb:

"Shiloh was labeled as feral after he was taken to an animal shelter when his caretaker died. Feral cats, also known as community cats, are those who are born wild and are often unsuited for life as an indoor pet due to extreme shyness or fear of people. Stray cats, who once had a home but were abandoned outdoors, are also sometimes mistaken for feral. The shelter ear-tipped him (a practice to let people know that a community cat has been spayed or neutered and will not add to the homeless cat population) and enlisted the help of Tenth Life Foundation to find him a safe outdoor home. But the barn home they found for him turned out not to be a good fit, and Shiloh turned out not to be feral at all! BrightHaven Rescue assisted Tenth Life in getting him some veterinary care he needed and networking him to find the perfect indoor home."

Leslie Cobb, Cat Artist
www.lesliecobb.com

Grateful acknowledgment to editor and friend, Rosalyn Newhouse, without whose encouragement and skill, this book would still be locked away in my laptop, and to Susan Landis-Steward, grade-school friend, who listened. Also thanks to the Oregon Humane Society, House of Dreams Cat Shelter, Pet Partners (formerly Delta Society) and Providence Hospice for inspiring me to make the most of my life.

Special thanks to all the cats, real and imagined.

THERE IS NO MORE COCKTAIL HOUR,

no fairy lights
no prism colors
no morning glances
no midnight soirees.

I am older and my world has shifted.
Soft fur, silent eyes.
I am the crazy cat lady, only I'm not crazy yet.
Not quite.

Chapter 1

My name is Lynley Cannon and I am the crazy cat lady, only I'm not crazy yet. I swear. Everything I say is true, though it may seem like the wildest fiction. It does to me, now that I look back, starting when Fluffs discovered the stone. But I'm getting ahead of myself. How are you to know what led up to that unfortunate find or its dire consequences? Why, at the time I didn't even know myself and could never have guessed.

I am fifty-eight years of age, and life in the slow lane has been pretty serene. Quietly happy, or happily quiet, whichever you choose. I'd had a good run in my youth—sex, drugs, rock 'n' roll—but I was over it. Too much trouble. Too much drama. I have better things to do.

Which brings me to the cats. I don't know where I got the reputation of being a crazy cat lady; I only have seven in my care at the moment. And two aren't even mine but fosters from FOF, Friends of Felines, the shelter where I volunteer. One is named Addison and he's here to recover from a kitty cold. The other is Fluffs.

Fluffs' is a sad tale gone good. Originally she came to me for a few precious weeks of hospice before she passed on. It had been so poignant, bringing home the dying cat, the scrawny gray with chronic kidney failure, to give her some last, best moments of TLC. But it soon became apparent that nobody had bothered to tell Fluffs her time was up. That was months ago and she's still going strong.

Fraulein Fluffs isn't the name I would have chosen for

a cat, but it was the name she came with and at twelve-plus, there was no going back. I accepted her as she was, though I admit to calling her Fluffo when no one else was listening. She allowed the silly pet name as long as it was accompanied by affection and food. I treated Fluffs as the treasure she was. And then one day she found a treasure of her own.

Mondays are always busy. Through a quirk of fate, I'm retired, but I seem to be busier than ever. I'm finally doing all the things I used to think about when I was at work but never did because I was always too tired when I got off. That Monday was no exception. After yoga and a brisk walk around the park with the senior ladies, I spent some time on the computer compiling my Scottish heritage, the Mackey family tree. Got to get it all down before I pop off in case anyone's interested. My daughter isn't—Lisa's too busy in the here-and-now—but maybe someday my granddaughter will take a break from her texting and her iPod and whatever else might be invented for sedentary self-gratification long enough to wonder where she came from. When that time comes, I want to be ready.

I was in the midst of a particularly difficult connection between a great-uncle and a third-cousin-once-removed when I heard a clink and then the clackity-clack of a sharp-sided object rolling across the hardwood floor. It stopped, then started up, then stopped again, creating just enough distraction to turn my attention from the quandary of my ancestors to the question of what was making the noise.

Cat toy, I thought to myself. But which one, and who was playing? *Can't be Red*—Big Red was seventeen pounds of muscled tabby dynamite; when he played, he sounded like a dancing elephant. Dirty Harry, the black and white, didn't play much anymore; he was getting on in years and preferred to sleep in his donut or his cupboard by the TV. And when Harry did sport around, it was with the little female, Little. Though Little, an all-black panther-shadow with daring yellow eyes, was half his size, they boxed and wrangled like tigers. Violet, who got her name from her gray-violet coat, didn't play at all because she was what veterinarians call morbidly obese, which for us laymen, translates into as wide as she was long. Solo was just that: a singular beauty. White as a ghost, she lived an almost-feral life out of sight of human eyes. Addison, the fourteen-year-old black male I mentioned earlier, was in quarantine. That left only...

"Fluffo?"

I tracked the enigmatic sound, not raucous enough to be the plastic bell-ball but too irregular to be the walnut. Down the stairs, through the hallway, and there she was, batting something small and glittery into a corner.

"What have you got?" I said softly as I crossed the room. When she heard me, she stopped dead in the middle of a serve and looked up with big, guilty eyes. Her paw covered the item, pressing it down with the gentle firmness she might have used on a baby mouse.

I bent over and scooped the object out from under her. Fluffs gave me a look that could have frozen fire and stalked off in the opposite direction.

"Fluffs," I called apologetically but I knew it was no use. She was miffed, and then she was gone.

Shaking the thing in my hand, I felt the smooth, oily heaviness of stone. Opening my palm, I glimpsed it for the first time.

I'd like to say I had a premonition of fate at that historic moment, a frisson of expectancy, a sense of *Things to Come*, but I didn't. My only thoughts on the brown agate

3

with the dark slash through the center were *How pretty!* and then *What's it doing in my living room?* since I didn't remember having ever seen it before.

A jangle of electronic church bells rose from the direction of the kitchen—my cell phone. The stone still in my hand, I went to answer it. This proved more difficult than expected since it wasn't where it was supposed to be: on the wooden tray by the real phone. The bell played merrily along, mocking me as I searched through my purse and rifled my coat pockets. Finally I found it under yesterday's mail just as it clicked over to message mode. With a sigh I waited for the caller's number to appear. When it did, I saw it was from the shelter.

I shot an alarmed glance at the Kit-Kat clock on the wall. Its switching tail and roving eyes confirmed my sudden fear that time had gotten away from me. My shift was about to start and I wasn't even dressed yet. My apron was still in the dryer. I hadn't even cleaned my own cats' litter boxes, and here it was time to do the forty-plus trays at FOF!

Without another thought, I tossed the errant rock into a catch-all basket on the kitchen table and ran to get ready. Maybe if I had been paying attention, if I were better at multi-tasking, if the phone hadn't rung right then, things would have turned out differently.

Maybe not.

Chapter 2

Cats smile with their eyes. That slow blink that exudes total contentment is their way of showing they trust you. If you blink at them, slowly and without staring, they will often blink-smile back at you.

"That was a good day's work," I said to Frannie as I unlocked the door and we stepped into my entrance hall. It was a routine we both knew so well we thought little of it.

Frannie DeSoto also volunteered at Friends of Felines and was also of a certain age. A small round woman with a chronic smile, her short platinum blonde curls contrasted with her brilliant lip color and blush. Eye shadow varied with her mood, anything from lavender to chartreuse, with nail polish to match—or not. I've never seen her without full war-paint whether she's out on the town or swabbing litter boxes. I, on the other hand, dabbed on a little lipstick in the morning and called it good. It takes all kinds to make a village, or whatever the saying.

Frannie was the closest thing I had to a buddy. She and I often got together after shifts. The thing I liked about spending time with Frannie was that I could be myself, cat hair and all. She, too, knew the joy of kittens, the sadness of euthanasia, and the fundamental wisdom of spay-and-neuter. She didn't mind stepping over cat toys, beds, and food bowls placed strategically around the floor. She was not repulsed by cat yack or litter mess. I never knew what she did with the rest of her life, but at the shelter, she dredged out kennels, scrubbed cat pans, washed blankets and towels. She always had a treat in her pocket and a laser light on her key chain. I had ultimate respect for her.

I took off my coat and tossed it on a chair. Almost before it landed, Little was up on it, kneading it into a bed. Dirty Harry wrapped himself around Frannie's ankles. He, too, thought she was the cat's pajamas, and for stoic Harry, that was saying a lot. Automatically she reached down and rubbed his sideburns, talking softly in cat-speak.

"Six adoptions and... how many holds, Lynley?" she said, disengaging Harry so she could walk again.

"Three, I think. Kanga, Zuzu, and who else?"

"Cat-erine the Great. That man and his son were really interested in her."

"I hope they come back," I said. "It seemed like a good match. Tea?"

Frannie nodded. "Sure." She followed me into the kitchen, giving Violet a pet on her head as she went by. Looking around, she asked, "Where's the rest of the brood? The hospice—Fraulein...?"

"Fluffs," I finished for her. "She's probably curled up on one of the chairs—watch you don't sit on her."

Frannie laughed her distinctive little chortle, carefully checking availability before seating herself at the kitchen table. I got busy with the tea things: pot, bags, kettle.

All of a sudden, I stopped dead. The kettle—it was on the wrong side of the stove! And the lid was tilted! I never leave the lid tilted. And I never put it on the left side of the stove either. That's where the big fry pan goes when it's not dirty. I glanced at the sink. The pan was there waiting for a bath after frying a chorizo-basil omelet for breakfast. Nothing strange about that. So maybe I had moved the kettle. And maybe I had cocked the lid without thinking.

Without remembering. I admit my memory isn't what it used to be.

I picked up the wayward pot, filled it with cold water, then thrust it onto the burner and lit the gas. *That'll show it for confusing me*, I thought with satisfaction as the wet bottom sizzled in the flame.

I turned back to Frannie and leaned against the countertop. She was playing string with Fluffs who had come on cue when she heard her name. Thankfully my friend hadn't noticed my momentary bout of paranoia.

"Are you going to the Volunteer Appreciation Dinner?" I asked as if nothing had happened. Which it hadn't.

"Most assuredly," she said, tickling Fluffs' nose with the ribbon. Fluff batted back with amazing speed and dexterity, clipping the thin green satin with a razor claw. "Wouldn't miss it."

"Yeah, me too. It's always nice to be appreciated. The place I worked before I retired was a little short on that, to say the least."

"I know what you mean. I wish I could have volunteered for a living."

We both chuckled. "I'd love to be rich so I could donate thousands of dollars to worthy causes like FOF," I said. "Get my name in the quarterly magazine with the rest of the philanthropists."

"You know who I really respect? The people who donate anonymously," Frannie declared. "I could never do that, I'm too egotistical. I like seeing my name in print." Fluffs jumped onto her lap and she paused as the delicate cat got her tiny self comfortable. "Even if it's down at the bottom of the page with the FOF Allies, the ones who can only manage a few hundred a year."

"Not everyone can afford to be in the Michael V. Smith Circle."

"No kidding," said Frannie as she gently rubbed around Fluffs' ears.

I could hear the purring from across the room and thought once again how lucky I was to have her in my life—Fluffs, I mean. Well, Frannie, too, come to think of it.

Turning to the cupboard, I got down two mugs with— guess what!—cat pictures on them. I put them on the table along with a pint milk carton and a sugar bowl. The kettle was beginning to whistle so I turned off the heat and went to get the tea.

"What would you like? Earl Gray? Oolong? I have herb tea, too. Chamomile, Peach Passion."

"Oolong sounds good."

"Oolong it is then." I flipped open the lid of the tin where I keep my collection of tea bags and for the second time, stopped short. The tin was empty.

I stared at the vacant expanse as if by sheer willpower I could bring back the little packets with their bright colors and spicy scents. It didn't work.

Frannie mistook my bewilderment. "Anything's fine if you don't have Oolong. You must know by now I'm not picky."

I looked up at her blankly, then back down at the tin. Unable to sum up in words the confusion I was feeling, I turned it upside down.

"Oops," Frannie translated.

"More than oops. Last time I looked, this was full, or at least partly full. I remember. This time I'm certain."

"This time?" she questioned. "What do you mean?"

"Well, a moment ago, when I went to get the kettle, it was on the wrong side of the stove. And the lid was off.

I'm almost sure I hadn't left it like that, but I couldn't think of another explanation so put it out of my head. But now I'm beginning to wonder."

Frannie's painted brows furrowed just the tiniest amount. I knew what she was thinking; at our age we're always watching for signs of the dreaded 'A' disease: Alzheimer's. In my grandmother's time, it was known as senility and seemed the inevitable end to anyone who made it past seventy. In those days, a little confusion or a few misplaced items, forgetting a name or a face, could land you in the nursing home to while away your remaining days watching soap operas and game shows with other such unfortunates. Now we're enlightened; we call it dementia and know there are several different forms. The nursing home has been upgraded to the assisted living facility; the nurse is now a care giver; you have your own TV where you can watch anything you like if you can remember how to turn it on. But no matter what you call it, those mental diseases are the pit of oblivion from which you never return.

"I didn't forget," I justified. "The kettle maybe, but I know there were tea bags here this morning. I had tea before I went to the shelter." I gestured toward the cup on the counter with the amber string hanging out of it in case she needed proof.

"Hmm," Frannie said softly. "What do you think it means?"

I wasn't listening. I was foraging in the condiment cupboard, pulling out crackers, raisins, corn starch, coffee, anything that might conceivably be hiding the absent bags. When that didn't yield any clues, I began on the next cupboard even though it only contained plates, bowls, and glasses.

"There are some tea bags there on the hutch," Frannie offered with sympathetic caution. She gently dislodged Fluffs and set her on the floor, then walked over. My gaze followed to a little pile of packets on the shelf. She held one up. "Are these them?"

I nodded like a zombie as I recognized the same lot that had earlier that day been in the tin: orange wrapper for peach; gray for the Earl; purple for Oolong; yellow for chamomile. All present and accounted for on the maple sideboard.

Frannie selected two of the purple packs. She ripped them open and pulled out the bags, placing them in the cups I'd set on the table. Going to the stove, she retrieved the kettle and poured the steaming liquid over the top. Then she picked up the cup with the black cat face on it which she knew to be my favorite and brought it over to where I stood like a stupefied deer.

"Here, Lynley. I think you need this."

Between the heat of the cup in my hands and the strong perfume scent of the steam, I revived and sat down at the table, checking the chair first for Fluffs. Frannie was staring at me with concern.

"Has this been happening often?" she asked.

"What? Having my stuff move around on its own? No, never. I mean, sure, sometimes I lose things. My cell phone or my keys. But then when I finally find them, it all comes back to me. This isn't like that. I didn't move these things. *Something's happenin' here*, as they said in the old song."

"Ah, yes, Buffalo Springfield," Frannie replied nostalgically, apparently ready to let go of my senior moment. "Those lyrics seemed so timely back in the sixties, right up there with all the greats. Dylan, Baez, Seeger."

10

"Remember Country Joe and the Fish? *'And it's one, two, three, what are we fighting for? Don't ask me, I don't give a damn; next stop is Viet Nam...'"* I paused. "What was the name of that song? I remember it was something absurd."

We both giggled and pointed at each other. *"Feel Like I'm Fixin' to Die Rag!"* we exclaimed in unison as the decades fell away.

"I wonder if the kids today have ever even heard any of the old protest songs."

"There have been a lot of remakes recently. Many of those topics are still timely, you know."

"I guess they are, come to think of it."

Frannie and I both jumped when the phone rang, and then pretended we hadn't. I went and picked up the receiver—it was the land line—poked the talk button and put it to my face.

"Hello?"

There was a click on the other end, and I thought it was going to be a sales call but then a person spoke. Plain English, I might add.

"Is this Lynley Cannon?" he asked flatly.

"Yes. Who's this?"

There was another click as the caller hung up.

"Hello? Hello?" I waited a few seconds to make sure it was a disconnect, then banged the handset back in its cradle.

"Wrong number or telemarketer?" Frannie asked with a knowing sigh.

"Neither. I don't know. It was a man. He asked for me by name—my whole name. Then he hung up."

I went back to my chair and narrowly missed Fluffs who had claimed it in the seconds I had been gone. Instead of moving her, I took a chair nearby.

11

"Maybe it was one of those credit card calls," Frannie suggested. "Sometimes they know your whole name."

"Those always sound like they're calling from India or somewhere. No, this was..." I considered. "I don't know what it was." Then after a pause, I added, "Really. I don't."

Frannie took a long draught of tea and then put her cup down. "I should probably take off. It's getting late."

I glanced at the clock: it was ten-thirty according to the white hands of Mr. Kit-Kat.

She got up and took her cup to the sink. "You going to the shelter tomorrow?" she asked with just a touch of awkwardness.

"I don't know. I'm not signed up, but I might stop in anyway." I smiled as I walked her to the door. "I love being retired!"

"Yeah, it's the best, isn't it?" She turned to me and her face sobered. "Maybe you should think about getting some rest, Lynley."

"Why?"

Her gaze dropped to the floor where Little—ever the polite hostess—was waiting to see her out. "You seem tired. Tired people can make all sorts of mistakes."

I bristled. "You don't believe me? About those things being moved?"

"Of course I believe you. But there has to be an explanation, doesn't there? We know they didn't walk around by themselves. I'm just saying you'll think better with a rested brain. You'll figure it out."

Retrieving her coat, she opened the door and started down the steps. Glancing back, she said, "Call me tomorrow?"

"Sure," I grumped, and then pulled myself together. After all, she was just looking out for my welfare, as friends do, even when their assumptions are dead wrong. "Think good thoughts about Cat-erine the Great and her maybe-new family."

"I will."

Frannie gave a wave and was off. I watched to make sure she made it to her car without being accosted, then closed the door, listening as the latch clicked into place. I hesitated, then flipped the deadbolt. Looking down, I saw Little standing by my feet. She was eyeing me with an almost quizzical stare.

"What?" I asked her out loud. I guess it goes without saying that I talk to cats in a proper and intelligent manner.

Little blinked slowly, which, for you laymen, is a cat's way of smiling. I smiled back.

Scooping her up, I held her close. The warmth of her body and the rumble of her purr were instantly soothing, but they couldn't quite offset the feeling that something had happened. Was happening.

It wasn't over yet.

Chapter 3

Many all-white cats with blue eyes are deaf. All-white cats are also especially susceptible to skin cancer, so it's best to keep them out of the sun.

After Frannie left, I went to bed. I realized how exhausted I was the minute my head hit the pillow. Still, I couldn't sleep. I couldn't get that blasted kettle and tea tin out of my mind. I tried really hard to make it into a slip of the brain, but it just wasn't working. I had nothing to do with those shifty little shifts and I knew it.

Which meant it was someone else. *Someone else!* This thought left me feeling paranoid and violated. Someone had been in my house without my knowing it, looking in private places, touching my stuff. Until I found out who it was, I would have no peace.

My mother had a key; maybe she'd dropped by without calling. Except my mother was eighty-three and doesn't drive. She does, however, stay up until all hours, so the best thing to do would be to call her and ask. If she admitted to the trick, I could rest easy. Then again if she didn't...

"Hello Carol?" I said when she answered her phone.

"Lynley! Nice to hear from you, dear. How are the kitties?"

"Kitties are fine, Mum."

"And how's the little deaf one? The one who's so shy?"

"Solo?" Carol had a soft spot for disabled animals, and when she learned that white cats with blue eyes often suffered from congenital deafness caused by the degeneration of the inner ear, the shy girl in her silent world became her favorite. "She's good."

"I love her eyes: one green and one blue. She has such an enigmatic stare. Do you suppose it's because she can't hear, poor dear?"

"I don't think she thinks of herself as a poor dear, Mum."

"No, cats don't, do they?"

The conversation lagged as I tried to compose what I wanted to say. How do you ask your octogenarian mom if she broke into your house? I took a deep breath, and faltered.

"Addison's almost over his URI and should be out in the general population in the next couple of days," I blurted.

"Addison? You have a new one?"

"He's a foster. He goes back to the shelter once he's well. For someone else to adopt," I added. "I thought I told you about him."

"I can't keep them straight, dear. I don't know how you do it."

"You'll have to come meet him. He's very sweet." I paused, feeling a flush across my face. "Or maybe you've met him already?"

"I really don't think so. When would it have been?"

"Um, today maybe?"

"Pardon?" She sounded genuinely surprised.

"Mum, did you come by today? Did you come in the house while I was out?" I hesitated. "Did you make tea?"

"Tea? No, certainly not," she huffed. "You know I'd

leave a note if I came by when you weren't there. It's rude to go into other people's homes without their permission, even if they are your daughter. And what's this about tea? You aren't making any sense, dear."

"Sorry, it's nothing," I sighed.

"It doesn't sound like nothing."

"I'll tell you about it tomorrow, okay?"

"Alright. I need to get back to my show anyway. Candy and I are watching Saturday Night Live. Betty White is the hostess. She has a bit of a potty-mouth but she's very funny. And we old people have to stick up for each other. Did you know she's even older than me?"

"That old?" I joked.

Carol harrumphed. "Take care, dear. Get some rest, you sound tired."

"I guess I am. Talk to you soon."

So it wasn't my mother. I put the phone down, briefly wondering if she might have come over and forgotten about it, but I put that idea out of my head. No one could accuse Carol Mackey of senility. She was sharp as an unclipped claw. Her years as a legal assistant had honed her into an extrapolating machine. Granted that was a while ago, but she refused to let her brain go to waste. She and her roommate, Candy, who had been a medical transcriptionist before that job became universally outsourced, were always coming up with mental exercises. Their ongoing favorite was to solve all the mysteries the media had to offer. Television, movies, books: Carol and Candy had the killer pegged before they were halfway through.

Maybe I should get them to solve mine, I thought despondently. I certainly had no idea what to do next.

I was feeling very sorry for myself which was getting

me nowhere. *What would Carol do?* I queried as I straightened my back and took a deep breath. First step: revisit the scene of the crime. Or was that what the criminal did? Whatever—it seemed as good a place to start as any.

I shrugged on my bathrobe after turning it around several times to find the armholes—is there a Murphy's law that says no matter how you pick up a robe, it's always upside down and inside out? I skipped the slippers—I just wasn't up for a wrangle with them too—and padded down the stairs in my bare feet. Stopping just inside the kitchen door, I flicked on the light. *I am Columbo!* I told myself, then amended it. *I am Marple; Fletcher; Ramotswe; Millhone! Peabody!* Or maybe *Nancy Drew?* I added wryly.

Squinting my eyes, I panned the room for clues, consciously ignoring the penetrating gazes of several hungry cats. Everything looked normal except for the little pile of tea bags on the sideboard. Even those had been so carefully placed that they didn't stand out, not as if the room had been tossed or anything. I had the feeling they were telling me something. If I just listened hard enough I could...

An urgent meow from the next room broke my concentration.

"Harry?" I called as I shook off my daze and went to find the big cat. He was in the living room in front of my makeshift entertainment center, a wide wooden bookshelf with my old analog TV set on top. The shelves held an ancient VCR and a cheap DVD player. To each side was a long cabinet that housed my meager collection of movies.

Both cabinet doors were shut tight.

"Did you get closed out of your cave?" I said to Harry,

who liked to sleep in the left middle cubby. It's so cute to find him there, just the white civil defense symbol markings on his face and the pair of glowing green eyes floating in the gloom. The DVDs on that shelf were pushed to the back so the big black-and-white could fit his considerable roundness into the small space.

Except they weren't.

As I swung the door wide, I saw that the contents of all three shelves were up front and center. I noted as I looked closer that they were also all mixed up. Some even lay in a flat stack which was just plain wrong. I always kept them upright, like records, back when there were records.

Another enigma. Instead of solving the mysteries, I was uncovering more.

Suddenly I felt angry. With a sweep of my hand, I dumped the whole lot of them on the floor. "There you are, Harry. All better," I said, much too loudly and with far too much desperation. Harry took one look at me and stalked back to his donut where he circled, lay down, and feigned sleep with his back to the offending cupboard.

I eyed the mess of plastic cases on the floor and was instantly ashamed of myself. What had Frannie said? There had to be an explanation. And like the proverbial light bulb going off in my head, I suddenly knew what it was.

* * *

I slept fine for the rest of the night with Red on one side of me and Little on the other and woke refreshed in the morning. My previous unease seemed like classic paranoia in the friendly light of day. My new theory of the relocated objects was a bit convoluted but altogether plausible, as the Mythbusters say.

You see, I have a granddaughter. She's fifteen. Need I say more?

Seleia spent a lot of time with me since now that she's a teenager, her parents are suddenly woefully uncool. For some unknown reason, Grandma was still okay. In my opinion, I'm far less cool than Lisa, her artist mother who travels all over the world showing her strange but beautiful work, and Gene, her architect father who commutes to New York every other week to consult on the rebuilding of Ground Zero, but I'm not about to dissuade her if she thinks otherwise.

For Seleia to hang out and watch a movie was easy to imagine. She probably pawed through the lot to find something besides my old-lady films. Seeing as I don't have a liquor cabinet for her to raid, she could have gone to the kitchen, put the kettle on the other burner, dumped out the bags to see what there was, and made herself a cup of tea. She'd been very careful, and if I weren't so anal, I would never have noticed the intrusion.

Yes, it had to be Seleia. The only catch was she didn't have a key. But I was young once and knew that to the teenage mind, obstacles such as that are merely challenges. She had plenty of opportunity to make one on the sly if she'd been so inclined.

Still, I wasn't mad at her. It was the natural order of things for young people to push the limits with their loved ones. I'd make her 'fess up and return the key. I would be stern. Convey to her that even Grandma needs her personal space. How would she feel if I went through her stuff, etc. etc.? She would get it. She was a good girl at heart.

No time like the present, I decided. I would take care of it right away, soon as I fed the cats. It was Sunday; she'd be home from school. I'd call—no, I'd just drop by. Catch her off guard and face to face.

I heard the rattle of the kitchen doorknob, and then a little tap-tap on the pane of the window. *Aha!* I said to myself, recognizing Seleia's personal knock. *Maybe I won't have to force a confession after all. She's probably here to tell me all about it.*

And if not, I thought as I went to unlock the door, *she's going to do it anyway!*

"Lynley, the door was locked," she said, bursting in with teenage exuberance almost before I got the thing open.

"Come in," I said after the fact. "Isn't it awfully early for you to be up? It's not even noon yet."

She gave me a wilting look, so sweet on the young face that I had to smile. "Lynley! I've got better things to do than sleep my life away." She went through to the living room and flopped down on the couch, swinging a long, Levied leg over the arm. "But did I wake you?"

I looked down at my robe and bright pink slippers, suddenly aware I hadn't even brushed my hair or washed my face. I hadn't even made coffee!

"Wait right here," I said, running back upstairs to get dressed. "Make us some coffee, will you?" I shot back over my shoulder.

She didn't answer but I heard the clink of the glass pot and the running of water.

A few minutes later I was clothed and washed and we were sitting in the living room with our beverages. Seleia had been twitching like a cat with fleas ever since she had arrived.

I looked her up and down, then said in my most solemn grandmother voice, "Do you have something to tell me, dear?"

"Oh, Lynley, how did you know?" She kicked off her glitzy loafers and squirmed her legs underneath her on the sofa. "I just couldn't wait. It happened yesterday!"

I felt relief wash over me. This was going well. I wouldn't have to wring the truth out of her after all. She knew what she'd done was wrong and was going to acknowledge it all by herself.

"Go on," I encouraged. "You know you can tell me anything," I added with compassionate magnanimity.

"I know," she said with a wriggle. "But this is kind of hard." She sighed. "Okay, here goes..." Another sigh, so cute.

"You know that guy I told you about? Vinnie?" she said with a blush rising in her face.

I frowned. I hadn't really minded Seleia breaking into my house, but it never crossed my mind she might have brought a boy. *Should I have checked my sheets?* I wondered suddenly.

"Well, Vinnie's a great guy," she went on, oblivious to my discomfort. "I've known him for quite a while now, ever since the beginning of term..."

Five months, I calculated. An eon in teen-time I supposed.

"...and he's really nice. He's a little older than me. He's a senior, only two years, that's not so bad, is it? I mean mom and dad are two years apart, and anyway you always tell me I'm adult for my age."

She looked at me with big, dare I say innocent, brown eyes. I couldn't help but smile. "Go on."

"Well, Vinnie's been helping me with my science. It's physics, which I love, but I have a problem with some of the theories—the quarks and gluons and stuff. So Vinnie's really good at it; it's what he wants to do, become an astrophysicist. Cool, eh?"

"Very cool," I agreed as she expected me too, though I was beginning to wonder where this was leading. I couldn't quite imagine the pair crashing my house to study particle physics. But she was off and running again.

"So Vinnie's got a car, an old Volkswagen—he knows how to fix it himself. It was his dad's back a long time ago, in the seventies I think."

"Definitely the dark ages," I commented.

"What? Oh, yeah. Anyway he's got this car, and we drove up to Skyline and took a walk in the cemetery—Vinnie likes cemeteries, too. He doesn't think they're scary; he knows a lot about the history of the people buried there and stuff. He's interested in history too, especially local, where the families are still around. He's into lots of things."

She stopped for a breath.

"They say an interested person is an interesting person," I threw out.

"Huh? Yeah, I guess. Oof," she grunted in surprise as Harry landed in her lap. "Where'd you come from, big guy?" she asked him, rubbing his sideburns the way he loved so much.

"They haven't had their breakfast. I was just about to feed them when you came." I stood up. "Do you mind? I really need to get at it before we're ripped to shreds. Go on with your story. I'm still listening." *Listening for the part about making a key and slipping into my house while I was gone,* is what I wanted to say, but I controlled the urge. It would be better if she told me herself.

I went into the kitchen. She watched through the doorway as I opened the tins of cat food and spooned the paté out into little bowls. Now that food was imminent, the cats were very vocal. Fluffs liked hers soupy and ate in my office so she wouldn't be distracted; Red had a room of his own as well so he wouldn't eat his and everybody else's. Dirty Harry and Little ate at the feeding station under the counter. Violet ate anywhere the food was but required a bigger bowl that she could get her pretty face into. I pushed Solo's under the couch. "I need to take Addison's. He's in the kennel. Be right back," I told Seleia.

I returned a minute later. The only sound was the slurping of cat meat and the soft tapping of Seleia's bare toe on the hardwood floor. The silence began to stretch out, so I asked, "Sorry about the interruption. You had something to tell me?"

She hesitated, then burst out all at once, "Vinnie wants me to go to *Destination Science* with him this summer and it's a science camp and it's in Salem and he'd drive us there in his Bug but mom says I can't go alone with him but I'm old enough to know what to do and can you please *please* talk to her, I really *really* want to go and it *is* science after all?"

She gave me the most pleading of looks, but I was no longer in the mood to be appeased. This Vinnie story had absolutely nothing to do with her home invasion, and I was a little miffed to say the least. I had so quickly accepted that she was going to tell me everything that I had stopped contemplating the confrontation that would come about if she didn't.

"Is that it?" I managed without sounding too upset.

"It, what?" Again the kitten eyes.

I took a breath. It didn't help. "Seleia, I know what you did. You might as well own up so we can get this out of the way and move on."

"What I did?" Suddenly her eyes became furtive, and the innocent act was supplanted by unease. "What do you mean?"

I slammed my coffee cup down onto the table. Little, who had taken up residence on my lap after her meal, leapt away in rebellion. "Don't play games with me, Seleia. I know you were here yesterday. I know you got into the house while I was gone, and since I didn't leave the door unlocked or the window open, I have to assume you have a key which you must have made without my knowledge or approval."

I collected myself and gave a resigned sigh. "It's not that I mind you coming around or even being here while I'm gone. I trust you—or at least I did, before this."

I paused. Seleia was laughing. The distress was gone now, and her air was one of relief.

"What's so funny about getting caught for a breach of propriety?" I grumped.

"But I didn't," she giggled.

"Didn't what?"

"I didn't come yesterday. And I certainly didn't make my own key. Though now that you mention it, it sounds like a good idea."

"Don't lie to me!"

Her face turned stony. "I'm not lying, Lynley. I thought you knew me better than that!" She bounced off the couch with much the same aggravation as Little. Scooching into her shoes, she stomped toward the back door. "Let me know when you figure it out."

I stood, watching her flounce away. "Seleia, come back. I'm sorry. I..."

She turned and looked at me, her shoulders slouched in that *get on with it* manner adopted by teens throughout the ages.

"Come back and let me tell you what happened."

"You can tell me from here."

I sank back into my chair, all my energy tapped out. "Seleia, something took place yesterday, something that, well, I guess it scared me. I thought maybe it had been you. I wanted it to be you. Because if it wasn't you, I don't know who it could be."

Chapter 4

Upper respiratory infections, or kitty colds, are the most common illness of shelter cats. URI can refer to any one of several feline viruses that cause cold-like symptoms. Usually URI's are mild, but they should be monitored for more serious complications.

I love the shelter! The buildings had been totally rebuilt some years ago, turning Friends of Felines from a dismal, depressing prison into a light, airy, friendly home-away-from-home for a large group of very lucky cats. Of course they would rather be living in their forever homes than in the two-by-two-by-four kennels at FOF, but we, the staff and volunteers, made it as nice for them as we could. It works both ways, too, because a happy cat is easier to adopt out than a traumatized, spiritless one. Last year our success rate was exceptional for a cat shelter. Ninety-eight percent went home.

Cheerful music wafted from the exam room where a pair of smiling young girls in blue scrubs chatted and cooed over a squirming kitten. It had been a good day. The man and his son had come back for Cat-erine the Great, and several other adoptions had gone through. I liked to imagine the people bringing home their new cat, or cats, for the first time. To a feline, every nook and cranny was filled with exciting possibilities. It's great fun to watch them explore their new world, making it their own.

The shelter was closed to the public for the night, and I had two more kennels to scrub, then the cattery staff could move some kitties from the back so they would have time to settle before tomorrow's opening. I was squeezed inside kennel B, spraying the stainless steel grid and walls with disinfectant to rid them of any left-over germs, when someone touched my shoulder. I jumped and nearly bumped my head on the door as I pulled out to see who it was.

"Frannie, you surprised me," I said, wiping my sanitized fingers on a brown paper towel. "I haven't seen you today. Where have you been hiding yourself?"

"Laundry room." She stuck out her pruney hands as proof. "It was a big job, but I'm finally finished," she said triumphantly.

"I hate to tell you..." My gaze slipped to a pile of soiled blankets and towels on the floor nearby.

Frannie rolled her eyes. "Shelter work is never done," she misquoted.

"But it can wait," I said.

"It's going to have to."

She ran her hand through her hair, and by magic, the platinum curls fell back into place as if she'd just left the hairdresser. I wish mine would do that, but I gave up long ago. Spending my formative years believing hair to be synonymous with self-expression, I couldn't quite give up the shaggy look, even though the locks are now more gray than brown.

"You want to come by my place this time?" she asked. "I promise I have no poltergeists."

"Sounds good. Just let me finish here and I'll be ready. Oh, hold on. I still have Cat-erine's kennel to do."

"I'll start it, then you can just throw in the paper and

bed when you're done with this one."

It took only a few more minutes working together to ready the kennels for their new inhabitants. We stood back and admired our work: spotless, gleaming steel with a colorful three-inch thick pad of bedding, a small litter box, a bowl of water. Staff would give the cat food when it moved in.

"Lookin' good," Frannie announced.

"One more thing," I said as I tossed a couple of toys into each of the empty confines. Clipping a hanging glob of neon-colored feathers to the grid wire, I said, "Perfecto!"

"What say we get out of here?"

I nodded—it was nine o'clock after all—and we headed for the locker room to get our things and check out on the computer.

In tired but satisfied silence, we spun padlocks, opened lockers, and began to prepare for the world outside.

"You ladies can't stay away, can you?" came a soft masculine voice.

"Denny," Frannie said jovially, "Sometimes I think I live here."

"Those cat beds are pretty comfortable," I took up. "If they were just a bit bigger, I'd probably never leave."

"You girls are great," said Denny, all joking aside. "The cats are lucky to have you."

"And animals everywhere are lucky to have you, Special Agent Paris."

Denny's cat-green gaze slipped self-consciously to the floor and a blush crept over his smile. I could almost hear him say, *Aw, shucks, ma'am,* in his smooth Washingtonian drawl, but modesty is only one notable thing about Denny Paris, Humane Investigator.

Denny was tall and broad, young and strong:

everything an officer of the law should be. He had passed his police exams but had aspired to do more than give parking tickets and bust druggies. And Denny had known right from the start exactly what that was: he wanted to help animals. Denny Paris wanted to be one of the three special agents commissioned by the Governor of Oregon through the Northwest Humane Society to investigate and enforce Oregon's animal cruelty laws.

It was a tough job. Where volunteers like Frannie and myself saw the happy side of shelter business—adoptions, love, healthy sleek cats, people with smiling faces—Special Agents Denny Paris, Connie Lee, and Frank Dawson were on the other side of the wall. They saw humanity at its worst, those cruel enough to harm the defenseless and neglect the needy. It was their task to bust puppy mills, free chained dogs, seize starving horses, uncover animal fights, rescue maltreated cats, and a plethora of other things that I know go on in the world but really don't want to put down on paper lest I give credence to such horrendous acts.

All three of the agents were amazing, but Denny was a real gem. In spite of the things he encountered in his investigations, he was always smiling, always optimistic. I once asked him how he stayed sane in the face of such depravity, and he told me it was because he knew he was making a difference. As long as those animals were still alive, as long as someone cared enough to step in and report neglect and abuse, he could help. Not all the stories had a happy ending, but he believed that with each personal perseverance against cruelty, the world became a better place, day by day, one creature at a time.

"What's new on your end?" I asked. "Should we be expecting a clowder of cats from a hoarder or anything like that?"

"I'm happy to say it's been a quiet week. Connie and I testified on Wednesday and Thursday. The breeder-gone-bad from Hood River. But she'd turned herself in when she realized how wrong things had gone so the fine was reasonable."

"I remember that one," said Frannie. "A few months ago. We got thirty-some Siamese mix. Besides a bad case of fleas, they were really pretty healthy."

I untied the bow of my green FOF apron and pulled it over my head. "She kept those cats in disgusting conditions. Crowded and filthy." I said with barely-veiled fury. "You'd think she would have caught herself before it came to that."

Denny shrugged. "I agree with you, Lynley. I have the pictures to prove it. The judge was duly horrified. She won't be allowed to keep animals anytime soon, let alone begin breeding again."

I balled up my apron with a harrumph and stuffed it into my pack. "Well, it's good to know you're on the case, Special Agent Paris."

Frannie was also stripping off her shelter apron and scrub coat. She pulled out a pair of street shoes, then stopped. "What ever happened with that mysterious drop-off we had last week?"

"The carton of puppies someone left by the front door?" Denny leaned elegantly against the jam, looking more like a male model than a policeman. "I don't know where those people got their information," he snickered. "This is a *cat* shelter, after all."

"The name should have given them a clue—Friends of *Felines*?"

Denny shook his head. "They knew what they were

doing though. They managed to elude all the surveillance cameras, which is no easy feat. That drop wasn't done randomly. They had to have known the location of the cameras as well as the routine of filming."

"Routine?" Frannie asked.

"None of the surveillance cameras run all the time. They fire in sequence. Oh, they cover all the angles alright; it's just that some views are more distant than others. Then they come around again for the close-ups. There shouldn't be any gap but obviously there is. Helen is looking into it with the surveillance service."

"I bet she is!" Helen Branson, our beloved executive director, though sweet when sweetness was due, was a lion when it came to anything that threatened her shelter.

"So you still don't know where the pups came from?" Frannie asked.

Denny grinned. "I didn't say that. We may not have caught them on film, but they did leave some evidence. We're processing that now and I think we're going to be able to issue a citation in the near future. It's still a crime to abandon an animal at animal shelter, a class C misdemeanor."

"Wow! CSI Humane Society?"

"You bet!" Denny assured.

"Hey slacker," came a jovial call from across the hallway.

Denny turned to the stocky, short-haired woman. "Just finishing up here, Lee."

Connie's face cracked into a huge smile. "Just kidding buddy. Hey, Lynley. Frannie," she said with a little wave. "How's the adoptions?"

"Cats are flying out of here," I joked.

"Glad to hear it. That's how it should be."

"Well, I'd better be getting on," said Denny. "You ladies have a good night."

Frannie and I shouldered our bags. While I waited for her to check out, I called to Denny who was striding across the lobby, "Special Agent Paris." He turned back to me as gracefully as a ballerina. "So what happened to the puppies?"

"They're going up to the County Animal Shelter in a few days."

"And 'til then?"

He gave a wide smile, showing perfect white teeth. "I got 'em at my place."

I nodded without the least surprise. "You're a good guy, Denny."

His eyes slipped floorward and the blush rose in his face. Though he was silent, in my mind I heard him say, *Aw, shucks, ma'am.*

Chapter 5

Cats have a unique olfactory sense organ called the vomeronasal, or Jacobson's organ. It's located in the roof of the mouth and connects to the nasal cavity so by drawing air through his mouth, a cat is able to perceive trace scents such as food and pheromones. Some people propose the organ also works as a "sixth sense," helping cats predict earthquakes, volcanic eruptions, and other unusual phenomena.

As planned, Frannie and I went to her apartment, a nice older suite with a gorgeous view of downtown, the Willamette River, and Portland's east side beyond. In the forties, the building was among the city's tallest and considered one of the most prestigious addresses. It had been well-maintained throughout the years and updated lovingly, but amid the crop of twenty-first century high-rise condos, the brick and stone neo-Renaissance structure was an anachronism. Still, it was its unique obsolescence that made it affordable to people like Frannie DeSoto, a retired widow of somewhat limited means.

Frannie had no cats; the building didn't allow it. That was one reason she volunteered at the shelter. She did have a pair of canaries that trilled with sweet abandon in their predatorless world.

We enjoyed a nice cup of tea—no poltergeists, just as she had pledged. I filled her in on the mystery of the rearranged DVDs, the talk with my mother, and the accusations I'd made toward my granddaughter. I felt bad about that now. The idea that she had broken in with the aid of the virile Vinnie had been ludicrous, and I realized on looking back that I had clung to it only because I despised the alternatives: One, someone had raided my home with malice aforethought (whatever that means); two, aliens had landed in my living room and perused my stuff to better understand humanity; or three, I really was losing my mind. That last option was seeming more likely all the time. A slip of memory was so much more conceivable than aliens, and far more comfortable than a break-in.

"It happens to the best of us," Frannie assured me. "No need to make arrangements with the old folks' home just yet."

We both laughed though neither of us found it all that funny.

I didn't stay at Frannie's much past the tea. I was tired and wanted to get back to my cats. I drove quietly across the river without a thought in my head, pulled up in front of my house with a little prayer of thanks that the SUV from across the street hadn't taken my parking place again, and got out, ready for a hot bath and bed. All I wanted out of life at that moment was to curl up with my kitties and nap and purr until morning.

* * *

'Twas not to be.

The first thing I noticed even before I made it up the front steps was the light in the bedroom. Suddenly I was wide awake, adrenaline pumping through my veins. I was instantly on alert. Had I been feline, my ears would have pricked up, my pupils dilated, and my mouth opened to let the clues in the air inform me through my vomeronasal organ. But I'm human, and my substandard instinct told me only to beware.

I paused, took a deep breath, and asked myself the burning question: Might I, just maybe, by pure accident or oversight, have left that light on myself?

The question was moot, because the next thing I noticed was my front door standing ajar. Just a crack, but that inch could have been a mile. There was no doubt in my mind the door had been closed—and locked—when I went to the shelter that morning. This time there could be no other explanation—my house had been violated.

I tiptoed up onto the porch and stood there for a while, trying to decide what to do. A little voice in my head that was my mother's said, *Don't go into a crime scene—the perp may still be there ready to kill you for catching him in the act.* It was probably sound advice since she was the reigning queen of mystery television. I thought about taking it but standing aside just wasn't in my nature. This was my home, after all. I needed to see.

Gingerly, I pushed the door open. It was old and squeaked in protest. I told it to be quiet but to no avail.

The light was off in the hallway and I could see nothing but black-on-black shadows. I reached ever so slowly inside for the switch which was just to the right of the door jamb, found it, and flicked it on. It snapped to like a gunshot, making me jump in spite of knowing the sound well. The light from the old hanging fixture blazed. I blinked briefly, and when my vision cleared, I reeled in horror.

If a hurricane had swept through that small and precise space, it couldn't have done more damage than what was before me. Everything that could be moved, thrown, dumped, or broken, had been. Books were askew on the ground, coats cast down and trodden upon. There could no longer be any uncertainty that my place had been tossed. With a freak sense of relief, I found myself glad I wasn't crazy. I'd abandoned the fantasy about aliens, so that left humans. Strange, bad, invasive humans who had no respect for other people's things.

Suddenly my mouth dropped as an even worse fear hit me. The cats! What had become of the cats?

Throwing my mother's telepathic warning to the four winds, I ran into the house, eyes wide, searching for any sign of them.

"Harry!" I called in desperation. "Little! Red! Fluffs! Solo! Violet??" How long had the door been open? Except for Dirty Harry who had his own cat flap, they were all indoor cats. Violet and Solo had never seen outside except through a window or the grill of their carrier; though Little and Red had been strays, that was a long, safe time ago. Plus, the break-in had to have been noisy and atypical, adding fear to the mix. They could be anywhere; they could be lost! I don't think I'd ever felt so forlorn before in my life.

Then I had a flash that took my breath away: what if they were hurt? What if the burglars were abusive or in a hurry when a cat got in their way? "Oh, no!" I cried, snapping into action to find (whatever was left of) my cats.

I crunched through shards of vintage Fiestaware and the detritus of an irreplaceable antique clock without a second thought. I threw aside ripped canvases that had earlier in the day been lovely original paintings. Nothing mattered but my babies.

I found Addison, still in his kennel in the back room, hunkered underneath his bed. I took a brief moment to comfort him, tell him it was okay now the bad people were gone, and explain that I had to go look for the others but would be back as soon as I could.

I stumbled through the house. Everywhere was the same: my precious belongings had been run through a blender and no sign of the cats. Finally, after a second round, I sank into a chair—miraculously still upright—and put my head in my hands. It was time to start looking outside, to go door to door with pictures. If I still had any pictures! A huge sob broke free and for a while all I could do was cry.

Something touched my ankle and I jumped out of my skin. "Little!" I yelped, grabbing up the black female and clutching her tightly to my breast. She squirmed in discomfort and then settled down to tell me all about it. I wished I were better at cat communication. She had seen the whole thing happen. She could point the finger—or in her case, the claw—at whoever had done this horrible thing.

But that's not how cats think. Though she had a lot to say, her recollection of the event revolved around her own fear, not the particulars.

I felt over her soft, small body for any sign of assault, but she seemed fine. Chances were, the cats had hightailed it into hiding the moment the ruckus began, and that the burglar hadn't cared a whit about them.

"One down," I said as I carried Little to Addison's room, the least chaotic in the house. "I'll be back," I told her, depositing her on the well-scratched easy chair. Before she could follow me, I closed her in and renewed my search for the rest.

It was a miracle, but in a matter of minutes, I had found the lot of them. Solo was in her hiding place under the sofa where she had probably been the whole time. In this case, I was thankful she was shy and knew how to care for herself. I left her where she was.

Violet had hidden behind a dresser in the bedroom. I heard her soft plaintive meow on my second sweep. She was safe but had gotten her big self stuck there. I helped her out and took her down to join Little and Addison.

Harry appeared out of the ether, acting as if nothing had happened. He went straight to his food bowl, which to his disgust, was upside down and empty.

When I was calmed enough to think, I knew right off where to find Red. And sure enough, he had skipped outside through the open door and run under the porch where he had lived as a stray before I took him in.

Fluffs had taken up refuge on the highest place she could reach, a tiny plate shelf in the kitchen, only a few inches from the thirteen-foot Victorian ceiling. I would have seen her before had I thought to look up.

Once I had them all, I collapsed on the floor by my purse where I had dropped it on the way in. I took a deep breath and called nine-one-one. After reporting the break-in and knowing that it was going to be a long night, I did what any normal fifty-eight-year-old woman would do: I called my mother.

Chapter 6

Fat cats are cute and cuddly, but obesity can cause serious health problems including diabetes, joint pain, and heart disease. Weight loss for cats is tricky however, requiring close veterinary supervision, because done too quickly, it can lead to life-threatening liver ailments.

Carol was great. First, she asked if we were okay—me and the cats. Then she told me to call my insurance company.

"Don't touch anything, but the minute you hang up, go around and take pictures with your phone."

"I'm not sure I still have a computer to download them to," I told her. I was beginning to grasp the impact of my losses and was feeling very sorry for myself.

"Don't worry about that now, dear. It'll drive you crazy. It happened—there's nothing you can do about that part so don't make it worse than it already is."

I wanted to ask her how it could be any worse, but I already knew the answer: We were safe, my little feline family and I, and that was what mattered the most.

"Are you listening to me?" Carol was saying, and I realized I wasn't. "Call a motel that takes cats and reserve a room. Make that a suite—your insurance will cover. Locate everything you'll need: clothes, toiletries, litter box, carriers, etcetera, but don't collect them yet. Wait for the police to finish. Then pack up, lock the door, and leave. Soak in a hot bath, go to bed, and be ready for an arduous morning. You know I'd have you here at the Terrace if I could," she finished apologetically.

"I know, Mum. Prissie would never approve."

"You know how she is. She gets so upset at the slightest change."

Prissie, my mother's elderly half-Persian, was spoiled, but that was her right at age twenty-two. It was, after all, Prissie's home, and spoiled or no, the mix of Priss and my brood would be pandemonium at the very least.

"I understand. Any other advice?"

"Don't forget your phone charger. And Lynley, don't take any chances. Make one of the officers stay with you until you're packed up and gone."

"Thanks, Carol. I don't know what I'd do without you."

There was silence from the other end of the line, then Carol said, "I love you, dear. Call me tomorrow with all the clues. If the cops can't find the perps, Candy and I will."

I laughed. "I almost believe you, Mum."

"Believe it! Now call the insurance company. They've got an answering service for emergencies. You can talk to someone tonight, don't let them tell you otherwise."

I was about to say goodbye when flashing red and blue lights strobed through the slats of my window blinds. "Cops are here. Call you."

A stampede of booted feet clambered up my steps. There was a perfunctory knock and then a different kind of chaos was set loose in my house. Uniformed and plain-clothes police swarmed into every room, every corner. They wore little paper booties over their regulation clunkers but not the full body covering you saw on crime shows, I guess because it wasn't a murder. I shivered as I realized the magnitude of that last thought and then shoved the idea out of my mind.

A nice if abrupt detective named Marsha Croft interviewed me in detail, taking down everything I said on a slim black laptop computer. I was a little hesitant to tell her about the happenings of the night before, but eventually I did anyway. Maybe it had something to do with the break-in, maybe it didn't. Not for me to decide.

With a slight accent I couldn't identify, Croft asked me if anything was stolen. I told her honestly I didn't have a clue. Patiently she took me around and asked all the right questions until we came to the conclusion that unless we had missed something minor, all was present. Broken, bashed and trashed, but present. For some reason, that only made me feel worse about the loss. I mean, why would anybody break in just to vandalize? It seemed ridiculous.

Croft and the others were very good at asking questions but nil when it came to answering them. Finally, at four in the morning, they were ready to call it quits, and I had no better idea of what had taken place than I had before they came. I guess they don't want to commit themselves until they have proof positive, and probably not even then. I had the sinking feeling that they'd never get to the bottom of this one. The strike seemed random, and unless the offenders re-offended, they might never be caught.

When the police were done, I packed my things and my cats. The officer who waited with me helped me to my car, transporting the cavalcade of carriers as if they were nothing—until he came to Violet. I saw the look of surprise on his face when he hefted her up.

"What you got in here? A Pit Bull?" he asked with a grunt.

"No, just a big cat."

He wedged her into my back seat with the others, then peered inside. "Wow!" was all he said.

I got in the driver's side and thanked the officer for his help. Reaching into the back, I stuck my fingers through the grid of Violet's carrier and scratched her soft white face. She went into an instant purr.

"Did you hear, girl? The policeman thinks you're 'wow'!" She must have liked that because her purr increased into a volcanic rumble. With a final caress, I started the motor and set out for our new home at the Residence Inn.

I remember thinking the worst was over.

I was wrong.

* * *

Needless to say, I didn't make it to the shelter for the next few days. I had my hands full with insurance, police, and the mess formerly known as my belongings. The neighbors were great though. Amy Allen, the virtual artist from across the street, brought me a vegan casserole; Janet and Daryl Johnson, the old couple next door, baked me bread and a Bundt cake; Patty Herbert, on the other side, offered to do my shopping. I thanked her but explained that I was fine and could still fend for myself. I'm sure there was a percentage of curiosity mixed in with their genuine friendly concern, but I appreciated the thoughtfulness just the same.

The detectives, on the rare occasion that I saw them, were always very busy. They seemed to be doing a thorough job of it, though, the results of which I knew nothing. As to insurance, I was glad I'd paid all those extra premiums, because as my mother had assured me, they covered just about everything. Besides paying for the hotel and promising a check to cover my personal property, they had a crew of sympathetic and competent eco-cleaners come to get my house back into working order.

I had lost a lot but not as much as I had first feared. I learned that computers are built stronger than I'd imagined, and books—even the antique ones—can take a lot of abuse. My little camera had skated under a table but had come up clicking.

My dishes were toast though some of the larger items that I kept far back on the top shelves had escaped unscathed. I thought maybe instead of replacing the vintage Fiestaware piece for piece, I'd buy the new ones which were actually very nice. I really didn't need to be eating off hundred-dollar plates, even if I had got them for a bargain thirty years ago.

The cleaners came in and I don't know how they did it but when they were done, not a stain was left on the carpet nor a scrape on the Marmoleum. Counters were spotless, certainly better than they'd been for a long time. Things looked a little bare without all my knickknacks, but it was kind of refreshing not to have all that lovely, dusty stuff lying around. A sort of Zen approach. I thought about keeping it like that but knew it wasn't in my nature: soon every shelf, every surface, every space of wall would be bedecked with some eclectic treasure.

Speaking of treasure, the strangest thing of all was that the burglars hadn't taken any of my jewelry. I owned some nice pieces: antique diamonds, a ruby pendant, and a good collection of amber, which I love. Though it took a while to corral it from around the bedroom, everything was there.

The cats had been skeptical of the new decor as well as of the new, way-too-clean smell, but all in all they were glad to be home from the motel. So was I, though a little thorn of mistrust had lodged itself in my heart and wasn't about to come out any time soon. I had seen what could happen for no good reason and when you least expect it. That would be hard, if not impossible, to forget.

And then there was always the nagging question ready to spring like a leg-hold-trap: What would have happened if I'd been home?

Chances are they would never have broken in had someone been in the house.

Right?

Right??

Because if I was wrong, would I still be here to tell the tale?

There were just some places I refused to let my mind go, and that was one of them. What was, was, and I needed to get on with things that were happening right now.

Like solving the crime. I had this idea that I couldn't let go until the creeps were caught, tried, and found guilty of wrecking my serenity. Every day I'd make an excuse to call Detective Croft or someone else on the force. Nothing ever came of it, though. Maybe they had nothing to go on; maybe they were just keeping it to themselves. For my part, I watched the papers, listened to the news, even cruised the internet for similar offenses.

Modus operandi as my mother called it. Carol and Candy were into the hunt all the way, so excited to have a real mystery to sleuth out. Carol called five times a day with a new theory, clue, or motive. The duo came up with some downright gritty scenarios, such as a pervert breaking in to steal my underwear—"He could be watching you this very moment, dear. Do you have all

44

your blinds drawn?"—or one of my old lovers back for revenge because I dumped him—"What about that boy you snubbed in the eighth grade? Maybe he's been plotting this for years (forty-five of them?) but couldn't act on it because he's been in prison for manslaughter." Some of their ideas weren't so far-fetched though, like the notion that the guy or girl—Carol and Candy know all too well that some of the most nefarious criminals are female—was looking for something specific, which would explain not taking the jewelry. "If they didn't find it, they'll be back. You did get that alarm system installed, didn't you?" Their stories might have made me nervous if they hadn't been so darned cute about it.

Bit by bit, I began to reclaim my life, though often I felt I was just going through the motions. Things were slightly skewed. The cats felt it too. They were quieter than usual and kept close to me whenever I was home. Harry even took to sleeping on the bed which he hadn't done since Red and Little commandeered his spot. One night I woke to an earthquake and realized it was Violet jumping up to join us. She lay on my feet until they both went numb, then I gently moved over but she just snuggled closer until my legs were off the bed.

Still all in all, things were getting better. I was actually beginning to feel like my old self. In the confusion, I had forgotten completely about Fluffs and the pretty stone.

Chapter 7

There are many theories as to the origin of the Maine Coon breed of cat. Some think they are descendants of cats that traveled with the Vikings; others speculate they were sent to America with the belongings of the ill-fated Marie Antoinette. Maine Coons are larger than the average cat; four to five times bigger than the smallest cat, the Singapura.

I have activities that don't involve cats, you know. I crochet, belong to a Scottish clan, keep a Facebook page, and on occasion I sell antiques and collectibles at flea markets and *junque* fairs.

I've always loved old stuff. My grandparents' attic was like a gold mine to me. I spent hours up there. Percy, the family Maine Coon, liked it too, and together we would explore—him for mice and me for the hidden worlds of the past.

That's where I began to appreciate my family history: great-great-great uncle William Ball who was a Major in the Civil War (a hand-tinted photograph in a box of family photos); his sister, Lois Ball Harley, who spied for the North (a series passes allowing her entrance into Confederate territory); Captain J. J. Gilbert who first mapped the Pacific Rim on the Pathfinder (a bound leather album of tiny travel photos); his brother, William Gilbert, U.S. Court of Appeals judge for the Western District back in 1892 (a grand oak gavel and a packet of letters between him and his daughter out East); and of course the Mackey line, which was to become the focus of my research later on in life.

But what I liked most were the forgotten and obsolete gadgets and gewgaws that had collected up there, too good to toss but replaced by something newer, better, or easier. There were at least six decades of radios running from a lovely nineteen-thirties cathedral console to a tiny mauve transistor type from the sixties. A dusty corner shelf held a century of toasters: a flapper style that was guaranteed to burn your bread, a sleek rounded model resembling an Air Stream trailer, and everything in between including some that were barely identifiable as kitchenware. The list goes on, but bottom line, I was hooked on the *junque* business from the start. I don't do much selling anymore but I'm still really good at buying.

It always relaxes me to cruise the antique stores, checking prices, looking for that perfect find, and feeling smug when I got the same thing for less. I have several favorite haunts but today I picked Antique Row, a mall in the basement of a restaurant on 42nd Street in Portland's Hollywood district. Unlike a store, the mall rents spaces to numerous people for their many and varied wares. You never knew what you might turn up.

This time, it was a vintage Mexican sterling cat pin for five bucks in a case with other jewelry and smalls. The piece was so tarnished, I could barely see the whiskers, but I knew the work, knew that under all that black was a delicately tooled piece. I debated whether I should buy it or not but quickly gave in. Five bucks? I'm worth it.

A tall, wispy man with a fuzz of bleach-white hair appeared over my shoulder. "Lyn-dear! You would like to see?" he said with an affected faux-French accent.

Gil, pronounced Ghee, was a permanent fixture of

Antique Row. I knew he couldn't possibly work all shifts, but I can't remember a time I've been there when he was absent. That included the sixteen months I rented a booth myself. Early, late, weekday, weekend, Gil was always around, always happy, always excited about something and everything. My day brightened whenever I was in proximity of the man.

"Hi, Gil," I said with an instant smile. "Let's see the kitty." I poked the glass case above the tarnished pin.

Gil's eyes grew big and round, showing off his long lashes and strange turquoise contact lenses. *"Le chaton! Bon choix,* Lyn-dear." He pulled a set of keys from the pocket of his puce vest and had the piece out in nothing flat. "Perfect *por tu!"* He placed it gently on a square of black velvet that he produced from who knows where. *"La dame du chat crazy.* Ze Crazy Cat Lady," he translated unnecessarily.

"I'm not crazy, Gil," I chuckled. "At least not yet."

I picked the piece up and turned it over. Bringing it close to my eye, I saw the mark I was looking for, confirming its age and the purity of the silver. "Very nice."

"C'est bon. You buy?"

"Sure," I told him. Why not? One more cat pin to add to my already considerable collection of cat jewelry couldn't hurt, could it?

He swept the piece, velvet and all, off the glass and we headed for the cash register.

"Sooo, Lyn-dear," he cooed salaciously as he rung me up. "I hear you have a *mésaventure,* how you say? A mishap *a la maison."*

I gave him a blank stare, but he nodded vehemently. *"Oui, oui.* News travels. *La petit madame pauvre!* 'Ow 'oirrible it must have been for you! *Très effrayant,* eh?"

I frowned. "I had a break-in a few weeks ago. But how

did you know?"

"Eet was in ze paper."

A little shock shot through me. "Really? When? I haven't seen anything. And I've been looking."

"*Aujourd'hui*, Lyn-dear. Eet talk about you, along with zee others."

I paused. "Others? Other what?"

"Burglaries, all near where you live. They think eet is because of *les diamantes, mon cher*."

"Diamonds?" Gil had lost me back at the mention of an article in today's paper. I mean, the thing had happened weeks ago which was like eons in the frantic pace of the news service. To run it today made no sense. 'Others' made no sense. 'Diamonds' made no sense.

"'Ere you are, Lyn-dear," he said as if he hadn't just dropped a bomb on my life. He handed me the little bag with my pin in it. When had he wrapped it? I hadn't noticed. When had I paid for it, for that matter? But I had; I still held the change in my hand.

"*S'il vous plaît*, be so careful out there." Gil gave me his five-star smile. "I be seeing you," he crooned as he flounced off toward another customer.

"Gil, wait!" I called after him. "I don't understand."

Gil just gave a little wave as he pounced on the next potential buyer like predator upon prey.

Clutching my little pink bag, I ran out of there, up the stairs and into the April sunshine. My face was hot, but it wasn't from those watery white rays. I'd completely lost track of what Gil had been talking about, but I knew how to find out. Today's paper, he had said. There was a news box just down the street.

I nearly flew to the scratched Plexiglas case while fumbling in my purse for quarters, but I was met with disappointment: the box was empty. It was afternoon; I should have known the morning edition would be sold out by now. I swore, trying to think where else I could go.

Turning on my heel, I went back to the restaurant. A waitress young enough to remind me of Seleia was on me the second I walked in the door.

"Need a table, ma'am?"

Cringing at the *ma'am* which most women of my generation find more offensive than respectful, I said, "No, *miss*, but maybe you can tell me where I could find a paper close by. Besides the box; it's empty."

The girl looked at me as if I were speaking Klingon. "Newspaper," I emphasized, suddenly wondering if she realized they still existed, what with all the electronic media these days.

Her face still blank as a bean, she moved behind the counter and pulled out a well-read copy of the *Oregonian*. "You can have this one if you want. Everybody's seen it."

I nearly jumped on it. "Today's?" I gulped.

"I dunno," she shrugged. "I never read 'em."

She tossed a raggedy, grease-splotched paper on the counter. "Sure you don't want something?"

"Actually, give me a coffee please." I slipped into the nearest booth where I could spread out my prize. She was off and running.

She was back in record time; I had only managed to find the front page and reunite it with page three/four and five/six. She dropped a thick green mug in front of me and filled it with steaming brown liquid. "Milk and sugar?"

"No thanks, this is fine."

"Anything else, ma'am?

I told her no thanks again.

"A menu?"

Nope.

"Some pie or a muffin? We have scones and cookies too."

I shook my head.

"Grill's about to close so if you want a burger, you should order it now."

I told her no burger. Thanks.

She rolled her eyes the way only the young can get away with. "Well, if there's anything..."

I watched her closely as she walked away, making sure she wasn't going to change her mind and present me with soup or salad or corned beef on a bun, but she breezed into the kitchen and disappeared. I was off the hook for the moment. With racing heart, I turned my attention to the paper.

There it was, on the bottom of page one, continued on page eight. *Fourth Laurelhurst Home Invasion—Homeowner on critical list, Police get break in case.*

I won't quote the entire article. Suffice it to say the press had taken a few generic facts and blown them into a two-column mystery-melodrama. But to me, any information was such a relief that it didn't matter.

These were the details:

There had been not one but *four* recent break-ins in my neighborhood, all attributed to the same perpetrator or perpetrators.

The most recent had been last night. The homeowner, a Mr. Daryl Johnson, had tried to stop the assailant and was assaulted for his efforts. He had been admitted to OHSU Hospital in critical condition.

A man was apprehended fleeing the scene, but he turned out to be the local peeper and was taken in on separate charges. Once in custody, he described someone he saw running down the street near where the crime took place.

Ergo, the police had a suspect.

I read the article three times, flipping from the front page to the eighth where the last few disembodied paragraphs had been stashed. As I read, I came up with a few details of my own:

One: I wasn't the only person who'd been invaded.

Two: The police knew more than they were telling me.

Three: Instead of explaining anything, this news left me with more questions than ever.

A separate matter had been cleared up by this info, however. I now knew what would have happened had I been at home that fateful night. The answer was right there on the OHSU critical list.

* * *

The more I thought about it, the madder I got. Why should the press, and as a result, the whole of Portland, get hold of information that directly affected me before I did? Why hadn't anyone bothered to let me know? Shouldn't the police have called with an update? My mother, if no one else—didn't she read the paper anymore? No, I had to find out from Gil, the local gossipmonger.

I was beginning to sweat and grind my teeth as a result of the resentment surging through my mind like a malevolent tornado. Everything I had worked so hard to overcome since the incident was rushing back, threatening to drown me in fear, mistrust, and self-pity.

The musty soap smell of the restaurant was suddenly suffocating; the cloying humidity from the boiling pots and the overworked dishwasher made me nauseous. I had to get out. I dumped a pile of money on the counter. It was more than enough for the coffee, but she hadn't brought the bill and I wasn't about to wait. I bolted through the door and didn't stop until I was well out into the open air. I knew of a little park at the end of the street where I could sit on a bench under a Japanese maple and gather my wits, what was left of them. All of a sudden, I felt very old. I wasn't up to this. Maybe when I was younger, when I was naive enough to confuse danger with excitement, but not now. I had learned my lesson. Danger was dangerous! It could hurt you, or worse! It could leave scars—mental, spiritual and physical—which might never go away. All I wanted was for the danger to pass. I wanted to go home where I could feel safe. Yet home was the very place my life had been violated. Not uptown or in some darkened alley—at home, where badness should never be.

I found I was crying; tears were rolling down my cheeks and I hadn't even noticed. Furtively I scrounged a Kleenex out of my coat pocket and tried to fix myself up before anyone saw—older people look awful when they cry.

I was too late. A wide-bodied woman in her early thirties was peering down at me with maudlin countenance. "Can I help, honey?" she asked sympathetically. "Drive you to a shelter or anything?"

I stared at her in disbelief, knowing that by 'shelter' she hadn't been referring to one for cats. Did I look that wretched? That destitute? Granted I wasn't wearing my best clothes, but really now. I guessed I'd better get my butt home, turn on the ADT, and grab some rest before I was picked up for vagrancy.

"I'm fine," I said in my most genteel voice as I pointedly looked the other way.

"Only trying to help," she harrumphed as she

lumbered off. In search of a more grateful charity case, I supposed.

Again the resentment. She really was only trying to be nice, and I had behaved rudely. It was time—past time—to get myself out of the public eye.

Picking up my purse, I realized I had left the newspaper in the restaurant. Just as well. I needed to get information from the source, not from some reporter trying to sell a story. I would call Detective Croft the moment I got home—heck, why wait? I had her number in my cell phone. I'd call her right now!

I whipped out my little phone, a basic model that is much passé now. It doesn't connect to the internet, play movies, or do my laundry, but it works and I like it. I would rather fancy a pink one with rhinestones, but not enough to go through the agonies of programing a new model.

Something hit my wrist—hard!—and the phone went skittering along the pavement. Out of nowhere, a strong arm came up around my throat, and a gloved hand clamped savagely over my mouth. I choked out a scream, but the sound never made through the glove. Instinctively I tore at what I could reach of my attacker, but he was well-protected; besides the leather gloves, he wore a heavy canvas coat like a Carhartt, armor of the workforce and nearly impenetrable.

I heard a low growl just before my world was shaken apart. It was the kind of shake that brings mad people out of fits and injures babies. The intention behind it was clear: fight and it will hurt.

The man—assuredly it was a man—dragged me backward into the azalea bushes. Ironically they were in bloom, creating a pink and white torture chamber. To my dismay, no one had seen us. This was a public park on a busy street for heaven's sake! Where was everybody? Where was that nice helpful lady? *Please come back!* I prayed. *I'm sorry I was rude. Please please please!*

The man wrenched my head around so hard I was sure he'd broken my neck except I was still very much alive in my pain. One more like that and I might not be so lucky.

This is it! I thought to myself. *Thank goodness I made arrangements for the cats!*

Hot breath exploded in my ear, and I felt more than heard him speak. The words made no sense though. He seemed to be asking directions, but that couldn't be. He wasn't exactly the tourist type. The hot words stopped for a moment, then he loosened the grip on my mouth by a micrometer.

"Make a sound and I break you," he hissed. I nodded acquiescence—what else could I do? The hand came away ever so slowly. "Where is the Babylon? Tell me now." This time there was no mistaking, and I knew I had to come up with an answer if I wanted to survive intact.

"In Iraq?" I whispered weakly.

Apparently that wasn't what he wanted to hear because the beefy arm clenched even tighter. He let me choke for a little while and then he asked again. "No jokes, Miz Cannon. The Babylon, the Eye—Where is it?"

"Look... don't... know... what... you're... talking... about," I hacked.

He paused as if considering what I'd said, but he must have rejected it because he came at me again.

"The stone—the brown stone."

Brown.

Stone?

Suddenly I had a vivid, detailed image of Fluffs batting

around a big brown agate. But why all this trouble over an agate?

Because it wasn't an agate, it was a...

"Brown diamond!" I gasped.

"See, you know the one. You thought you could keep them for yourself? Well, we got the Burma, and we'll have the twin, too, if you know what's good for you."

"Twin? You mean there's two?"

"Cats have two eyes, don't they? You ought to know with all those varmints running around your house!"

Varmints? Even in my unhappy state, I bristled at this jerk calling my lovely felines varmints!

"The infamous Cats' Eyes diamonds," he went on, his voice softer, as if he were talking to himself more than me. "The rarest uncut chocolate diamonds in creation. Worth millions.

"Where is it?" he snarled, clasping my neck, back to his old nasty self again.

"I don't have it. I only saw the one," I squeaked. I considered telling him that Fluffs was tossing it around like a catnip mouse but thought better of it. "I didn't know what it was or how it got there. Honestly."

Whether he believed me or not, I'll never be sure. I heard voices nearby and coming nearer. He heard them too because the hand came up over my mouth again.

I saw my chance and began to struggle as hard as I could, grunting against the glove, kicking out at the bushes, anything I could do to attract attention.

I heard that growl again. "You'll be living in misery until you give us the stone!" he threatened. "We'll be in touch, Cannon." His grip loosened, then there was a reverberating crack, and my vision went white with pain. I screamed, my mouth free now. Clutching at my shin which felt as if it were a toothpick snapped in two, I fell forward in a writhing, damaged heap. He had hit hard with something heavy, a pipe or baseball bat, and I knew without a doctor's opinion that the bone was shattered.

Someone was at my side, arm under my elbow, helping me up onto the bench. Someone else was asking what happened.

I was attacked! He's wearing a canvas coat and leather gloves. Quick, get him—he can't have gone far! I shouted as loud as I could. Except in my agony, I was mute—my articulate description came out a gargled, senseless splutter. I couldn't catch my breath. I was sobbing; behind tear-filled eyes I was blind. Excruciating pain pulsed with each beat of my heart, renewing itself again and again.

Through ringing ears, I heard several voices now—must have attracted quite a crowd. They were all talking at once.

"Call nine-one-one!" someone shrilled.

"What happened? Is she drunk?"

"I got your purse, sweetie." I recognized the voice of the woman who had tried to help me before. I managed a nod of thanks which was about all I could do before I sank into the safeguard of oblivion.

Chapter 8

Spraying is a natural behavior for cats. They use their urine to mark territory and communicate with each other. Although spraying is most common with unaltered males, altered males and females are just as capable. But don't give up hope; there are many ways to discourage spraying behavior, from removing triggers such as competitive cats to vet-prescribed drug therapy.

I woke in a hospital bed, feeling fine. Too fine: I'd been drugged for sure, and with the good stuff. I went to sit up but my body was far too heavy to move. Especially my left leg, which in the long leg cast the orthopedic surgeon had slipped on me while I was sleeping, felt like it had confronted the Medusa and been turned to stone.

Suddenly I remembered getting cracked in the shin and in spite of the medication, shivered with pain. It was all coming back: the attack, the grilling, the threat. I needed to tell someone what happened! Get the police out there looking for the guy! I wanted him off the streets before I got out of emergency since I didn't like the idea of *living in misery* until I gave him the stone that I didn't have. If it were anything like the misery he'd wrought so far, I was in big trouble.

Again I struggled with my unresponsive body, and this time managed to squirm enough to set off some kind of alarm bell. A male nurse in teal scrubs was at my bedside in a heartbeat, checking machines, feeling my pulse, and taking my blood pressure with a device that fits over a finger instead of throttling your arm like a military tourniquet.

"How're you doing, Lynley?" he asked in a pleasant voice, a nurse's voice—they may not be female and wear white dresses anymore, but that half-caring half-condescending tone hadn't changed since Florence Nightingale's time.

If I hadn't had a thermometer in my mouth, I might have answered. Instead I grunted until he got the thing out. "Someone has to feed my cats!" I erupted. Then, second in importance, "I need to talk to the police."

As it turned out, they were way ahead of me. The police had been alerted and were on the scene before the paramedics had picked up my broken body and put me in the ambulance. The admitting doctor had filled out a medical report, stating that my injury, a tibial shaft fracture, was the result of blunt-force trauma by an unknown but heavy instrument. Detective Croft had been my first visitor at the hospital, after interviewing people at the site. Since I was unconscious at the time, she'd arranged to be notified when I woke up.

Now she sat with her laptop on her knees. "Just tell me what you remember, from the beginning."

"I... I..." *Aye yi yi!* I stuttered, my mouth as dry as cat sand.

"Take your time."

I scrunched my head back into my pillow and closed my eyes. Get a grip, I told myself; I took a deep breath, then another. Finally the words came pouring out.

I told her everything: about Gil and the article in the paper and how frustrated I was that no one had warned me or even *told* me what was happening because since my neighbor Daryl Johnson whom I had known for at least a decade was on the critical list, it was no longer a harmless little break-in, but then she already knew that and why oh why hadn't she informed me of what was going on?

I told her that I'd been just about to call her when I was grabbed from behind and terrorized and my phone fell on the ground and did anybody pick it up because otherwise it's still in the park or *stolen* and someone could run up a huge bill ordering porn or something—well, not porn because my phone didn't have internet, but sexting or one-nine-hundred numbers—

Detective Croft interrupted long enough to assure me the phone had been found and put with my purse which was safe in the hospital locker room.

I apologized profusely for getting sidetracked. *Profusely!*

She said that was fine but now please get on with my statement. "Can you tell me anything about your assailant?"

Well, she asked so I told her.

It became clear about halfway through my description of every thread in his coat, every stitch in his leather glove that the drugs were making me chatty. "Wow. I'm sorry. I can't get my brain together. I think they've given me something." I waved a general hand toward the nursing station outside my cubicle.

Croft's stern eyes softened. "I imagine they have. But you are doing fine. A very detailed report."

I gazed up at the detective. She really was a nice lady, reminding me a little of my cousin's husband's niece. I don't know why I hadn't noticed it before. She was a pretty woman, though she didn't seem to know it, or maybe she just played it down for the job. The silky black hair would look gorgeous worn long instead of in that widow's bun; her dark eyes barely needed makeup but something softer than that shade of blood red lipstick might look more becoming. Her bulky suit tended to make her look fat, but she was probably just muscular. Probably strong as a lion.

"Please, Ms. Cannon, go on," Croft directed, and I realized I'd been wool-gathering.

"Sorry, again," I mumbled. Fact is, I didn't want to dwell on the next part. I shuddered just thinking about it. "It was the scariest thing that's ever happened to me in my life," I said with a sigh that hurt all the way down to my injured leg.

"I am sure it was. Now think carefully. Did he say anything, and if so, can you remember the exact words?"

I closed my eyes; the little zaps of neon lightning coming out of the ceiling were distracting me. They were still there with my eyes shut but it didn't seem so befuddling. What had he said? Something about...

My eyes popped open, and I wrestled myself into a slouch before my leaden leg got the better of me. "He asked me about a stone. This is going to sound really crazy, but he said it was a brown diamond, extremely valuable. For some reason, he thought I had it. The thing even had a name: Babylon."

"Babylon?" she broke in. "Are you sure?"

"Yeah. I'm a Babylon-5 fan," I added to prove my credibility. She gave me a funny look. "I know, the show's been off the air for years, but it's a classic. Like Star Trek. Well, nothing's quite like Star Trek."

"Anything else?" *Besides old sci-fi TV?* She didn't have to say it; I heard the glimmer of impatience in her voice.

I shook my head meekly.

Her demeanor had taken on an urgency at the mention

of the stone, which made sense if the thing really was a priceless diamond. Crazy, I thought to myself. This whole situation is downright nuts.

"And do you have this stone, Ms. Cannon?"

"Of course not. Well, I mean, I don't know exactly — Detective, I don't understand any of this. I just want to go home and be with my cats. Little will be wild with worry by now, and Harry will probably spray if no one lets him out. He's really a good boy, but one of those cats who needs his space, and with six others around he gets a tad upset."

"Ms. Cannon, let me tell you something," Croft put in. Her voice was brittle as flint. "If this man is seeking the Babylon diamond, then it is no joke. It is all too real, as your broken leg can attest.

"Let me tell you a story." Her tone mellowed a little, and I thought I saw a ghost of a smile on the ruby lips, but it might have been a drug-induced hallucination. "You should enjoy this, being a feline aficionado."

I was all ears.

"This diamond, Babylon, and its twin, Burma, are a perfectly matched set of chocolate diamonds called the Cats' Eyes. As you may know, brown diamonds are relatively common, even at this size — sixty-three and sixty-five carats — but these are special. They have nearly identical inclusions, small needles that mimic the pupil of a cat's eye. Once cut and faceted in the Marquis style, they will resemble the copper-brown eyes of their owner's prize cats for whom the diamonds were named."

"What kind of cats?"

"Pardon?"

"What kind are they? Brown eyes are uncommon in cats."

"That makes sense. This person would have nothing that was not rare and expensive. But I am afraid I do not know the breed."

Had I heard a note of envy in her brusque tone? Why not? The guy probably spent more on his prize cats than a cop—even a detective—made in a year. Not that pampering your cats is a bad thing. I began to drift into fantasies of how many kitty toys I could buy if I were a millionaire.

Croft shifted in her seat, readjusting the computer on her lap. "Ms. Cannon..."

I blinked innocently.

"Are you listening?"

"Yes, ma'am," I replied, banishing the company of colorful catnip mice skittering around in my head.

"I cannot tell you any specifics of the case, but the Eyes disappeared on their way to a Portland gem cutter. If the theft can somehow be tied to your assault," she nodded toward my mangled leg, "then it may be the breakthrough we've been looking for."

"Glad to be of service," I mumbled.

Her brow furrowed and her face was grim. "Do not be glib. People are willing to kill for lesser gems than the Cats' Eyes." She looked at me squarely, as if she were delivering a death sentence, which in a way, she was. "So far, you have gotten away with merely a fractured tibia. If you have the stone, you must tell me, before things go any farther."

Okay, I was scared now. I glanced around the cubicle, afraid I'd see a gun poking through the curtain or a man with a knife hiding behind the monitor machine.

"So these stones are real?"

"Deadly real."

"I had no idea."

For a moment, I was silent and she let me be. Then I gravely met her gaze. "I might have had the twin for a while. I didn't know what it was. Honestly. I mean, how could I? My cat was playing with it on the floor. I thought it was one of the agates we'd brought back from the beach years ago."

She sat forward in her chair. "When was this?"

"I don't know."

"Before the break-in?"

I thought for a moment, then nodded.

"How did your cat get hold of it?"

I shrugged. "I don't know that either. She just suddenly had it and was batting it around like a hockey puck."

"Could she have brought it in from outside?"

I shook my head vehemently. "All my cats are indoor cats. Well, except Harry, and I only let him out when it's nice and I have time to look after him."

"So you would have seen if he had picked it up?"

"Well, no, not necessarily. I mean, I don't watch him every minute." I felt like the worst cat mom in the world and vowed to finish the cat fence in the back yard as soon as I was well enough to manage a hammer.

"Where is it now? What did you do with it?"

"I don't remember."

"Try."

I though back. Fluffo... Oh, I missed her so much! I still didn't know if anyone had cared for her and the others since I'd been in the hospital. "What time is it?" I asked abruptly.

Croft, with the tolerance of a saint, said, "Three-thirty. AM."

"I need to make a phone call. I need to get someone to look in on the cats."

"We will be done here in just a minute and then you can make arrangements. Now please, the stone. Try to recall."

I pictured it in my mind: Fluffs was playing; a stone, pretty like an agate; I picked it up and... "I put it in the basket in the kitchen," I said triumphantly, congratulating my brain on its great achievement. "But I don't remember ever seeing it after that."

I guess my brain wasn't finished with its miracle of memory because another snippet flashed into the forefront. "Wait! Yes! He said he had that one. I remember now!"

"Who said he had the one?"

"The man who..." I gestured helplessly at my cast.

"The man who attacked you told you one of the stones was already in his possession?"

"Uh-huh." I nodded as vigorously as my fuzzy head would allow. "Do you think he's the one who broke into my house?"

Detective Croft hesitated, then she abruptly stood. "That will be all for now, Ms. Cannon. I will let you get your rest."

I grabbed a corner of her jacket, the full measure of my fear seeping through the pink Percocet haze. "What happens now? He threatened to make my life miserable unless I gave him the twin. He said he was coming back for it—*they* were coming back for it. But I don't have it, I swear! What am I going to do?"

"We will keep surveillance outside your house. If he comes around, we will see him." She gave a brief smile. "Take care of your cats and try not to worry. We will talk again once you are home and settled."

I nodded in resignation. My leg had begun to throb, and the pain was increasing exponentially.

"Would you like me to call the nurse?" she asked.

"Is it that obvious?"

"I have been where you are, more than once. I recognize the signs."

I watched her walk away, stopping as promised at the nurse's station. The nurse was nodding soberly, then looking on the computer at a chart I assumed was mine. He nodded again and Detective Croft disappeared beyond my sight.

Nurse Dave, as I read on his ID tag, breezed in with quick efficiency. "Officer said you need some more pain meds?"

I nodded weakly. In a matter of minutes, the pain had gone from a one to a seventy-five on the one-to-ten scale.

"Don't worry, Lynley, we'll look after you while you're here."

That's great, I thought to myself, *but what happens once I'm gone?*

Chapter 9

Rule of thumb for litter boxes: one per cat in your household, plus one. If you have three cats, there should be four litter boxes placed throughout the house. Now, if you have eleven cats, twelve boxes are probably overkill. Then again, if you have eleven cats....?

It took every bit of restraint I could muster to keep me from phoning Frannie at four in the morning to have her run right over and take care of my cats. Cats are stoic, however, and when I thought about it seriously, I knew they could wait until a decent human hour to get their fix of wet food and love. They had kibbles after all, an endless supply of them in a fancy timed feeder, and plenty of fresh water from the fountain. The litter boxes would be getting a little ripe by now, but there were several of them around the house and hopefully the brood could hold on without any stinky protests.

I couldn't get the things Detective Croft had told me out of my mind. It was like some wild story that happened to someone else and not to me. The thought that I'd had a priceless diamond in my hand without any inkling of its value seemed impossible. The idea that there was someone lurking out there ready to do me harm if I didn't come up with a second one was beyond comprehension. It was all too much, and I was glad when the painkillers and whatever else they had given me began to weave their intoxicating magic. My cares and woes drifted in a soft furry haze, and next thing I knew, I was out for the duration.

When I woke again, it was much later. The hospital was bustling with early morning urgencies. I had been brought from my slumber by Nurse Dave unhooking me from the machines. A doctor young enough to be my grandson was smiling benevolently down upon me. He pulled a rolling stool up to my bedside.

"You're almost ready to go home, Lynley," said the doc. "We just need to make sure you're not too groggy from the medication."

"I feel fine," I fudged as I tried to get the two of him to fuse into one.

"That's good. You're going to have a certain amount of pain for a while. Ashleigh will send you home with a prescription for Vicodin. You will have limited mobility; that leg is fractured in two places and even with the cast, you'll have to avoid placing weight on it for several weeks. Your orthopedist will take periodic X-rays to ensure the bone is healing properly, and if all goes well, the cast may be removed in six to ten weeks. It will probably take five to six months of restricted movement for the break to heal completely."

Six months? I thought in alarm. *I'll be hobbling around until Halloween?*

"Ashleigh will set you up with the physical therapist who will adjust your crutches to your personal specifications before you leave the hospital. Do you have someone who can help you around the house?"

"Maybe my granddaughter," I said. Big maybe but I wanted to go home, and I had the feeling that 'no' would have been the wrong answer.

"Ashleigh will make a follow-up appointment with an

orthopedist. You can tell her your preference, or we can refer you to one in our group."

I nodded and mumbled a generic thank you.

"Ashleigh will go over your discharge summary with you right after we finish here. You should heal up just fine as long as you're careful and follow your instructions conscientiously. I can't emphasize enough how important they are for your recovery. It's not a bad break, but as one gets older, there can be complications. We've done the basic work; now only care and time can do the rest. Any questions?"

I shook my head, sure that I would think of some the minute he left, but that was okay; I could always ask the ever-efficient Ashleigh.

"Thank you, Doctor..." I squinted at his name tag but couldn't make it out.

"Doctor Manghirmalani," he said—no wonder I couldn't read it.

"Thank you," I repeated, omitting his name because in my drugged state, I wasn't sure I could wrap my mouth around anything greater than two syllables.

He grinned, nice bright teeth in the face of a Grecian god. Obviously I wasn't the first patient to have trouble with Mangy-whatever.

No sooner than he had gone, Special Agent Denny Paris stepped into the cubicle. "Your ride awaits," he said with a grin.

"Denny! What are you doing here?" I stammered, suddenly feeling like an old hag in front of this sweet young thing.

"Frannie's helping your ma Lynley-proof your house." I gaped at him in incomprehension. He pointed to my cast. "You don't think you'll be dancing up and down those stairs, do you?"

"I guess you're right. I hadn't thought that far. And I appreciate you coming to pick me up."

"Gotta take care of our volunteers, you know. Precious commodity there."

If I'd had the energy, I might have blushed.

"I guess they got a few more things to do with you before they let you go. I just wanted you to know I'm here so you wouldn't worry. And yes, Frannie's been by your place twice and the cats are fine. They're all asking for you."

* * *

I don't think I've ever seen anything as beautiful as that sunny April afternoon. It was warm enough to hang my arm out the window of Denny's Silverado truck and let the cool, if not quite fresh, Portland air flow across my face. I refused to think beyond getting home and seeing the cats. I could picture them clearly: Little would be at the door to greet me, talking up a storm; Red would be slinking somewhere behind her, craving affection but too shy to come right up and get it; Dirty Harry would be in his donut or maybe sulking on the DVD shelf; Solo would be solo; Violet would stick her nose up to sniff my scent in the air, then drift back to sleep wherever she was. And Fluffs, dear old Fluffs—you could never tell with Fluffs. She could be in one of several favorite spots. Fraulein Fluffs owned the world, at least according to her. Frannie had taken Addison back to the shelter earlier in the day since he was over his URI. I missed saying goodbye, but it was for the best since I would have enough trouble keeping up with the six.

Denny gave me my space which was great because I

just couldn't answer any more questions. The whole thing seemed like an unfortunate dream and I was so ready to wake up now. It wasn't until we got to my house that I could even open up enough to say thanks for the ride as Denny wished me well and drove off into the sunset.

Frannie and my mother were there to greet me, along with Seleia who was ever-so-solicitous. I dreaded the inevitable third degree I would get from Carol but still I was glad to see her. After what had happened, I was happy to see anyone who was neither an assailant, a detective, nor hospital staff. I take that back: I was extremely happy to note what had to be an unmarked police car parked down the block with two efficient-looking officers sitting inconspicuously inside.

It took all three of my helpers to get me and my new gear up the steps and into the house. Though I had gone in with nothing but my purse and clothing, I was coming away with crutches, wheelchair, bath accessories, and the pink plastic tub, pitcher, and cup set that come complimentary with the hospital stay. The tub would make a nice little litter pan, I thought.

My reunion with the cats went pretty much as I had anticipated except I was laid out on the couch with my leg up and they had to come to me if they wanted to say hi. They all did with the exception of Solo whom I didn't expect to see until everyone else had gone away.

I must say my steadfast crew had done a great job of making the big rambling three-story house handicapped-accessible. Furniture had been pushed aside and knickknacks, what was left of them after the break-in, were picked up so I could get around unimpeded. They had moved the single bed from the sewing room and put it in my downstairs office which happened to be conveniently next door to the bathroom. I didn't want to know what they'd done with the piles of ironing, mending, sewing, and miscellaneous flotsam that had been stacked on top, but I wasn't going to find out any time soon since those twenty-seven stairs had become as unmanageable for me as Mt. St. Helens.

Through the kitchen doorway I glimpsed grocery bags on the counter, and someone had made something that smelled like heaven. Apparently I wasn't going to starve.

It was the funniest thing: In spite of the many, many years between, I suddenly felt like a kid again. We sat around the living room with our meal of hearty chicken and vegetable soup, oyster crackers, and hot chamomile tea, chatting about nothing in particular and especially not about my misadventures. There was a warm fuzziness to it. I supposed having Red beside me, Little on my lap, and Fluffs on the back of the couch behind my head might have added to the fur factor. But right then, at that moment, I felt safe and warm and loved.

After dinner, everyone cleaned up for me as I lay around feeling pampered and guilty all at the same time. Then Carol and Frannie said goodnight. Seleia had agreed to stay over to make sure I was okay. She really was a good girl and I would have to talk to her mother about letting her go to Science Camp with that boy, Vinnie. Any girl who would give up her time to babysit her grandmother without even being asked is responsible enough to make some decisions for herself.

It was only eight o'clock, but I was exhausted. Seleia helped me to my office-cum-bedroom where I dutifully oohed and aahed over the magnificent job they'd done. They'd put a lovely set of straw-colored linens on the little bed, with a dusty-gold down comforter on top. Fluffo was curled up right in the center like a furry silver donut which made it all the more attractive. On my desk sat a small television; the remote lay on the bedside table along with a glass of water, my painkillers, a random selection of cozy murder mysteries from Carol, a candy bar from Seleia, my cell phone, and a vase of spring lilacs. Wow, had anyone ever been so blessed?

My green plush bathrobe was spread across the foot of the bed, and at the head was a whole collection of pillows. I couldn't imagine wanting more.

"Can I get you anything else, Lynley?" Seleia asked for the third or fourth time.

"I don't think so, dear. I'm just going to lie down for a while. I don't know why I'm so sleepy."

I sat hard on the mattress, still unused to my leaden appendage. Setting my crutches on the floor, I hefted my leg up and let out a little cry of pain.

Seleia nearly jumped to my side. "Are you alright, grandma?"

"I'm fine," I said with confidence I didn't really feel, but I saw right away I was going to have to be careful or I'd be overwhelmed with a glut of good intentions. "I'm fine," I repeated, in case she hadn't got it the first time. "I really appreciate your staying over."

"That's okay. I was just hanging out at the Terrace while mom and dad are away."

"They're off again?" I asked. Lisa and Gene were gone so often that Seleia had her own room at Carol's condo.

Seleia gave me a little nod-shrug-sigh. I knew exactly what she meant.

"Well, I'm glad to have you here. You know that, don't you?"

"Sure Lynley. I like it too."

"Now why don't you go watch a movie or whatever you like. I'm just going to take a little rest."

She looked at me doubtfully, and for a scary moment, I thought she might insist on watching me as I slept, but then her face cleared. "I've got some homework. I'll be in the living room if you need me. Just call, promise?"

"I promise. Oh, there is one thing," I said as she started for the door. "Would you mind very much cleaning the cat boxes? They don't like using dirty ones."

"Already done," she laughed. "And the feeder is full, and the fountain is clean and has fresh water in it and I don't know what else, but Frannie said she did all the cat stuff before she left. Is that okay?"

I let myself fall back on the pillow hill and sighed gratefully. "That's wonderful. See you in the morning, love."

She made to leave and then turned back, shuffling her feet nervously. "Um, Mom's called twice to see how you are, you know."

"Oh?" was all I could come up with off the bat. My daughter and I are not on the best of terms though I don't think it goes far enough to affect the love between us. We're just very different people.

"She's really worried," Seleia continued.

"She is? Well, I hope you told her not to be, that everything's fine."

"I let Carol talk to her about... well, about what's going on and all."

Suddenly Seleia seemed to regress about a decade, back to when she used to come to me to ask the big questions. You know, like *Where do kittens come from?* and *What makes the lights work?*

Why is there air? Why is grass green?

74

Why do mommy and daddy fight all the time? Is it because of me?

She flopped down beside me. "She and dad are in Santa Fe for a gallery opening or she would have come by."

"I'm sure she would have." I put my hand over my granddaughter's. "But you don't have to make excuses for her, you know. Your mom and I have our own kind of relationship, just like you and I do. What happens with us is our business and our problem, nobody else's." I paused, realizing those were true but harsh words. "I know how much you care, honey. I'll call her tomorrow and catch her up on things, okay?"

"Okay," Seleia said, much relieved. She gave me a little hug and hopped to her feet. "Goodnight, Lynley."

"Goodnight, dear."

She left my door ajar so the cats could inspect the new arrangements and visit their long-lost cohabitor during the night. I listened to her bare feet pad across the hall into the living room. A few moments later, the vague, hidden tinkle of iPod music started up. I knew since I could hear it all the way through her ear buds, she was playing it too loudly. *Homework?* I thought to myself. But that's the way they did things these days. Teens couldn't concentrate unless they had at least four things going at once.

I closed my eyes and said a little prayer of thanks to the Powers That Be for my family and my life. *And please, God*, I added, *let me never hear the words Babylon or chocolate diamond again so long as I live, amen.*

Chapter 10

Abuse of an animal is a serious offense. Every state in the US has laws prohibiting cruelty to animals, and forty-one states plus the District of Columbia have felony provisions for animal cruelty which include heavy fines and even jail time. Yay!

It was a real comedy act, complete with slapstick, to get out of my clothes and into my bathrobe. I hadn't realized it before but besides the broken leg, I had a sore wrist where Mr. Badass had grabbed me and a huge and painful bruise on my throat from his not-so-gentle choke hold. Whenever I moved my head wrong it hurt like a mother bear. My chest ached too, as did my arms, my hips, and the balls of my feet. Face it: the fifty-something body isn't as resilient as it once was. Stifling a groan, I popped another painkiller—it had been almost four hours, after all.

Fluffs had moved just enough to allow me to lie straight on the bed and now I was mindlessly rubbing her head as she purred her little heart out. Solo had also granted me one of her rare audiences. She lay at my feet where she could dive into hiding if anything threatened, like the shadow of a tree outside the window or the lights of a passing car. I felt relieved, safe. The alarms were set; if anyone tried to break in now, ADT would have the cops on them in an instant. I almost wished they would; I'd love to see Badass's face as they hauled him off to jail.

I tried watching a little TV but nothing really grabbed me; the few shows that looked promising couldn't hold my interest past the onslaught of inane commercials. The book assortment wasn't much better. Carol was well-meaning, but at the moment, murder was the last thing I found entertaining. *There but for the grace of God* and all. Finally I owned up to the fact that I was just plain tired and shouldn't attempt anything more complicated than sleep. I reached over—ouch!—and turned out the light.

* * *

It was dark and I was hearing church bells. No, it wasn't the angels come to get me but my cell phone—I made a mental note to change that ringtone to something a little less ethereal. I tried to sit up, then remembered that to do so would cause me great pain. I could see the phone, blinking on the side table. Carefully and with minimum exertion, I managed to get it to my ear.

"Hello?" I panted.

There was a pause, then the voice on the other end of the air said, "Lynley Cannon. You know what I want."

This time I did sit up, the adrenaline scorching through my veins and the cold gut fear that had seized my body overriding everything else. I would recognize that voice anywhere, for the remainder of my life, but I said in a whisper, "Who is this?"

"You know who it is," came the disembodied hiss. "Are you ready to get down to business now?"

My heart was beating so hard I thought I was going to die. I felt like I should be doing something—asking the revealing questions or keeping him on the line so the call could be traced—but it was all I could manage just to draw breath.

"I told you before," I said as evenly as I could, "I don't have it. I don't know anything about it. I don't even know how the first stone got into my house. You've got the wrong person." That last was a sob, but it didn't get me any sympathy from Mr. Badass.

His silence was even more threatening than his words.

"Look!" I gasped. "Leave me alone. The police are watching. If you try anything, they'll—"

"Now listen carefully," he interrupted. "Get rid of the cops—if you don't, you will suffer. Be ready to bring the stone; if you don't, you will suffer. Don't tell anyone about this call. If you do, we will know, and *you will suffer!* We hold all the cards here, Cannon. You'll see."

"See what...?" I began, but he had already rung off.

I stared at the phone's glowing display, then tossed it down on the bed as if it were a snake. I flicked on the light and picked it back up. I looked at the caller ID, but not surprisingly it was a restricted number. With shaking hands, I brought up speed-dial and pressed the key for Detective Croft, then flipped the phone shut before it connected. What was I doing? He said no cops. He said I would suffer. Maybe he was bluffing, but I should probably think this through before I did anything I couldn't take back later.

Suddenly the front doorbell rang, and I jumped out of my skin. In the silence, it seemed as loud as a fire alarm. Who would be dropping by at this hour? I checked the clock—it really wasn't that late, a little after nine. I must have only been asleep for a few minutes before getting the call.

"Don't answer it," I called out to Seleia, but from the telltale squeak of the hinges, she was already opening the door. There was muffled conversation. I strained my ears for the sound of screams or a struggle, but all seemed quiet.

Seleia's barefoot shuffle came across the hall and then she knocked lightly on my door. "Denny's here, Lynley. He says he needs to talk to you."

Denny Paris? What would he be doing here at this time of night? I reluctantly quashed the thought of a romantic assignation with the hunky investigator.

"Tell him I'll be right there."

"You need help, Grandma?"

"No, I'll be fine. Got to get used to this, and no time like the present, eh?"

Her footsteps retreated and again there was the soft buzz of dialogue in the other room.

I won't go through what it took to get myself up and at 'em. Luckily one of my thoughtful female friends or relatives had left hairbrush, lip gloss, and a hand mirror on the desk so I didn't have to look like the Wicked Witch of the West's grandmother when I went to greet my visitor. Not that it would have really mattered much—he had seen me at my very worst at the hospital—but women, of any age, have their vanity.

Denny Paris was standing just inside the door. Stumping into the living room on my new crutches, which in spite of having been professionally adjusted to my height, weight, and size, seemed clumsy as tree trunks, I gave him a brave smile. "What's up, Special Agent Paris? Please, have a seat. I'm sure we could convince Seleia to make us a cup of tea."

Denny gazed at his feet, but this time it wasn't the *aw, shucks* look. He was frowning.

"This isn't a social call, Lynley." Suddenly he looked like he was about to cry.

Alarm bells went off in my head. "What is it? What's happened?" The only things I could imagine that could account for Denny's anxiety were bad—really bad. Had the shelter burned down? Had someone died?

He squared his shoulders and looked me in the eye. His own face went unaccountably blank. "Lynley Cannon, as a humane investigative Special Agent for the state of Oregon, I am following up on a complaint against you for animal abuse in the first degree." He produced an official-looking paper from his jacket. "I have a warrant here to search the premises and to confiscate all animals until this charge can be looked into and either dismissed or brought to trial."

I made a little strangled cry as my knees buckled out from under me. I would have fallen had Denny not jumped to my rescue with his strong though official arms. "I'm so sorry, Lynley!" he blurted as he ferried me to the couch. "I know this whole thing is a pile of crap, but I still have to do it."

I stared at him in disbelief.

"It's my job..."

"Who made this ridiculous complaint?" Seleia demanded. "No one in their right mind could think my grandmother would hurt one of her cats. She'd be more likely to..."

I gave my well-meaning granddaughter a cautionary look, not wanting whatever she was about to say, which was probably something like '... *more likely to commit murder*' to go on record. Then my glare fell accusingly on Denny. "Answer my granddaughter's question, please, Special Agent Paris."

He squirmed and I almost felt sorry for him, but I was feeling a whole lot sorrier for myself. "You know that's confidential." He paused, then crumpled into an armchair and leaned close to me. "Lynley, I hate this. You have to know I do. But I've got to do everything by the book or it compromises the job and creates a loophole for real abusers to get away with their crimes."

I knew he was right, but I wasn't about to make it easy for him. "You have to give me something, Denny. We've been friends for a long time."

"Okay, but what I tell you can't go beyond these walls. Promise?"

I nodded.

"I think, well, I *know* this is a bogus charge. It was called in anonymously. They were very graphic in their supposedly eye-witness description of the abuse though. Look, the way I see it, we'll take the cats to Northwest Humane; the vet will check them out; she'll discredit any accusations of abuse and the whole thing will be over. Think of it this way—your cats'll get their annual veterinary check-up for free."

"No way I can get out of this?"

"I'm afraid not."

"Do you have to take the cats? Can't Dr. Siles come here to do the examination? I know she would if you asked her."

"I know she would too, but that's not how it works. Cats have to go in. And there's one more thing. Dr. Siles has left for the night and has a conference tomorrow morning. She won't be back in the shelter until late afternoon, but I'll call her and make sure she knows it's an ASAP priority. Sorry, Lynley. You know we'll take good care of them."

"You bet your flyin' fanny you will! Because I'll be right there seeing that you do!"

Denny made a little coughing sound. "I'm afraid that won't be possible."

"Why not? I can walk. See?" I slammed the rubber feet of my crutches onto the ground and pulled myself up to a wobbly stand.

"It's not that. You've probably never been in this situation before..."

"Of course she hasn't," Seleia grumbled.

"No, of course not. But when a complaint's brought against someone, they're not permitted to come within fifty feet of an animal shelter until they're cleared. Sorry, Lynley."

"I can't see my own cats?" This was getting worse by the second.

"We can get this resolved the minute Dr. Siles has a look at them. I'll bring them right back myself, I promise. In the meantime, why don't you just relax? Get some rest. You've had a nasty accident."

"It wasn't an accident!" I blustered, "And how can I rest knowing my poor cats are in kitty jail for a crime I didn't commit?"

Denny looked helplessly at Seleia but she, wonderful and loyal girl that she was, just made a little harrumph sound and left him to interpret it as he saw fit.

"Might as well get this over with," he mumbled more to himself than his decidedly hostile audience. He turned and went outside, returning with an armload of carriers.

From the moment he said they were taking my cats I was in shock. I had only just been reunited with them after a harrowing experience, and now we were to be separated again! What had I done to deserve this?

The answer regurgitated itself from my brain like a hairball. *This was Badass's handiwork! The suffering he had promised!* He certainly couldn't have thought of a crueler gesture, short of...

Oh, no! What if he found a way to hurt them? Was this merely the beginning?

"You watch out for these cats, every one of them!" I commanded. "I have reason to think they might be in danger."

Chapter 11

Cats have been a favorite subject of fine jewelry from Bast (ancient Egypt) to Laurel Burch (twentieth-century California).

I stared forlornly at the cat pin I had bought at Antique Row before my life went down the toilet. It had shined up nicely, but I wasn't sure I'd ever be able to wear it without dredging up memories I hoped someday to forget. Maybe I'd give it to Seleia for helping out. I touched the sleek silver body, the sweet, detailed face. Denny had assured me he'd have my cats home as soon as they were released, but when that would be was anyone's guess. The house was so quiet without their meows, their purrs, their rambunctious play and stampedes across the hardwood floor like a pride of little lions.

Seleia had gone to school. She said she'd drop back by afterward to see how I was but couldn't stay long because it was Chess Club night. Chess Club? I didn't know they still had Chess Club. I asked her if it was played on an X-Box. She assured me it was a good, old-fashioned board with little carved men. Apparently Vinnie was a chess champion which explained the draw. She offered to return for the night, but I told her not to bother. Fact was, I didn't want her here. I wasn't exactly scared for her life or anything, but after Mr. Badass's threats and the subsequent abuse charge, I couldn't take any chances. I hadn't told anyone about the phone call or the intimidation. Was I scared? Sure. But mostly I was confused. Until I was certain the cops could protect me, I had to play it safe.

The phone rang—the normal, boring brrng-brrng of the land line. It took me a minute to get myself up and over to the phone table, but I was becoming quicker with the apparatus of my new disability all the time. Luckily the land line was programmed to ring forever before the computer girl took a message.

I reached for it, then wavered. What if it were him again? Fear makes me mad, so I grabbed it from its cradle and barked a gruff greeting into the mouthpiece. There was silence on the other end.

It *was* him! I knew it! What meanness was he going to threaten me with this time?

I was just about to shout some colorful expletive when I heard the voice of Detective Croft. "Lynley Cannon? Are you alright?"

"Detective, sorry. I thought maybe it was..."

"Was whom?"

"Nobody," I said quickly. "Sorry, I didn't mean to sound abrupt."

"You did not sound abrupt, you sounded afraid." She paused, but I didn't take the bait. "Is everything alright?"

Alright as it can be with a broken body and my family ripped from my aching breast, I thought, but there was no use complaining to the hard lady cop. "Fine," I clipped. "What's up?"

"I know how upset you were when we did not keep you in the loop before."

"Did you catch him?" I exclaimed.

"No, not yet, though we are doing everything we can, I assure you. Actually the news is not favorable. We have nothing on your assault. Though several people recall seeing you after the attack, not one noted the attacker himself. As for the home invasion, we took a suspect into custody based on the witness's identification from our booking photographs, but the man was released last night."

"There was a witness?"

"Correct. The voyeur—the original suspect that we brought in from the scene."

"Oh, right," I said. "I'd forgotten. Rats."

"My thoughts exactly. The new suspect seemed a good lead, but his lawyer got him pulled—not enough proof of involvement to hold him," she said sarcastically. "We will be watching him like an owl, though. You can count on it. If he slips up at all, we will have him back, even if it is for jaywalking instead of robbery and aggravated death."

"Death?"

"Correct. That is the other part of the bad news—last night Daryl Johnson passed away in ICU."

* * *

The next time my phone rang, I wanted to run the other direction—I just couldn't take any more—but it was my cell and the display assured me the call was friendly.

"Tell me something good, Frannie, or I'll hang up this minute!" I yowled in lieu of hello.

"Whoa, don't shoot the messenger," she snapped back. "Besides, this is good—very good! Two things: Addison got adopted. I knew you'd want to hear right away."

"Yay!" I whooped, picturing the sweet old cat I had nursed through his kitty cold. "Do you know who took him?"

"I did the adoption myself," she announced proudly. "I think it's a great match. They were an older couple—I mean around our age. (That gets me every time! When did we become our grandparents?) Anyway, they really loved him and all the more because he was fourteen. Dr. Angela told them all about his finicky stomach, and they said sticking to the special diet would be no problem. They looked well-off, able to afford prescription cat food. It was blessed, Lynley, I tell you."

"Great! I'm so glad. I love Addison. He's got such a positive personality in spite of his disadvantages."

"Yes, he does. Sally did her usual brilliant job of counseling them on the ins and outs of a new cat, and she'll do a follow-up call next week to see how they're getting along. She told them how much we all cared for him and encouraged them to send us an update once in a while."

"Oh, I hope they do. I love to hear the success stories. Sometimes they send a picture. It's so great to see the kitties all settled in their new homes."

"I bet Addison will pork out a little with regular love and care," Frannie observed. "He didn't like shelter life — too noisy and too many other cat smells."

"He was beginning to calm down while he was here at the house," I recalled.

"And that surely had a hand in why he was adopted so quickly. Fosters always go fast."

In all the joy of Addison's adoption, I'd nearly forgotten she had said there were two pieces of good news. "Well, that's great, but what's the second thing?"

"It's the one you've been waiting for, Lynley. Your kitties are on their way home *as we speak*!"

* * *

For the first few days after that joyful homecoming, I

wouldn't let the cats out of my sight. Well, not literally because no one can keep exact track of six free-roaming felines in a house as big as mine, but I came as close as humanly possible. I can't tell you how many times I went running—or in my case, hobbling—around looking for Little or Red or Fluffs, only to find them in some new haunt, blinking out at me innocently as if to say, *What's all the fuss? I know exactly where I am.*

Dirty Harry was miffed that he'd lost his outdoor privileges. I tried to explain about the danger and Mr. Badass, but he couldn't see the problem. I finally had to fall back on the rude and unsatisfactory statement that our mothers used on us: "Because I said so."

During that time, I was always looking over my shoulder, jumping at every little sound. I had heart failure whenever the phone or the doorbell rang. I lay in bed at night, meditating on my death—and not in the Buddhist way but the scared American paranoid way that leaves you cold and breathless and empty.

And every time I was beginning to get a handle on things, there would be another interview or another debriefing, and I would instantly be back to that fear place again.

I had finally, sheepishly told Detective Croft about the phone call and the threats. I got what I deserved when she admonished me for impeding an ongoing investigation and risking danger to myself and others—she didn't mention the cats, but it was implied, at least that's the way I took it. Thankfully once she said her piece, she got on with it, adding the new details to the scant list of clues.

It had been established that the break-in and the attack in the park were related, and they had everything to do with the Cats' Eyes diamonds. Everybody was doing their utmost to find both perps and stones, and I would have loved to have helped, but once I'd 'fessed up to the forewarning phone call, there was nothing more to add. Contact with the police dwindled, then petered out altogether.

Somewhere in the midst of that taxing time, I had a birthday, bringing me one year nearer the big six-oh. I ignored it completely and commanded that no one around me speak of it: not a card; not a gift bag; not a single note of the traditional Happy Birthday To You.

My leg healed without any surprises and the cast was removed in early June. I felt like I had wings once it was off, though the doctor told me not to go out dancing for at least another month. The same went for jogging, high-jumping, and rock-climbing, which I could easily promise since I did none of them in the first place. I returned to an abridged version of my yoga program and the senior walk in the park, but the doc assured me both were good for my rehabilitation.

June is beautiful in Portland, once the Rose Festival gets out of the way. The annual celebration of our city flower is well-known for its rain, since by the grace of Murphy, most of the activities which included three elaborate parades were held outdoors. But that was past and now the sun could shine its little heart out, at least until the Fourth of July, another holiday seemingly doomed to drizzle in the lush Pacific Northwest.

Frannie and I were sitting in my back yard in the leafy shade of the fig tree. We wore summer frocks and sandals, indulged in lemonade and iced shortbread cookies, and all was right with the world. I had nearly finished the cat fence—or I should say Seleia and a group of her friends had nearly finished the fence, since they were doing the work while I 'supervised' from my lawn chair. I was letting Dirty Harry out again but still only during the day when I was there to watch over him. He couldn't stray without preforming a series of jumps that would have been a piece of cake for Little or Red, but Harry was large, elderly, and somewhat arthritic: the chance of him launching five feet in the air for the great escape was unlikely if not impossible.

Times like this, I found myself forgetting the Incident, as I'd dubbed my terrible experience. "Life is good," I commented as I took a sip of my frosty cold drink, then clinked it down on the glass-topped table.

"It's fantastic to hear you say that," Frannie commented. "It's been a long time coming."

I sighed. "I know, but somewhere along the way I got sick of waiting for the trap to snap. Besides, what good will it do to worry about things than may never happen?"

Frannie gave a little chuckle. "That's very Zen of you."

"I think so," I boasted. "But that's not going to get the FOF Annual Benefit Show and Sale planned, now is it?"

"I suppose not." She picked up the yellow lined pad and a flamboyant green pen. I noticed it matched today's choice in nail polish. "Where do we start?"

I considered. "How about a recap of what we've already got? Then we can fill in where things are a little thin. Let's start with the show. So far we have music —,"

"Benny and the Vets, the all-veterinarian band." She wrote it at the top of the blank page.

"And Trudie, the animal care tech, is going to sing. Show tunes, I think. Something from the musical, Cats."

Frannie added Trudie to the list. "My, we are a talented bunch, aren't we?"

"We sure are."

"Ginger, one of the new volunteers, is getting her friend from the Comedy Club to do part of his act."

"Oh, is that a for sure?"

"I think so. Sounded like it last time I talked to her."

"Know his name?"

"Not yet. I'll just put down 'Ginger's friend' for now."

"And don't forget Mr. Marcus, the emcee. He's a comedy act in himself. He's going to be doing the auction too."

"He's always good." Frannie examined her handiwork. "Looks like a show to me!"

"It's getting there. I'd still like to see some dancing. Dancing's the hot thing these days, what with the *Dancing with the Stars* craze."

"I don't watch it."

"Neither do I—I'm boycotting that station since they canceled my soap opera after forty-one years on the air—but we may be the only two people in America who don't."

"Dancing," Frannie wrote, then put a big curly question mark behind it.

"Okay, that's about all we can do for now. Let's move on to the auction."

"Everybody's gathering donations, anything from a massage to pet sitting to original works of art. I don't know who's going to be in charge. You're doing the rummage sale, though. Right?"

I nodded. "This year I'm going for quality versus quantity. All the really good stuff will be set out on nice table coverings with prices to match and pretty cards to remind the buyers that the entire amount goes for the cats. The not-so-nice stuff I figure I'll sell by the box. It's easier for the cashiers that way."

"Good idea. They won't need to add up an interminable list of five- and ten-cent items."

"Nothing under a dollar, or maybe even five dollars." I smiled. "It is for a good cause, you know."

"You bet it is!"

"More lemonade?" I asked.

"Sure, but let me get it."

Before I could reply, she was up and halfway across the lawn with our glasses. "Thanks," I called as she slipped into the cool dark of the house.

With Frannie gone, I sat back and studied my garden. I hadn't been able to keep it as well as I liked because of my leg, and it showed in the weedy edges, but at least it was all green and some of the weeds were really very pretty. The grass was cut, thanks to a helpful neighbor, and the geraniums that ringed the narrow stone patio were beginning to open their generous brick and coral blossoms. The little water feature, actually an extremely low-tech contraption of black plastic, sand, pebbles, and a hose, was gurgling away. The birds liked to drink from it, as did Harry. He was there now, his pink tongue lapping deep into the cool. His black back glistened with brown highlights and his white ruff and petticoat gleamed like the sun itself.

As if he knew I was watching him, he turned and gave me his enigmatic green stare. Then he peered back at the stream. For a few moments, he contemplated. Cocking his head to get a different view, he very carefully reached a paw into the water. Instantly he pulled it out again and shook it off, offended by the wetness, but apparently what he wanted was more important than a doused paw. Deliberately he reached back in, this time hitting his mark. Slowly he drew something out, then with a deft move, flung it across the patio as he chased close behind.

It skittered to a stop a few feet in front of me.

I looked down at the sparkly brown stone.

My breath caught, and suddenly I was back there again, back in the murky turmoil I had tried so hard to forget. I snatched up Harry with one hand and the stone with the other and started for the house.

"Frannie!" I cried out.

There was no answer.

The panic button in my head went off again and again. "Frannie? I think we got a problem!"

I stopped dead in the kitchen door. Frannie was splayed out on the Marmoleum, her fingers still clutching a broken tumbler and a dark red stain expanding from underneath her blonde hair.

Harry squirmed.

The diamond felt cold in my hand.

Something moved in the shadows. Without thought, I pivoted and ran—right into the clutch of Mr. Badass himself.

I screamed and let Harry drop; he'd have a better chance on his own. Before I knew what had happened, I was face down in the grass.

I'd forgotten about the stone until my fingers were savagely pried apart and it was wrenched from my grip. "Okay," I grunted into the lawn. "You got what you came for, now go away and leave us alone." It was a futile gesture of bravado for two reasons, the least of them being that my words were all but unintelligible with my mouth full of dirt. The other, I didn't want to contemplate because it was all balled up in the fact that I had seen what he looked like. After what they'd done to Frannie, I had little hope of them departing like gentlemen now.

A booted foot came down on the back of my neck, driving my face farther into the grass. Would I ever feel the same about the fresh scent of a newly-mowed lawn? I seriously doubted it.

Maybe if I'd been younger, if I didn't have that bad back and hadn't been recovering from a fractured leg, I could have reached around in some prehensile karate move, gripped his ankle and flung him to the ground. But I was old and feeling older every minute. As the heel of his boot ground down between my shoulder blades, I knew I was completely helpless. It was a feeling no one should ever have to experience, because it never quite goes away again.

Badass began to speak to his partner in the shadows, but the throbbing in my ears was so loud I could barely make it out. I could tell they were arguing, though, by the intonation as well as the liberal use of blasphemes. Words I caught clearly were *stupid, dimwit,* and *screw-up.* Badass was doing most of the talking and I got the impression that the upset had to do with Frannie and me. I heard something about not leaving witnesses. I hadn't known my heart could beat any faster, but it did.

The foot let up a little and I wondered if he were getting ready to stomp my head into oblivion, the obvious solution to the witness problem. Instead, he pulled me roughly to my knees.

"You're coming with us," he growled.

Yanking me the rest of the way up to a teetering stand, he whirled me around and shoved me toward his partner. Surprised, the stocky man caught me in a mock-embrace.

"My brother will take care of you, since he prefers action to stealth."

Brother Badass quickly rallied to his new assignment. I

saw the baton coming up over me, and the moment before the blackout, the old Beatles tune tinkled teasingly through my mind:

Bang Bang Maxwell's silver hammer came down on his head; Bang Bang Maxwell's silver hammer made sure he was dead...

Chapter 12

According to medical studies, petting a cat can reduce blood pressure, slow heart rate, and create feelings of well-being and comfort in their human companions. The low-frequency vibration of a cat's purr is said to induce bone growth, promote pain relief, and aid in the healing of tendons and muscles.

I quit getting loaded decades ago when I finally smartened up to the fact that the punishment for excessive inebriation inevitably fit the crime, so when I woke with the worst hangover of my life, I admit surprise. My head pounded with the thunderous regularity of the engines in the Battlestar Galactica; my mouth tasted like dirty litter; I was so nauseated I wondered why I wasn't vomiting.

The room around me churned up and down like the crab boat on Deadliest Catch. It was dark, but somewhere above me undulated a lighter patch—a window. I knew better than to sit up fast, so inch by dubious inch, I lifted my head until I could see out. What I discovered sent me back onto the bed with a thunk.

There was a reason I felt queasy. I get seasick in a hot tub and here I was surrounded by the pitching Columbia River. At least I assumed it was the Columbia; too big and wide to be the Willamette, the river that runs through the heart of Portland, splitting east side from west in more ways than mere geographics. Automatically I put my hand out to pet a cat, my proven and preferred stress reliever, but all I got was a fistful of crusty flannel. I scrunched my eyes shut, pulled the gritty blanket over my head and concentrated on breathing.

Two things burbled to the surface of my groggy mind: first, this was no hangover—it was the indicator of some powerful and probably illegal drug, and second, last thing I remembered, I hadn't been on a boat. The drug was making it hard to concentrate—to be honest, stringing two coherent thoughts together seemed to be an insurmountable task: By the time I made it to the second, the first would have sunk into the two-point-eight pounds of sludge that was my brain. I pictured what it would look like in a PET scan—none of the blue dots connecting anymore and the neon pink lit up like a Mardi Gras parade.

For the umpteenth time, I tried to focus. I remembered sitting in the garden with Frannie. I remembered Frannie, out cold on the floor. Then I was down too. I reached up and touched the back of my head. Sure enough, there was a sticky, painful welt the size of a muffin.

Finally, panic made it through the drug-induced dark matter, so clear, like skywriting across my senses: I was in big trouble! The nausea was suddenly gone, quashed by pure adrenaline. I think I preferred the nausea.

I waffled between the Serenity Prayer and the *Bene Gesserit* Litany against Fear. *I must not fear; fear is the mind-killer...* I chanted, but it didn't help—no matter how I tried, I couldn't get the fear to pass over me and through me and out the other side. It just stayed and stayed.

Wallowing in my terror wasn't going to get me anywhere, a little voice in my logical mind mewed. It was time to learn the facts.

Pulling myself together, I made a brief study of the cabin. Though I recalled nothing about how I got from my home to this tossing tin can, I had no trouble filling in the blanks. I had been taken—kidnapped?—by the Badass brothers, and now my duty, as I had learned from a surplus of spy movies, was to escape.

I couldn't see details, but my vision had adapted enough so at least I managed to differentiate shadows. The space was small, as are most cabins, aren't they? Boats were not my forte, what with the *mal de mer* and all. I was on the bunk, a flat wooden surface with a thin pad and a few musty blankets. Around the sides and underneath were built-in shelves and drawers—stowage? A clock glowed dully in the corner, but it read eight-forty-five which was wrong for so many reasons. Across a little stretch of floor was a built-in dinette. A doll-sized sink and stove perched against the far side. I peered down the walkway and saw a blacker square that was probably the head. In the other direction was the ladder that led topside.

I crept unsteadily to the ladder and with a concerted effort, mounted the four rungs. I fully expected the hatch cover to be locked and was surprised when I felt the click as it gave way. I peered through the crack and heard the snarl of raised voices. I couldn't make out all the words over the engine rumble, but it was the Badass boys for sure. One of them said something like, *Why not... over the side, Larry?* and the other answered, *No way, George, ...not... murder on my hands.* Neither of these statements made me feel any better about my situation but at least I now knew their names.

Suddenly I heard footsteps stamping toward me. I dove for the bed as the hatch cover burst open and booted feet clamored down the rungs. Someone grabbed my arm. I felt the needle stick, and before I could count backwards from one hundred to ninety-eight-point-five, I was out again.

* * *

The next time I came to, the boat was docked at a remote landing and I was being hauled like a sack of cat food off the side. My mouth, hands, and feet were bound with what felt like, and smelled like, tee shirt. It was still nighttime but there was a twilight glow on the horizon. With the cloud cover, it was hard to tell where it originated but I had the feeling it was morning. At least that was what my bladder told me.

I began to squirm and yell through my gag. I must have made an impression because my captor put me down. I sat in the gravel and begun to whine like a puppy, one of the few sounds easily made with a mouth full of cotton.

"Shut up or I'll punch you into tomorrow," the guy—it sounded like George, the one who wanted to drown me in the river—hissed. He punctuated his threat with a little kick to prove he wasn't kidding.

I screwed my neck around to find Larry who at least didn't want to kill me.

Larry Badass stood a little way away by a beat-up old station wagon watching me. This was the first time I'd been able to study my captor in toto and was surprised by what I saw. I had known he was tall and of a good build— I could tell that much from being wrapped in his arms— but until now, I hadn't been able to fill in any of the details.

In the half-light, his skin seemed almost translucent; his eyes were mere shadows in the long face, but dark eyebrows bushed out above them. The hair was dark as well, straight and a little long over the collar. The chin descended into a small point that must have been a goatee or whatever they call those scraggly little beards these days. I couldn't determine his age—I've never been good with ages—but he was young, thirties maybe, which is a spring chicken to me. He still, or should I say again, wore the canvas coat, indeed the Carhartt brand, and pants of some unidentifiable origin: not jeans, not Dockers, just pants.

I began my squirm-and-yelp show for him. He let me go on for a while, then said to his partner, "It looks as if she wants to tell us something."

As a reward for his astute observation, I redoubled my efforts. George raised his foot to kick me again, but Larry stopped him with a dirty look. "Is that all you ever think about?" he chided. "Violence is for those too stupid to do things any other way."

"Yeah, whatever." George spun around and engaged his intellect in kicking gravel.

Larry came over to me and unbound my mouth. "I have to go to the bathroom!" I whimpered. I couldn't spit the words out fast enough.

Larry wasn't expecting that.

"Please! Please! Please!" I chanted.

George was laughing. "Jeez, what a deal," he muttered.

"Please?" I mewled like a lost kitten.

Larry Badass made a grumbling sound, then hauled me to my feet. "Not much in the way of facilities out here," he said, stating the obvious. "Go over there." He nodded toward a corner of the small parking area edged by forest trees.

I think he expected me to complain about the lack of privacy, but I was too desperate to care. "Untie me?" I asked, holding out my hands.

He paused, then reached down and fumbled with the knot at my feet. When it wouldn't give, he pulled a four-inch jackknife from his pocket and sliced through the stretchy material.

"What about my hands?"

"You got a dress on, you can manage. Now go before I change my mind."

I didn't argue.

I wish I could say I used the moments out of his close proximity to concoct a surefire plan of escape, leave a help message for someone to find, or fashioned a weapon from gravel and sticks, but it was all I could do just to relieve myself. Still, it was a positive move in more ways than one. First of all, he had given into my needs which meant he had feelings, and second, it would be a lot easier to think now that I'd done my business.

I loitered at the edge of the lot, wondering about running away, but besides the dock and a small road that disappeared up the hill into wilderness, it was bush in all directions. I had no idea where we were: no longer on the Columbia, that much was clear. We must have taken one of the sloughs that parallel the big river and could be anywhere. I couldn't even tell if we were on the Oregon or the Washington side. No, running in the dark in the wilds wouldn't get me very far. I had a better chance seeing things through with Badass.

"Come on," Larry yelled. "You're done, come now or I'll send my brother to get you."

I glared at the other man, who was doing a flawless impression of a bulldog ready to pounce, and my heart fell. One look at George told me the whole scary story. Though he had the same dark hair as his brother, he was short and most likely had a short man's complex. The burly physique contrasted with the baby face, though whether he was truly as young as he looked, or his features were just built like the Pillsbury Doughboy I couldn't be certain. If I'd seen him on the street, I wouldn't have given him a second look. No horns, no pitchfork, just the average Joe. He might have been a sheetrocker or a roofer—some sort of honest physical labor where he could work out his aggressions on wallboard and lumber. But something had gone wrong. Here was a man with no compassion, no concept of good or bad: a true sociopath. Even in the dark, I could see his eyes: there was no mercy there.

Wordlessly I crossed the gravel and delivered myself of my own free will into the hands of the enemy.

* * *

I guess Larry's moment of magnanimity was over. Without a glance in my direction, he swung himself into the driver's side of the old Ford, leaving my installation to brother George. George moved to the back of the car and opened the trunk. For a moment I thought he was going to stuff me in it, but he just grabbed a pile of sleeping bags and clapped it closed again. He came back around, and grabbing me by the hair, shoved me roughly into the back seat.

"Ouch! What did you do that for?"

"Lay down," he menaced, "Or I'll lay ya down myself."

I did as I was told.

He tossed the sleeping bags in on top of me, slammed the door shut, and went around to the other side. Positioning himself in the shotgun seat, he peered over at me. In that moment, I realized to my horror that the malice in his eyes bordered on insanity.

"We should give her another hit, Larry," he told Badass with a leer.

Larry reached over and thunked him hard on the arm. Don't use my name, you twit," he growled.

"You used mine," George said reproachfully, rubbed at the bruised muscle.

"No, I didn't."

"Yes, you did. A bunch of times."

"No, I didn't. Now hurry up and let's get going."

"But shouldn't we tie her up again?"

Apparently the answer was negative on the restraints, for which I was thankful.

I tried sitting up to see where we were going, but that was pushing it. George turned instantly. "My brother may be a pansy when it comes to *necessary force*, but I'm not."

He began to rustle in the glove box. "Ouch!" he yipped, drawing back, then attacking the box with a vengeance. Papers went flying; maps hit the floor until he found what he wanted. He turned toward me with the fierceness of a wounded Doberman. I had just enough time to see what it was before the needle stabbed into my arm. "Lay down, lady. And stay down."

I managed one last look around before I fell back into the sleeping bags. It was getting a little lighter now but there was nothing to see besides the lush canopy of the Pacific Northwest forest: Douglas fir, huckleberry; arbutus trees. Out there somewhere were mule deer, elk, chipmunks, and red squirrel—maybe even a cougar, but we'd never get a glimpse of her.

Suddenly I was very tired. Even though it was summer, the morning was cool, and I appreciated the warmth of my grubby cocoon. My eyelids slipped closed in spite of myself, and I was asleep before the big engine varroomed to life and the tires squelched out of the parking lot so I never got to see where we were going. If I had, it probably wouldn't have made me feel any better.

Chapter 13

Cats have more than one hundred vocal sounds, while dogs have only about ten.

I was in the garden with my cats. The air was filled with their song—everything from Violet's tiny mew to Little's percussive maow-maow-maow to Harry's basso profundo yowl. They were all happy sounds though, a sort of feline symphony.

I didn't think it strange that they were outside; I was in the moment. Harry and Little chased each other through the bayberry bushes—it was always so good to see the old cat play. Red was stretched out on a sunny flagstone like a great orange tiger. Violet had found a perfect hideaway under the broad leaves of a hosta, her considerable bulk hidden in the lush green shadow and only her sweet white and gray face in view. Solo was on my lap, purring up a storm. As I stared lovingly down at her, I realized how remarkable an event this was. She rarely came out of hiding, let alone onto my lap. I stroked her silk milk fur, just thankful for her presence.

Suddenly I tensed. Where was Fraulein Fluffs? I looked around but there was no sign of her. I realized I hadn't seen her all morning. Had I taken her back to the shelter for some reason unrecalled? It didn't seem likely; I had no memory of doing anything like that.

I didn't want to upset Solo, her visits were so precious, but my concern for Fluffs wouldn't quit. It wasn't just the fact that I couldn't see her; there were hundreds of hiding places in the garden for a tiny gray cat. It was more than that. I had the gut-twisting feeling she was in trouble.

Solo must have sensed my apprehension because she sprang from my lap and hightailed it into the house through the open sliding door. I stood, scanning for Fluffs but to no avail.

Everything was quiet, too quiet. Where were Harry and Little who had a moment ago been wrestling in the grass? There was no sign of them either. Had they followed Solo into the house? If so, I hadn't noticed. My bad feeling was beginning to morph into full-blown anxiety. I figured I'd better get Red and Violet into my care before they both ran off as well.

My eyes surfed the patio, but Red's sunny spot was empty. Violet was no longer under the hosta. I surveyed the yard in panic: Not a cat in sight!

Suddenly I noted that the gate was wide open. It hadn't been that way before, had it? I couldn't have made such an oversight. Could I? But done is done, and now the cats might be anywhere—out on the sidewalk, in the street!

I was running for the gate, but as I pushed through, I slammed into someone I hadn't noticed before. Rough arms held me prisoner; though the face was a blank, dark blur, I knew instantly who it was.

"Let me go! I need to find my cats."

"Don't bother," said the smooth voice. "Your cats are gone."

"Gone where?" I wailed in terror.

"Gone forever," he replied, solemn as a judge.

I came too with a start. I was stiff, hot, and beginning to suffocate underneath the sleeping bags. As I battled to pull them off and found my hands bound together, it all came back to me. Even so, I was relieved. It had been a dream; even being carried off by the Badass brothers was preferable to the shattering loss of my cats.

We were still bumping along what seemed to be a rough gravel road. From where I lay on the seat of the Ford, I could see the backs of the two men's heads, one matted as an unkempt Persian and the other sleek and dark as a panther. And these guys were brothers? Maybe the fraternal reference had been only a figure of speech.

My eyes moved to the window and what little I could see from my disadvantaged vantage point. More trees, more forest, but the dark fir fans had given way to lacier long-needled pine. This meant we were moving up in elevation. Where could they possibly be taking me? They had the stone, both stones as far as I knew. If it had been my caper, I would have been long gone by now.

George glanced back at me and I quickly closed my eyes to feign sleep. No need for him to know just yet that I was awake and ready for more abuse.

"Darn it, Larry. Why'd we have to bring her along?" George sniveled. "I could have just done her right there."

The high, slightly feminine whine didn't jibe at all with his nasty character. I might have found it amusing under different circumstances.

"You're not *doing* anyone anywhere!" Larry proclaimed. "We're not murderers."

"Yeah, but this is a pain in the rear. And she could still identify us, long as she's alive."

"No, she can't. You gave her enough temazepam to scramble her memory good. It's all going to be a fog by the time she gets out of here. We wouldn't have this problem if you'd got the diamond back the first time around."

George grumbled something unintelligible.

"Yeah, I know," Larry acquiesced. "That pond was a better hiding place than you thought—even you couldn't find the rock. It took a cat..."

"Shut up," grouched George.

"A little pussy cat," Larry taunted.

George swung around and for a moment, I thought he was going to punch the other man. "Shut up! I had to be fast. Someone could have recognized me."

"If you hadn't got yourself picked up by the cops," Larry snapped, "it wouldn't have been a problem. That lawyer cost us half our get-away cash, you know."

George's anger deflated in a hiss of beer breath that I could smell all the way in the back seat. "He got me off, didn't he?"

"It is what it is," Larry sighed.

I waited to hear more but apparently the conversation was over. We jogged ahead in silence until my body betrayed me and I sneezed. Just a tiny a-choo, but there was no more pretending.

"Good morning, Miz Cannon," Larry said as politely as if he were greeting me at a breakfast meeting.

I harrumphed back, then added a curt *good morning*. Being kidnapped is no excuse for rudeness, I told myself.

"Did you sleep well?"

"Where are we?" I asked as I tried to wriggle upright. I kept an eye on George for any type of tackle, but he seemed to be asleep now or maybe just powered down like a robot.

Badass didn't answer. He kept his eyes on the road, for which I was thankful, seeing that it was really just a narrow, rutted path climbing straight up the side of the mountain. The view was stunning. Far below, a silver

ribbon wound its way through the deep green valley;
boats, tiny as fleas, dotted the bright water. *Roll on,
Columbia, roll on.*

My heart raced. This place made the middle of
nowhere look urban, and here I was with not the choicest
of company. I should probably have stayed quiet but the
curious cat in me wanted answers.

"What are you going to do with me?" I demanded,
trying to sound ever so composed, but "Please, please let
me go!" burst out right afterwards, blowing the whole
brave facade.

Larry didn't answer. The car slid to a bumpy stop. Out
the front window, I could see an old traffic barrier, its
black and yellow paint flaked and peeling. Beyond that
was only bush and more bush. We had come to the end of
the road.

After a moment, Larry turned to look at me with dark,
emotionless eyes. "That's just what we're going to do."

"Huh?"

He nodded to the door handle. "You want out? Then
get out. Go!"

"What? Here?" I asked incredulously.

He reached around and pulled the handle himself. The
heavy door swung wide, and I nearly tumbled onto the
dry clay roadbed. Awkwardly I righted myself.

"Okay, sure." I held up my hands.

He stared at them blankly.

I shoved my bound wrists in his face. "Aren't you
going to untie me?"

He pushed them aside. "You're a smart old lady. You'll
get it off in no time. Now here's the thing." He took a deep
breath. "We're not murderers. All we wanted were the
diamonds. When we get them into the hands of our buyer,

our work is done. That will be very soon. Then we'll disappear, and neither the Portland Police nor the FBI nor you are ever going to see us again."

"You sound pretty sure of yourself."

"Oh, I'm sure. Very sure. I'm also sure that while we're doing our deal, you'll have your hands full..." He laughed, a hoarse snort, and flicked a long finger at my bonds. "Excuse the joke. You'll be busy making your way back down the mountain. It's a better solution than some, don't you agree?"

Better than being thrown over the side of the boat, I guessed, but hiking would be no easy task for me either. "That's ridiculous!" I said before I could stop myself. "I'm still recovering from a broken leg, as you very well know since you're the one who put me in the hospital."

Larry draped his arm over the seat and coolly clasped his hands together. He looked me in the eye as if I were a colleague. "I have to say I'm sorry about that, I really am. If you'd only handed over the Babylon, none of this would have happened."

"But I didn't have it. I didn't know it was in my pool until today—I mean yesterday?" I shook my head as a wave of absolute confusion swept over me. "That first one..."

"The Burma," he said almost reverently.

"If you say so. It just appeared out of the blue. It was a complete mystery to me." I didn't mention that for all intents and purposes, the mystery had been solved when Harry pulled the second stone out of the water. His discovery gave new meaning to the old adage, look what the cat dragged in.

"I believe you... now. But at the time, we thought otherwise. Again I apologize."

"What were they doing there anyway? The stones."

"We really have to be going," Larry sidestepped. "You should be able to make it to the bottom of the hill before dark. There's a pay phone at the boat dock. Don't bother looking for the boat, it's long gone."

He swung back around into driving position and punched his partner on the shoulder. George woke with flailing arms and a mouth full of oaths. His noxious breath wafted through the air like poison.

"Get out and help me turn around," Larry commanded. He looked over his shoulder, all geniality gone from his face. "If you don't want George's assistance, you'd better start moving."

George grinned lasciviously at me before he jumped out and went around behind the big Ford. I took the cue—I didn't want that thug anywhere near me. Standing shakily, I balanced my weight against the car, trying to get all my stiff parts functioning and my head out of the benzo cloud. With a little impetus I stumbled behind the road barrier. Feeling slightly safer with a substantial obstacle between myself and my nemeses, I turned to watch.

Larry had got the car swung sideways with the old back and forth technique: back a few feet, turn the wheel, forward a few feet, repeat *ad nauseam*. George shouted directions but from what I saw, they weren't all that helpful—the big Ford landed in the bushes more than once, where it took great revving of engines and spinning of tires to get it back out again.

Finally they had made the circle. George slung himself back into the car and they were off bouncing down the hill in a puff of dust. Such a strong sense of relief flooded over me I almost passed out.

Bracing myself against the barrier, I took the next few

moments to burn everything I knew about Larry, George, and their car, a green Ford station wagon with a mud-caked—and therefore unreadable—license plate, into my Swiss-cheese memory. One thing the Badass boys hadn't reckoned with was my previous experience with drugs. (I think I mentioned I'd been somewhat of a flower child back in the day?) Though the *downers*, as we called them in the Summer of Love, had made me tired and groggy, I knew how to *maintain*, which is Hippie for *keep my head together*.

As the crunch of the tires receded, the chatter of birds took its place—that, and an echoing silence so profound it hurt my ears. I looked around. The relief dwindled as I fully comprehended where I was, which was nowhere. The Badass brothers said I could reach civilization, or at least a telephone, by nightfall, but they were young and strong—what did they know of limitations like a bum leg and a diminished sense of balance? And if I didn't make it? The day was lovely—warm sun, blue sky—but night would be a whole different story. I wasn't really afraid of being eaten by bears, and it might almost be worth it to be confronted by a wild cat just to catch a glimpse of such a beautiful feline. No, I was mostly afraid of myself. Imagination can do strange things to the psyche. It had been a long time since I'd camped out. Moss and leaves could not compete with my Memory Foam pillowtop mattress; nuts and berries, of which there were few to none until later in the season, were no match for the piece of Chinook salmon in fresh yogurt dill sauce that I had waiting in my refrigerator; and I won't even get started on the bathroom situation.

There was only one thing to do—get going and get to that phone, the sooner the better. First, though, I needed to free my hands. My balance, as I mentioned, was not that of a ballerina, and navigating down the steep, bumpy hill would require equilibrium. Besides, my hands were turning an odd shade of mottled mauve from having the blood cut off at the wrists. Trouble was, I needed my hands to untie the knot that tied my hands. See the problem?

Maneuvering myself onto a fallen log, I examined my dilemma. Sure enough, the ties were jersey, probably a tee shirt in a former life. Jersey was a stretchy fabric, but it had been pulled tight and wound in figure eights around my wrists. Luckily I'd had myriad experiences with tangles throughout my lifetime: afghan yarn, fishing line, kids' shoelaces. This knot actually looked pretty basic. Whoever had done it—George I guessed—had substituted quantity for quality. Once I managed to pull apart the first loop with my teeth, the rest were easy.

I stuffed the strip of tee shirt in the pocket of my summer dress—you never knew when you might need to tie something—and began the weary trek back down the way we had come. At least I wasn't going to get lost; the clay track that turned into a gravel road somewhere along the line should take me directly to the dock.

As I had predicted, the going wasn't easy. Though it was a straight shot, the roadbed was pitted and strewn with loose gravel, making the steep incline even more precarious. More than once I nearly fell on my bum, which may be comic on America's Funniest Videos but in real life was no laughing matter. My leg hurt and I hadn't been kidnapped in hiking shoes. The little pink sandals were reasonably sturdy but certainly never intended to see terrain more challenging than my back yard. Which is where I'd still be if I had my way.

I thought of Frannie lying on the kitchen floor.

I thought of my cats and my dream.

It was about then I decided to stop thinking. No good was going to come of it.

I managed to get into a rhythm, timing my steps with my breathing as I'd learned to do back before walking was a challenge sport. With the help of frequent rest stops, I felt like I was making good time. I won't say it wasn't taxing; that would be a lie because it was. I hadn't had so much exercise since last year's Walk for the Cure. But there was no point in complaining and no one to complain to except myself, and I hate complainers!

The sun had hit high noon and was now declining toward the west, but by my calculation, there were still several hours to go before it set. My fear of not making touchdown by nightfall was evaporating the farther I got, and beneath the tiredness, I felt a sort of elation.

It had been a while since I'd had a glimpse of the river, so I couldn't gage my actual progress. The curve ahead looked promising though. If there weren't too many trees in the way, I should have a good view of the valley.

As I rounded the sharp bend, I stopped and stared, but it wasn't at the view—it was at the road. *Roads.* Ahead, the track suddenly diverged into two, one aimed downward and the other veered off to the right. I must have been passed out when we came by before, because this was a total surprise, throwing all my calculations to the wind. It had never occurred to me I would have to make a choice.

I walked to the crux of the Y and gazed both directions. It seemed like I should be able to tell which one we had come up, see traces of the big Ford's passing, but the dry clay was aggravatingly clear. The only tracks were old ruts from back when the road was muddy. I'm sure the CSI team could have figured it out in a heartbeat, but to me, the layperson, one was as likely as the other.

Okay, what would Horatio Caine do besides stand there and look cool in his black sunglasses? Process the information. That's what I had to do: process the information.

I walked around the Y, checking the place where the road bisected. Studying the tread marks, I noted a continuous track curving around from the right-hand side, but that only proved it had been used sometime last spring. It seemed more logical to take the downward way since down was where I wanted to go.

Down it was then, and I was off and running, figuratively speaking of course.

Chapter 14

You don't often hear about cats who save the day, but there are plenty of feline heroes. In documented incidents, cats have rescued humans from fires, snakes, sexual assault, carbon monoxide poisoning, heart failure, seizures, and dangerously low blood sugar levels. There is even a case of a cat dialing 911 when his owner fell from his wheelchair.

I tried to view the intersection as a good sign. I was reaching a road more traveled. With renewed energy I picked up my pace. I was so ready to get the whole thing behind me and move on to safer things, like reading a book with a cat on the lap. That would be heaven! I couldn't keep my mind from wandering though, no matter how hard I tried. I was tired of walking, my leg was killing me, I had a headache from whatever—no food, no water, being drugged, take your pick, but instead of feeling depressed by my misfortune, I was getting madder by the moment.

How could those creeps have done this to me? What did I ever do to them besides mess up their plans, which wasn't my fault or intention? Boy, when I got to that phone, first call would be to the police—Detective Croft! No, nine-one-one! This was an emergency, after all. Someone needed to pick those guys up before they vanished into thin air. And someone needed to pick me up too. I waffled as to which should be first on the list.

I was so caught up in my hissy fit that I didn't notice

how steep the grade had become until my legs slipped out from under me and I went skidding down a few bumpy yards on my backside. Landing in a pothole, I saw now what I should have noticed before. Not only was the road heading precariously down at a slope unlikely to be managed by anything other than an ATV, but it had also gotten much narrower as well. Glancing back the way I'd come, it seemed now more like a runoff than a road. The ruts had gone from two to one, from tire tracks to watershed. With a shock, I realized no car, let alone the big Ford, had come this way today or any other day. I had made the wrong choice.

That's when I finally put my head in my hands and cried. I'd made it through the abduction, the bondage, the terror of being left alone at the top of a mountain with a broken leg. I'd toughed out the long trek down, ignoring the multitudinous pains and pushing the panic aside. But now I'd have to go back, retrace my steps—and some very difficult steps at that since from where I sat, the road seemed steep as a ladder—and start all over again. The sun was already low in the western sky; at this rate I'd never make it back before dark. I suddenly had this perception of myself as a tiny, near invisible pinpoint in a very large domain, extremely insignificant in the order of things. I couldn't have felt any smaller had I been a dwarf star at the edge of the universe, which made me weep all the more.

And then it happened, the little miracle that instantly restored my faith in a power greater than myself. It came in the form of a tiny sound that meant everything to me.

I heard a meow. The quiet little prrrfp of a cat in greeting. Looking up through my tears, I saw her, a wiry tabby shorthair with a smiling face and curious green-gold eyes. She rubbed her sideburns against my knee, then gazed up at me, cocked her head and gave another little prrrfp.

She jumped in my lap where she immediately curled up and began to purr. I was elated, and it wasn't just because I loved cats—this was sure to have its practical side too. The tabby was no feral; a feral cat would have come nowhere near me, being deathly afraid of humans by nature. And a feral wouldn't have a little green collar with a gold heart-shaped tag that gave her name as Tammy. I discarded the possibility that she was as lost; she was well-fed and groomed and obviously cared-for. No, this cat belonged to someone, and that someone was nearby.

"Tammy," I croaked, my voice surprising me with its roughness. "Where did you come from? Are you here to help me, sweetie?"

With a little yow, she hopped to the ground and began to saunter along the road, black-ringed tail held high in the air. After a short way, she stopped and looked back at me.

Now, I don't pretend to be a psychic or even a cat whisperer, whatever that might be, but communication is communication, and I knew cats well enough to get that she was going somewhere, and I was invited to come along. Since I didn't have anything else on my agenda, I accepted. Wherever she was headed, it had to be better than where I was now.

Hefting my aching body off the ground, I carefully picked my way down the hill behind her. I didn't for a moment think she would lead me astray. No, most likely she was going home to where the food was. And where her people were. And a phone and some water and a chair where I could rest on something softer than clay and pebbles until someone came to take me away. Obviously anyone who cohabited with this beautiful feline would be nice and sympathetic and helpful, and then all my troubles would be over.

Tammy was a great scout leader. She didn't run ahead, and when I lagged; she waited for me. Soon we left the road for a well-trodden path that broke off at an angle, and the walking became easier. Suddenly the pain seemed to lift. Once again I saw the beauty of the dappled sunlight through the trees and heard the quiet wonder of the wilderness. I could hear something else too. Rushing water. The sound grew closer, the path grew lighter and then we were there.

I can't describe the pure joy that overwhelmed me when I saw the house. I don't know if it was my compromised state of health or a leftover effect of the drugs in my system, but the place glowed with the inner light of a Kinkade painting. The low wood and stone cottage, the blooming Japanese lilac tree, the babbling brook that ran behind—it all seemed enchanted. For a moment I wondered if the whole thing was a dream, and I was still sitting in a pothole in the middle of nowhere. Then all wondering ceased and so did my consciousness. I remember slumping in slow motion, deflating like a balloon until I was lying on the thick grass. A wet nose touched my cheek, and a big green-gold eye blocked my view. My own eyes slipped closed. The river sounds intensified until they became the rushing of my blood and the beating of my heart. When they receded again, I was down for the count.

* * *

I woke on a sofa in what had to have been the living room of the little house. Tammy was lying on my chest, purring merrily. Someone was trying to lift her off and I instinctively reached up to stop them.

"Let her stay," I whispered.

I felt pressure as Tammy settled back down.

"She's awake," said a male voice, and I found myself staring up at a young paramedic.

"How do you feel?" he asked.

"Okay I guess. Kind of dizzy. And my leg hurts," I added.

"We're taking you to the hospital now, is that okay?"

I wasn't sure what to say: if I consented to go to the hospital, I would have to leave the cat behind, and I was really loving her curative attention. On the other hand, I probably could use a check-up after what I'd been through, and Tammy's family might not want me as a permanent fixture on their couch. "Okay," I said, then added, "What hospital?"

"Longview General."

"We're in Washington?"

The paramedic exchanged concerned glances with his partner. "That's right, ma'am."

"Oh. Well then, thanks," I said. "And thanks to you, Tammy, for rescuing me." I held her close as I sat up, watching with amusement the doubtful look on the young man's face.

"I talk to them all the time," I said to put his mind to rest, but it seemed only to confuse him all the more.

"To who?" he asked.

"Cats, of course."

He stared at me and then shrugged. "Don't worry, ma'am. We'll have you to the hospital in no time. Make sure you tell the doctor all about this when we get there."

* * *

I won't bore you with the ambulance ride or the black comedy of trying to check into emergency without an advocate or an insurance card. Or any other ID for that matter, since the Badass brothers had forgotten to let me collect my purse before they spirited me away. Actually it's all a little hazy anyway. I remember being grateful beyond measure that I was safe; I kept saying thanks to anyone and everyone who came near me until finally they gave me something for anxiety which put me into a deep, restful sleep, for which I was also very thankful.

They kept me overnight, during which time a parade of law enforcement officers came to take my statement. I was happy to turn the whole business over to them. If I never heard of Larry and George Badass again in my life it would be too soon. Of course I knew that wasn't to be; I'd have to testify at the trial. That idea brought a whole plethora of revenge possibilities to contemplate in between naps.

Special Agent Connie Lee came to pick me up in the Humane Investigations van as soon as I was discharged. She was perfect, first letting me know that my cats were fine and that after a few hours' observation at the ER, Frannie had been sent home with a Band-Aid and a headache—head wounds bleed a lot and it had looked far worse than it was. For the rest of the hour's drive down the I-5 freeway, she shut up and let me think my thoughts. I had given her the condensed version of my adventure, the same cut-and-dried report I gave the police. Being plucked like a helpless kitten out of the sanctity of my own home had been psychologically devastating. I wasn't ready to delve any further into the ramifications of what had happened to me just yet, and maybe never.

Connie had my key and let me into my house. Little

met me in the front hall, telling me all about her experiences, thoughts, and dreams since she last saw me. I scooped her up and held her close, but she wasn't ready to forgive me for abandoning her and leapt away, using my chest as a springboard. Even the sting of her sharp back claws felt like bliss.

Connie came in with me, picked up my mail, opened the blinds, and checked unobtrusively for burglars. It felt a little weird to have someone else doing for me what I should be doing for myself, but I was mentally and physically exhausted, so I let her futz around the place like a mama hen.

"Can I get you anything? Make some tea?" she asked.

I was still standing in my hallway, breathing in the scent of home and wondering if I could ever trust it again. "No, Connie. I just want to take a bath and lie around with my cats. Thanks anyway."

She nodded. "I'll see ya at the shelter then." Hefting her utility belt higher on her substantial hips, she went to the door. "I know it's like closing the barn door after the mare's escaped but make sure you lock up and set your alarm when I leave."

"I will—I promise. I'll probably be scared to go outside for a while." I gave a feeble laugh.

"You'll be fine soon enough," she told me. "Give yourself time."

"Thanks for the ride. I really appreciate it. Longview's a little out of your way."

"Na, not at all. I was up in Kalama anyway, a deposition in an interstate abuse case. He's goin' down!" she added with a smile and a fist pump.

I watched her jog down the steps to her van, wishing for a moment that I were as fit as the young agent. Then the Badass Boys wouldn't have had a chance!

I closed the door on my fantasy. With the click of the latch, the street sounds, birdcalls, and hum of the city cut off, and in the pulsing silence, a cold tendril of paranoia wormed its way into my mind. I shook my head to dislodge it; there was no way I was going to let those hoodlums back in—to my mind *or* my house! Ferociously I punched the alarm into activity and felt slightly more empowered. Time to locate the rest of the cats.

Red had ventured out to greet me now that the scary Connie had left; he really was a one-person cat. I didn't bother to reach down to pet him because I knew he'd just run away. He only liked to be petted when he couldn't see my feet, such as while sitting on a couch or bed. I could extrapolate what that behavior implied for the one-time stray but would rather concentrate on the fact that he now had a good home and would never have to fear feet again for the rest of his life.

"Hi, everybody. I'm home," I called.

Red jumped on the couch, looking back at me as if to say, *Come pet me now.* I gave him a rub down his long back and tail, for which he shivered with ecstasy.

Dirty Harry was in his donut. He looked up sleepily, purred when I scratched his head and then bit me softly to welcome me home. I felt better already!

Little had curled up on the striped Mexican blanket that hung over the back of the couch and was giving me the cold shoulder.

"Fluffs? Violet? Solo?"

With a petite mew that belied her voluminosity, Violet waddled out of the kitchen licking her lips. She studied me with her lovely eyes then turned and retreated back from whence she had come. I followed her and saw her motivation: Someone had fed the cats in my absence, and by fed, I meant gave them great heaping bowls of kibbles and three full plates of wet food. The contents were well-diminished now, but that's where Violet was headed. I let her go. Diet tomorrow, I figured. Today we celebrate.

I was relieved to find the cleaning fairies had cleansed Frannie's blood from the kitchen floor. I couldn't even see where the deed had been done, though I admit I didn't get down and inspect with a magnifying glass.

After a short lovefest with Violet, I went to look for Solo and Fluffs. Solo was a cinch, ensconced in her favorite hiding place under the couch.

"Hi, sweetie," I said. She blinked her blue-green eyes at me in a cat smile that told me she was glad I was home.

Only one to go. I wasn't sure where Fluffs might be— she changed spots with great regularity—but after a cursory and unproductive search downstairs, I had a feeling I knew where to find her.

As I pulled myself up the long flight of steps, I realized how sore I was. The pain killers must have been wearing off because every muscle ached, every joint felt as if it had been packed with sand. Somehow I made it to my bedroom and sure enough, there she was, curled into a perfect fluffy circle on the velvet quilt. I flopped down beside her with a sigh of relief. All cats present and accounted for; I was home in one piece. As I stroked the silken fur and listened to her soft but potent purr, I could think of nothing else I wanted in the whole wide world. A million dollars would have only detracted from the moment, and don't even get me started on diamonds. Brown, white, or unicorn-purple, I wouldn't be comfortable with that precious stone again for a long, long time.

Chapter 15

Some cats like to take walks. They can't wait to don harness and leash because they know it means a trip outside. Others, once the harness is on, act like they've been put into a strait jacket. I had a cat who could escape any harness with one quick Houdini twist. Start them young so they get used to the feel, and always purchase quality equipment.

The annual Portland Highland Games were held on the third weekend of July. My clan, Clan MacKay, had a booth in the upper field of the Mt. Hood Community College campus, along with forty-some other sons and daughters of Scotland.

MacCay, MacGaa, MacKee, McKee, Mackie, MacQuey, McCoy, McKay, Mackay, Mackey—I didn't know much about my ancestors on the Scottish shores, but the American faction were descended from my fourth-great-grandfather, John McKy of Lothian, who came across the pond in 1726. His gravestone, a seven-foot granite slab, still lies in the Timber Ridge Cemetery in Rockbridge, Virginia, though I've never seen it myself. Because of this, my grandmother had always considered herself a Scot even though she was born in Ridgefield, Washington and only one of her line hailed back to the bonnie highlands. I was raised with a love of all things Scottish: the Highland Fling, the tartan and thistle. Granna was long gone now, but my membership in the Clan MacKay Society keeps her close to my heart.

The clan society was founded in 1806 and claims to be one of the oldest in Scotland. Our little twenty-first century Portland order was somewhat less impressive: aside from our genealogical studies and a few talks at schools and luncheons, we of the motto *Manu Forti* (With a Strong Hand) were basically a social club, enjoying a modicum of charity work with a few ceilidhs and dinners throughout the year. Our grand event was the Highland Games where we passed out flyers on Clan MacKay, offered ancestry tips, and generally chatted with anyone and everyone who looked interested.

There were four of us manning the small open-air tent: Erin McKee, a young PSU student with lovely green eyes and curly hair the color we used to call strawberry blonde; Gordon Jones, a freelance architect, forty-five and a hunk in a kilt; and my old friend, Halle MacKay Pratt, a sixty-eight-year-old crime lawyer from Portland who also thought herself a hunk in a kilt.

Halle expressed her personal diversity by wearing full manly Highland garb instead of the usual ladies' skirt and sash, and I loved her for it. She was my liaison with the law, always there to answer questions and give legal advice, though I was glad to say I had not yet needed her in her official capacity. I saw Erin occasionally at the cat shelter when she brought in strays she had found, or should I say strays who found her; cats knew instinctively she was a soft touch for a meal and a bed. I'd only just met Gordon, but he seemed like a bright young man, and I was looking forward to getting to know him better.

I had brought Little with me to the games because although she's an indoor cat, she likes traveling and meeting new people. She's a great draw for the crowd, sitting by the glossy brochures or basking in her tartan bed like a queen. I always put her in a harness and leash in case something scares her and she tries to bolt, but she's amazingly unflappable and there hasn't been a problem yet.

I liked our location because it was close enough to the heavy athletics area for us to watch the competitions: the Throwing of the Hammer; the Tossing of the Weights and Sheaf; the Putting of the Stone where brave and burly Oregon-Scots threw big boulders around the field as if they were skipping rocks across a lake. The average stone weighed between sixteen and twenty-six pounds, but the signature event was the pitching of the ninety-six-pound Portland Stone, harvested from the local Sandy River. Really.

The Mac MacTarnahan Memorial Challenge Caber Toss was held in the main field below, and each year our group would draw straws for who got to go watch. This was my lucky year, and leaving Little in Erin's capable hands—she and Little had a thing going—I hurried down the walkway and into the sweeping grandstand. The bleachers were full, the Tossing of the Caber being a high point of the games, right along with the Kilted Mile and the Salute of the Massed Pipe Bands, but I managed to find a seat by the aisle halfway down. I scrunched my pleated tartan skirt underneath my bum and scooched into the hard wooden pew. A kilted gentleman with an incongruous orange Mohawk gave me a nod of greeting and moved over a few inches. I smiled in thanks, even though he wore the red, green, and gold of a Cameron, one-time enemies of the MacKays. At the Highland Games, all animosity was left at the gate. Men in skirts and women with daggers in their aprons had to stick together, no matter from which burgh or shire their ancestors hailed.

The Toss was already underway, and I had no idea who was the favorite, but I didn't care. I just liked to watch those beefy guys in their Scottish finery heft trees into the air. Who wouldn't? It was mid-July, ninety degrees in the sun; the caber weighed around fifty kilograms which translated into over a hundred pounds. I shook my head, wondering again how such a thing could be done.

Clan MacKay usually offered a contender, Don MacKay, but he was down with a cold. Isn't there a platitude about the lion being brought down by the mouse? Or is that the elephant? I don't remember right now. Anyway, our bonnie lad had been felled, not by a broadsword but by a microscopic virus.

There were several other worthy contestants though, eight in all. Some were the same men who had been throwing the stones, hammers, and weights earlier on, and it seemed they should be tired by now, but you'd never know it by watching them.

Tossing the caber is harder than it looks, and it looks impossible. First, from a crouching position, the thrower has to lift the pole by lacing his fingers underneath the stump. He carefully hefts it to his waist; then, running to build momentum, he launches. For it to count, the base must rise at least nineteen feet straight up in the air. The goal is to get it to pivot or turn on its top, then fall over in a straight line away from him, the base at the twelve o'clock position. I'm always amazed that they can get it up in the first place, and for every good throw there were many bad ones.

I was just mulling over the question of where one might practice for such a sport—it's not like you could go down to the local gym—when I felt a tap on my shoulder. I looked up and saw Erin. Her young face held a worried frown.

"Lynley?" she shouted over the enthusiastic roar of the crowd. "You need to come back to the booth."

I stood automatically. "Why, what's happened? Is it Little?" I asked in a panic.

"No, it's nothing like that." She looked around guiltily. I found the fact that never once did her gaze fall on the caber toss or the lovely men doing the tossing more alarming than her dire summons.

"Just come," she charged, then turned and started back up the steps.

This time I followed without question.

When we got out of the stadium and the noise died down enough to talk, I caught her arm. "Okay, Erin, what's going on?"

She spun around to face me. "Oh, Lynley! It's the police!"

I sagged with relief; as usual for the human species, I had envisioned the worst, and a chat with Portland's finest wasn't it by a long run. I'll admit I hadn't been too hot on cops when I was a young hippie—back then, it was us versus the Establishment—but I'd got over my paranoia somewhere around the same time I quit smoking pot. Funny how that happened.

"I'm sure it's nothing to worry about, Erin. I've had plenty of interaction with the police since the, uh..." I still had trouble talking about my incident with the Badass brothers. "You know. They probably need a signature or another go-around about what happened. Something like that."

Erin looked doubtful. "I hope so," was all she said.

Wordlessly we continued up the path. Something was nagging at the back of my mind, having to do with the lameness of what I had just told her. Sure enough, I'd seen my share of the cops lately, but if a signature were needed, wouldn't they have called on a weekday? And as to another go-around, why would they have bothered to trace me all the way to the games?

My uncertainty grew when I got to the field, and it virtually blossomed as I trod across the dry grass to our booth. When I was close enough to see the look on the officers'—there were three of them!—faces, uncertainty became apprehension and apprehension quickly morphed into alarm. There was something different about this crew. In all my recent run-ins with the long arm of the law, I'd never felt this vibe before.

One of the officers broke from the rest as I approached. "Lynley Cannon?" she said, her expression an absolute deadpan.

"Yes?"

"I'm Officer Mae Wong and these are Officers Bob Sterling and Chuck Lewis." In perfect synchronization, the three whipped out identification. The laminated cards flashed briefly in the sun before being returned to blue uniformed obscurity. "Will you come with us please?" Wong's words were polite, but the tone indicated in no uncertain terms that this was a mandate, not a request.

"I'm sorry but where is it you want me to go?" I thought it was a perfectly reasonable question, but she looked at me as if I were resisting arrest. "To the downtown station," she begrudgingly informed.

"The station?" It sounded like something out of a cop-drama. "But why?"

This time I guess the question wasn't worth answering because she just stood there as if I'd never spoken.

I wasn't about to give up. "Now? You mean right

now?"

She nodded affirmation.

"Well, really I can't..." I stammered. "I mean I'm working here. I can't just leave everybody shorthanded. And what about Little? My cat," I added, gesturing to where the small panther was curled up in her bed, golden eyes fixed on Officer Wong's shiny badge.

"I apologize for the inconvenience." Back to the veil of courtesy.

I looked helplessly at Halle; as an attorney, maybe she had some notion of what was going on.

Halle stepped up to the brochure table, crossed her arms over her generous breasts, and eyed the crew. Her highland-red spiked hair glittered in the sun like the flame of justice. "Can you tell her what this is concerning?"

Officer Wong turned to the older woman. "And you are?"

Halle stood to her best five-foot-two. "Halle Pratt, attorney at law. I'm Ms. Cannon's lawyer."

Wong rolled her eyes, then looked back at her fellows. "Her attorney. Isn't that convenient?"

It was Sterling who answered. "This is regarding the suspicious deaths of George Sinclairii and Lawrence Sinclairii."

Halle's gaze shot to me and then back to the muscular policeman. "Suspicious deaths? You mean murder?"

"Alleged," said Wong.

"Is my client under arrest?" Halle's voice had become cold and formal. I could easily imagine her in a courtroom giving her best Perry Mason defense.

Wong glared at the lawyer. "Not at this time, no. We just have a few questions, that's all," she added dryly.

There may have been more dialogue; I'd stopped

listening. At the word *arrest*, I was off in a different sphere.

Lynley Mackey Cannon, you are under arrest on suspicion of the murder. You have the right to remain silent, but anything you do say can and will be held against you in a court of law — I'd heard it on every TV police show from Dragnet to Blue Bloods. Next would come the pat-down for weapons, the smooth steel of the cuffs.

Then something else struck me. "They're dead? The Badass... I mean the men who kidnapped me are dead?"

The officers were infuriatingly unforthcoming. I looked pleadingly at Halle.

"You'd better go with them, Lynley. If it's a murder case..." She let that last hang in the air like fly paper.

"What about Little? And you? The booth? The games?" I gestured feebly around the field. "I can't abandon the clan."

"I don't think you have much of a choice," Halle told me.

"I'll take care of Little," Erin volunteered. "We'll be fine. Won't we, Gordie?" She gave the brawny man a nudge.

"Ah, sure we will," he said. "Yeah, Lynley, no problem. Do what you gotta do."

It wasn't really the answer I wanted. I'd have preferred he said, *Don't go! We can't go on without you.* And then Officer Wong would say, *Well, I see you're really busy here. We'll come back later.* Or maybe even, *Sorry for wasting your time. We've changed our minds and won't be bothering you again, ever,* but I knew that was not to be.

"I'll come down when the games are over," said Halle.

"Okay," I replied without conviction. I'm not sure whether the assurance that I would be accompanied by a criminal lawyer made me feel better or worse.

I looked at my watch, the gold one that hung from the brooch on my sash. "But it's only three o'clock now. The games don't end until seven. You don't think I'll be there that long, do you?"

Halle said nothing which was answer enough.

As I was escorted off the field, I glanced back at the booth. Erin, Gordon, and Halle were gathered close; Little sat tall in her bed, watching me go. It was a perfect Scottish vignette in blue and emerald tartan. Their troubled faces said it all.

Other people were looking on as well; even the contestants on the heavy athletics field had paused their sport to follow my progress with the uniforms. I gave a shaky wave goodbye and tried to smile, telling myself it would be over soon. I'd just answer a few routine queries and that would be the end of it. We could all look back and laugh.

But in my head, a tiny voice screamed it might not be so easy.

* * *

Being a *person of interest* showed me a whole new side to the criminal justice system. Everyone had been so pleasant, sympathetic, and gracious when I had been the victim of a crime; now they were stoic, if not verging on hostile. Where before they had bent over backwards to expedite my needs, now it was a whole process of hurry up and wait just to go to the bathroom.

I found it really hard not to panic. There's something about being in police custody that automatically makes a person feel guilty. I hadn't killed anyone—I knew that much—but I was sure I'd done something illegal in my life, and maybe now the time had come for me to pay.

Though they had rushed me to the station, a massive concrete fortress in the heart of downtown Portland, as if it were a matter of life or death, once there I was taken into a spartan interrogation room where I sat, and sat, and sat. Well, it wasn't quite that simple. Before they could allow me in the area, I had to go through the metal detector to check for knives, guns, or screw drivers, then be patted down and my clothing inspected in case I wore exploding shoes.

I waited alone for over an hour in the close, quiet space listening to the tick-tick-tick of my antique watch. The sounds outside were muffled and vague like a television playing in another room. I could almost feel the isolation and despair of those who had come before me. Finally, just when I thought I would fall asleep, in came the detectives, a man and a woman wearing slightly tatty business suits. With great drama, they slapped down a sheaf of papers and a small tape recorder. The woman held a paper cup of water which she put in front of me. I eyed it warily, wondering if it were spiked with truth serum.

"They always ask," she said, reading my thoughts. "Figured I'd get it out of the way now so we don't have to interrupt the interview."

"Thank you," I said politely, but it fell on deaf ears.

"I'm Detective Dean," she said disinterestedly.

"Detective Soo," the man took up like an echo. "Our department has been brought in on this case by the Cowlitz County Prosecutor's office."

Then the two fell silent.

I restrained myself from asking what we were waiting for; I'd learned long ago in my counter-culture youth not to volunteer a single word to the police beyond what was asked. Times have changed and I hadn't thought of the law as an adversary for many decades, but at the moment, caution seemed best.

The door clanged open and in walked Detective Marsha Croft carrying her ever-present laptop. I sighed with relief to see the familiar face. She had been so compassionate when I was beaten and then kidnapped. She knew my story; if anyone could straighten out this mess, it was Croft.

"Marsha...," I began with a smile.

"Detective Croft, please, Ms. Cannon," she said stiffly as she skidded out the metal chair and sat down across from me. There was no compassion in her face now.

Chapter 16

A cat's brain and a human brain have many similarities. Both have identical regions responsible for emotion.

I had nothing but questions, but so did she, and her questions eclipsed mine. Luckily Halle showed up about the time the interview got past name, date, and other mundane statistics. She had left the games early, enlisting an unsuspecting cousin to take her place. Though I felt guilty for being the cause of this fiasco, I was sincerely thankful she was there.

I thought we looked a great pair in our full Highland dress, though it didn't seem to intimidate our interviewers. The police had confiscated Halle's Sgian Dubh, the black knife she wore in her stocking, somewhat muting the *Ladies from Hell* ferocity that marked the kilted regiments as they charged across the heathered hills, bagpipes blaring; sporrans swinging; broadswords, dirks, halbard axes, and the infamous two-handed Claymore to the fore.

Though on television the interrogation is portrayed as the crux of the investigation where the detectives shout and the perps bluster and deny, then waive their rights and finally confess their crimes, real life was a whole different matter. My interview was a monotone of repetitive questions, some puerile and brainless, others so complex and bizarre they were impossible to answer. I hadn't been Mirandized since I wasn't officially being held in police custody, but Halle advised me to cooperate. Each time a question was posed, I'd look at her; she'd either nod or shake her head. If she nodded, I answered with full disclosure; if she gave me a negative, I graciously declined.

The detectives asked all the obvious ones: Did I know the victims? Did I own a gun? Did I know the location of two very valuable chocolate diamonds? They also quizzed me on things that had nothing to do with the brothers Badass as far as I could see, such as when was the last time I'd been out of state and what make of car did I own, as well as a number of personal queries that, in my unofficial opinion, were none of their business. Detective Croft made me go through the kidnapping once again, from sitting in my back yard with Frannie to waking up in Longview General.

This went on for three-and-a-half hours, not including the periodic breaks which were required by law. I was asked oh-so-politely to submit a voluntary DNA sample for their records. Halle objected on the grounds that I wasn't under arrest, but I overruled her, allowing an oversize Q-tip to be swabbed across the inside of my mouth which, in spite of the drinking water, was dry as kitty litter.

I'm not sure why I did it. I guess I hoped my cooperation would hurry things along. It didn't. By the time I was released, my belongings returned to me, and the obligatory mandate given that I was not to leave town, it was after ten o'clock at night.

* * *

Coming out of the station onto the brightly lit city streets, I felt a sudden blaze of gratitude for my freedom. You'd think I'd been in lock-up for the relief I felt upon pushing through those heavy metal doors. I skipped down the marble steps into the neon night. Everything was wonderful; even the bums in the park across the street seemed to be smiling.

I hit the sidewalk at a run, my tartan skirt swishing and my sash fluttering in the breeze.

"Lynley, hold up," Halle called. I stopped and turned to see the older woman shuffling breathily toward me. Halle, though basically healthy for her age, was a teeny bit portly and maybe just a speck out of shape.

With fond amusement I watched her chug up the sidewalk, a short Scottish steam engine puffing away. "Sorry, Halle," I said. "Just couldn't get out of there fast enough. What the flibbertigibbet was that all about anyway?"

Halle must have considered the question rhetorical because she didn't reply, and we set off to the car park at a more leisurely pace.

There's a popular local bumper sticker that reads *Keep Portland Weird*. I laughed, thinking we fit right in, costumed as we were. Then I noted the others on the nighttime street: the young rebels left from the Occupied protest; loud and fearless bands railing against society— what little they knew of it; the disenfranchised, lugging great bundles of plastic grocery bags, recyclable cans, Goodwill blankets, and sometimes a pet—everything they had on this earth; the loners slinking, head down, hands in pockets, from doorway to doorway—Artists? War veterans? Serial killers? Who knew? Those kinds of weird seemed a lot more solemn than a couple of old ladies playing dress-up.

Halle and I made it to the car without being mugged, murdered, or solicited for sex. I phoned Erin first thing to check on Little; Erin said she was set for the night and not to bother coming to get her until morning. That out of the way, I lapsed into a mindless daze. I was exhausted. It had been a long day, and though the interview was over, I had the nagging feeling it wasn't anywhere near finished yet.

Halle drove in silence as we sped across the Willamette River, clattering on the metal grid of the Hawthorne Bridge. I watched the lights stream by: Burgerville, Safeway, the Hot Dog Hut. The scenery grew more eclectic as we traveled up the trendy boulevard. Sign boards and security spots gave way to fairy lights and Japanese lanterns; warmth and color glowed from unique shops and restaurants that catered to a generation or two after mine.

We stopped at a red light beside the neon brilliance of the Bagdad Theater. A throwback to the flamboyant twenties, the vintage Arabian Nights-style movie palace had recently been refurbished into a theater brew-pub. The sidewalk tables were filled with happy imbibers, a new addition since I was a kid. Their youthful laughter wafted in through the open car window like honey on the tongue.

Farther on, the new New Seasons grocery was lit up like a rhinestone, but after that, the density waned. The grade began to steepen as we neared Mount Tabor, a dormant volcano masquerading as a small lump of grass and trees smack dab in the middle of southeast Portland. A few blocks before Hawthorne morphed into a one-lane road that wound its way into the hill park itself, we turned left onto a residential side street. Halle slowed, watching for cats who might dart out from behind parked cars, and other urban hazards. The houses lining the narrow lane were old, mostly Victorian though not the gaudy style that's come to be associated with the era. These were solid laborers' houses, remodeled, restored, or left to proudly decline in their old age.

Halle veered to the curb in front of my place, killed the engine, and sat, staring out the windshield at the night. "Lynley, what's going on?" she finally asked. Her voice sounded brash in the quiet.

"I don't know." I gave a little sigh. "I don't know anything about what happened to the brothers. And I really don't care," I added with all the spite I could muster in my wearied state. "I really haven't a clue why the police took me in."

She turned to me. I could see only her spiky silhouette against the streetlight. "They detained you because you're a suspect in a murder case." She paused. "Lynley, I think I'd better come in for a minute. We need to talk."

* * *

Tea and cookies with an old friend is usually a pleasant affair, but this was the exception. The Oolong tea was tasteless, and the shortbread cookies felt like dust in my mouth. The combination of exhaustion and anxiety had set off an unpleasant reaction in my nervous system, a sort of adrenaline angst that began as whiskers in my stomach and tickled out to every part of my body. My hands ached, my head was foggy, and I couldn't feel my toes. Even having Red on the back of the couch like a big orange pillow, Harry in his donut at my feet, and Fluffs curled up on my lap didn't make me feel better. Violet gazed at me from across the room, her eyes sad, as if she knew everything I was feeling. Drama is great fun when you're young, but there comes a time when a person grows up and sees it for what it is: an inconvenient pain in the rear that threatens one's quest for serenity.

I don't think Halle was faring much better. Her red spikes were wilting, her suntanned face was pale, and no amount of concealer could have hidden the worried bags under her eyes.

"I'm sorry to bring you into this," I told her for the umpteenth time.

"It's my choice, Lynley," she replied—again. "Not only are we proud descendants of the great MacKay clan; we're friends, and friends don't let friends go to jail if they can help it!" She smiled, but only for a moment. "Seriously, Lyn, I'm afraid this may become big trouble. I imagine they're going to want to speak to you again."

I'd had the same feeling, but still I asked, "Why? I've already told them everything I know."

"But they don't know that. As far as they're concerned, you could be lying through your teeth. That wasn't just some random query to see if you could assist them with their case; that was a real live suspect's interrogation. Which means they must have some kind of evidence that ties you to the murders."

"But what?" I exclaimed, sloshing tea onto my tartan skirt in my exuberance. "Bother! Now I've got to get it dry cleaned."

Halle dabbed the spot with her napkin. "Saltwater will take it out. Or a drop of mild shampoo. It's on the black, you'll never see it."

I set my mug on the table for safety; the tea was cold anyway. Halle dabbed at the spot, then tossed the soggy napkin in a handy waste basket. "Did they say what they had on you?"

I shook my head. "They were too busy asking me questions I couldn't answer."

"If this goes any farther, I'll make sure you know. As your lawyer I can do things like that."

Halle was trying to put on a good face; optimism was

as much a part of her innate personality as her crimson hair, but it wasn't working this time.

She absentmindedly petted a cat or two. "Lynley, think. Is there anything—anything at all that happened when you were up on the hill that you might not have mentioned, passed off as meaningless, or maybe even forgotten? You'd been doped, after all, to say nothing of being scared to death. I mean, if you had killed them, it would only have been a matter of self-defense."

"I didn't kill them!" I rose, shifting Fluffs to the couch so she wouldn't get dumped onto the floor. "Now I almost wish I had!"

"Don't say that!" Halle cautioned. "Not even to me. If you're going to plead innocence, you need to act it—mind, body, and heart. Okay?"

"Yeah, sorry." I picked Fluffs up again and sank back into my corner of the couch. The little gray cat had had enough however; she indignantly sprang away and headed to the kitchen for a snack. Red thought that was a good idea and leapt down like a tiger, landing with a thud as he hit the floor.

"Lyn...?" Halle urged. "Anything. Something that could tie you to the victims?"

"I'm thinking!" I snapped. "Sorry," I added the minute the rudely toned words popped out of my mouth. She was on my side, for heaven's sake, and I'd be stupid not to remember that.

So think I did. "Well, the car, for one thing," I offered reflectively. "Obviously my fingerprints would be all over the inside of it."

"Your abduction is on record; they'd expect your prints there. No, it would have to be more specific."

"DNA evidence, blood, hair, saliva? Same thing, but..."

I stopped mid-sentence. "Halle, I just thought of something! Did I miss it, or did the detectives skip the part about just how the brothers were killed? And when and where—all that stuff?"

Halle raised her fleecy eyebrows. "They never told you? I assumed they'd covered all that before I came in. Shouldn't assume, should I?" she giggled. "As my mother used to say: it makes an *ass* of *u* and *me*."

I had to laugh at the old adage. Women of our mothers' generation were great for platitudes like that. Obviously we were as well.

"No, Detective Croft never said a thing, and I didn't ask. Or maybe I did, but I never got an answer."

"Well, I'm sure it's not a secret. Where's your computer? I bet we can find out."

"It's upstairs. You really think it'll be on the internet?"

Halle gave me a sly look. "Everything's on the internet, hon, if you can just figure out where."

I led her up the steep stairs to one of the spare bedrooms—the vintage house had four. This one I had turned into a combination storage, hobby area, and media center for my family tree project. The computer was old with only a near-obsolete Windows program, but it worked fine for my purposes. I sat down, turned on the monitor and clicked the mouse to bring up the screen. My wallpaper was a group shot of my cats sitting on a brightly colored afghan—what a surprise!

Little had followed us as I knew she would. In a single bound, she vaulted to the top of the computer desk and draped her lovely black self above the monitor, tail trailing like a twitching feather boa in front of the screen. I tucked it back underneath her and grasped the mouse.

Once I connected with the internet—something I had

to do the old-fashioned manual way—I looked over at Halle who had pulled up a chair. "Where do we start?"

She leaned forward. "Let's try Sinclairii and see what happens."

I filled in the Google search box and punched the little magnifying glass. I was rewarded with a page of suggestions, blue underlined links to websites that the computer thought might be what I was looking for. The computer doesn't always think the way people do, however: for my efforts, I got *Meryta sinclairii,* a large leaved evergreen tree endemic to New Zealand; Species *Phellodon sinclairii,* a ground fungus; *Acianthus sinclairii,* an orchid; and the anti-obesity effects of *Isaria sinclairii.*

"Lots of botanicals," I observed.

And then there were the usual advertisements: Purchase Sinclairii on eBay; Best prices for Sinclairii at Amazon.com; Find Sinclairii and all your old friends for only nine ninety-five unlimited access.

"Scroll down," Halle instructed.

I scrolled, but though several pages were listed, the search veered increasingly off the mark the farther I went.

"Try... what's his name? Leonard?"

"Lawrence," I corrected. "And George."

"Try them both, Lawrence George Sinclairii."

I did as told, and this time I got somewhere. I scanned through the new set of links: lots of Georges, even George Lawrences, mostly connected to genealogy sites, but only one contained all three names. I clicked and was taken to the *Oregonian* news media website: a big flashy header, a border of blinking animated ads, and a tiny little box of text buried obscurely in the center.

The article had run in the newspaper a few weeks previous. The headline was as short as the article—*Two*

Found Dead—but both Halle and I peered at the words on the screen as if they were the Holy Grail.

It went on to say that the bodies of Lawrence Sinclairii and his brother George Sinclairii had been discovered in their car by some hikers on a Washington back road. The place was described only as a 'rarely traveled dirt road west of Longview'. They had been dead for some time.

I looked at Halle with concern. "But when they dumped me on the mountain, Larry said they were going to hit the highway and disappear. I got the impression he meant Las Vegas or Florida or even the Caribbean, not off in the boonies somewhere."

"Maybe they didn't get that far," she offered solemnly.

"What are you saying?"

"Maybe they died before they had a chance to get away. Maybe they never got off the mountain. You may have been the last person to see them alive—besides the killer, as they say in the movies."

I didn't like the sound of that but it would explain why the police were interested in me.

"Hey, I just thought of something!" I exclaimed. "In the interview, Detective what's-his-name said they'd been brought in on the case by the Cowlitz County police. The mountain's in Cowlitz County."

Halle beamed. "See? I told you that you knew more than you thought. It's the way the mind works."

I read on. The article didn't say how they were killed, though it did say the deaths were being considered suspicious. The police requested that anyone with knowledge of the brothers' movements on that or the days prior to their demise should come forward. They were still seeking next of kin.

I scrolled down, but the only thing after was a list of

related articles, none of which were remotely related to the case. "That's it?" I said with disappointment.

"That's it. Go back to the search and see if there's anything else we can look at."

I clicked the back arrow, retrieving the Google page, but none of the other entries were connected to the Sinclairii brothers.

"Try an obituary search; that sometimes brings up some new sites. Just put in the last name and *obit*."

My fingers faltered, reversing the *l* and the *a* in Sinclairii. "Good grief!" I muttered as I backspaced to change it.

"You're tired, Lyn." Halle peered at the little clock at the bottom of the computer screen. "And it's late. We can do the rest of this tomorrow if you'd rather."

"Let's finish the obituaries first. If we could just figure out what happened, maybe..." My statement fizzled.

"Maybe you'd feel more on top of things?"

"Yeah, that. Knowledge is power, so they say."

Nothing came up in the obituaries. I was disappointed but not really surprised.

"Got any other ideas?"

"Not a one," said Halle. "My brain is fried. But we got somewhere, didn't we? At least we know where it happened, and when."

"Sort of. Maybe," I added dubiously.

Halle rose. "Lynley, I've got to go home. If I don't get out of this kilt, I'm going to go crazy."

I hadn't thought of it all evening, but other than taking off our sashes and Halle unclipping her sporran, we were still in full dress. "And I should get my tea stain soaking before it sets. Thanks for all your help."

"You'll get my bill in the mail," she said.

I stared at her blankly, then saw the twinkle in her eye and realized she was kidding. "No, really," I stammered. "Of course I'll pay you as my lawyer."

She waved a hand. "This one's a freebee. If the case gets more involved or, heaven forbid, goes to trial, we'll talk about fees then."

I disconnected the internet and turned off the monitor to conserve a few watts of energy, and we trudged back downstairs.

Halle gathered up her things. "Call me in the morning?"

"Oh, I'm okay. I don't want to bother you."

She reached up and took my shoulders in her hands. "You aren't bothering me. I'm your attorney, remember?"

I nodded reluctantly, not wanting to admit to myself or anyone else that I might need one.

"It'll be good to rehash everything in the clear light of day."

I nodded. "You're right. I'll call. Not too early though."

"Fine. Then I'll talk to you tomorrow." She moved to go, then turned back and gave me a hug. "Try to get a good night's sleep. And don't worry about things."

"Okay. Thanks for everything."

Halle sashayed down the steps, her kilt swishing across the backs of her knees. As I watched her go, I wondered if she had told me not to worry because in her professional opinion, I had nothing to worry about, or because even though I was now in deep doo-doo, worry would get me nowhere.

Chapter 17

Calico- and Tortoiseshell-colored cats are predominantly female.
Only one in 3000 is male. The males are usually sterile.

In the morning, after an unexpectedly deep and dreamless
slumber, the events of the previous day seemed like
fiction—a television show I had been watching too late at
night, or a book I had fallen asleep reading. I enjoyed that
feeling of denial and I wanted to perpetuate it, so instead
of calling Halle and going over my legal problems, I put on
my kitty socks and my volunteer apron and went to the
shelter.

It had been several days since I'd been there, what with
the Highland Games and being detained by the police, and
there was a whole raft of new faces. Some of the old faces
were absent, having been adopted over the weekend.
Though I missed the kitties I'd gotten to know throughout
their stay at Chez FOF, I was happy for them and wished
them the best in their forever homes.

The FOF volunteers were an autonomous bunch, rather
like the cats themselves. There was no set routine;
everything requiring a schedule such as feeding and
medication was done by paid staff, leaving us free to play
or groom or help potential adopters, whatever struck our
fancy at the moment. Since my fancy wanted desperately
to run away and hide, I had taken Pumpkin, a feisty
tortoiseshell who had been there way too long, into the
Real Life room for an opportunity to stretch her legs.

Pumpkin needed some serious socializing. She was a conundrum that was all too common in shelter life: petulant to begin with, she had not shown well to folks looking for a friendly family pet; the longer she languished in her little metal prison, the more cantankerous she got, making her even less appealing. Some of the other volunteers and I had taken on the project of reintegrating her into society which involved, among other things, as much people contact outside the kennel environment as possible.

The Real Life room was a brilliant contrivance for just that purpose. It was exactly what it sounds like: a room designed as much like your living room as could be pulled off in a shelter environment where everything has to be disinfected between feline visits. There were soft chairs, a coffee table, cat toys, food, water, and even a TV that ran Animal Planet and other cat-friendly shows. As I lounged in one of the low chairs, Pumpkin could hide, play, eat, or sleep, whatever she wanted. I just let her be, talking to her and every so often inviting her to come take a treat from me. Socializing cats isn't terribly interactive since most things cats like to do they do on their own, but they appreciate the company and the chance to blatantly ignore you. And every once in a while, they have a breakthrough that makes it all worthwhile.

Pumpkin swaggered up to me, her round tummy swaying—there's a reason she's called Pumpkin besides the bright orange color in her coat. She looked me straight in the eye, then with no further ado, jumped onto my lap. She kneaded my leg for a few minutes which was relatively painless since her claws were well clipped, then turned in a circle and laid herself down. She looked at me once again, blinked a quick kitty smile, then put her head on her paws and went to sleep. I petted her cautiously—I didn't know if she'd like it, but she began to purr, so I did it again, then not wanting to press my luck, left her alone.

I relaxed into the chair; it looked like I'd be stuck there for a while. Animal Planet was playing a show on fauna of the Outback, not my favorite subject but interesting all the same—anything that kept me from my own thoughts. Soon I found my eyelids drifting shut. I listened absentmindedly to the Australian narrator until his words flowed together in a pleasant monotone and I began to fall asleep.

Just when he reached the part where the wallabies were flying off to meet the dragons—at least that's what they were doing in my dream—the top part of the Dutch door swung open and Pumpkin and I woke with a start. We both glared at the intruder, but it was Frannie and she was always welcome.

"Oh, look who you got!" she cooed, smiling benevolently at the great Pumpkin.

"Come on in," I said softly. I wasn't sure how the tortie would take the intrusion, but surprisingly enough, she lay her head back down and returned to her cat nap.

Frannie came and sat in the other chair, quiet as a cat herself. "How's it going? Long time no see."

"I know. What's been happening around here? I saw King Henry's kennel was cleared out. Did he get adopted?"

"He sure did!" Frannie's perfectly plucked and painted eyebrows rose in excitement.

King Henry was a special case, an elderly gentleman who had come to us after his person had passed away. He was one of the Friends Fur-ever cats, a program where the owner made arrangements, along with a nice donation, for

FOF to assure a good home for their pet after their death. I love the people who plan ahead for their pets. You wouldn't go off and die without making provisions for your children, would you? Well, to some of us, pets are children too, and sometimes even less able to fend for themselves.

I frowned. "Do you know where he went?" He was a fragile boy in delicate health; it would take a certain sort to appreciate his unique qualities.

"I did the adoption myself," Frannie beamed. "It was an older lady who had been watching him on the website since he came in. She has two senior cats already and knows all about their needs."

I sighed with relief. "That's great, Frannie. I thought about adopting him myself, just to get him home where he belonged. I really loved him, but Lord knows I don't need another cat."

Frannie snickered. "Not just one more?" she joked.

"If I get anymore full-timers, I won't be able to foster."

"It's good to know your limits," she said with a smile. "There's a fine line between helper and hoarder." She reached over and gave Pumpkin a gentle pet. "So what have you been up to?"

I grinned slyly. "You want to hear the latest in the Lynley Cannon story?"

"Oh no, what now?"

"It looks like the brothers Sinclairii went and got themselves murdered."

She gasped. "The guys who kidnapped you? You're joking!"

"No, but that's not the worst of it. Guess who's a suspect?" I let the question hang in the air.

She stared at me in shock. "Not... Not you, Lynley?"

I nodded with perverse satisfaction. "Yes, me. Can you believe it?"

"Well, no, as a matter of fact, I can't. Don't they realize you were the victim in that whole mess?"

"Of course they do. I have no idea what makes them think I did it. Proximity maybe, or revenge for breaking my leg. As if a night in the hospital would be worth throwing my whole life away."

"I can't see it, but I suppose in a society where you can get killed for cutting someone off in traffic, anything can happen."

"My friend Halle is a lawyer. She's helping me out."

"You need a lawyer? Wow, Lynley. This sounds serious."

I sighed. "Yeah, I guess it is."

We both got quiet, me petting Pumpkin who was sleeping like a kitten, and Frannie staring out the top of the Dutch door at the people passing by.

"Hey, Denny!" she called, catching sight of Special Agent Paris in the hallway. "You've got to hear this!" She looked sheepishly back at me. "Sorry, I hope it wasn't a secret."

"Not anymore," I grinned.

Denny ambled over and leaned languidly against the door. "What's up, ladies? Haven't seen you around lately, Lynley. You too busy hanging out with your boyfriend?"

"I'm going to have to get a new one now," I bantered. "Frannie tells me King Henry got adopted."

Denny laughed. Being young and lusty instead of old and jaded, he didn't realize how close to serious I was. If it didn't have four legs, whiskers, and a tail, it was getting nowhere near my bed.

"So what's the big news? Someone win the lottery?"

He gave us his gleaming smile.

"Lynley's a suspect in a murder investigation!" Frannie blurted with twisted glee.

"A person of interest," I corrected.

"Okay, whatever. Anyway, she was just about to tell me the whole story."

Pumpkin, insulted by all the activity, lurched off my lap and scuttled behind my chair to sulk.

Denny raised an eyebrow, Spock-like. "What happened? You finally get your hands on one of those animal abusers?"

"You'd better come in, Denny, and close the door," I nodded toward the crouching cat, "in case she decides to become a flying Pumpkin."

Denny did as he was told, hunkering down beside us. I could smell his man-scent and for a moment wished those days of pursuit and retreat weren't quite so far in my past.

As I told the two what had happened—the embarrassing apprehension at the Highland Games; the long interview at the police station; the few facts Halle and I had dug up on the internet—I began to realize just how bizarre the whole thing sounded. When I finally finished, I felt like I should be saying *The End.* But this wasn't fantasy and it wasn't happening to someone else. It was on record, for ever and ever in the bowels of some computer file: me, Lynley Mackey Cannon, killer alleged.

"So what happens now?" Frannie asked.

"Nothing, I hope. I hope I never hear from Detective Croft or any of the rest of them again in my life."

Denny was quiet, not a good sign.

"What do you think, Denny?" Frannie asked. "You've been with the police; you know how those people think."

He gave a little laugh. "*Those* people?"

"I'm sorry. I know they're only doing their job."

"*To serve and protect*—you," he pointed out.

"Yes, but you've got to admit that sometimes they get it wrong. Lynley's no killer."

"Granted." Denny shrugged nonchalantly though his knitted brows gave him away.

"Come on, Special Agent Paris," I prodded. "What are you not telling me? Is it bad?"

"Bad?" he repeated thoughtfully. "Can't say I'd call it bad. Sounds like they really don't have enough on you to make an arrest, but..."

"How could they?" Frannie interrupted. "She didn't do it, obviously."

"But what?" I pushed.

Denny looked out the window, suddenly obsessed with the birds flitting carelessly in copper bower of the Japanese maple.

"But *what*...!?"

"Well, the next step would be for them to gather more evidence."

"More evidence?" Frannie demanded. "Against Lynley? And just how do you suppose they're going to do that?"

I wanted to hear his answer, but church bells began to chime in my apron pocket. Denny looked like he had been literally saved by the bell. I pulled out the cell phone and checked the display. It was Carol.

"Hi, Mum. Can I call you back? I'm at the shelter..."

Carol's answer, which I had expected to be *Sure, dear. Call me later whenever you get the chance*, was instead a garbled series of unintelligible words and phrases with a few obscenities thrown in.

"Carol, slow down. What is it? What's wrong? I can't

understand a word you're saying."

I heard her take a deep breath on the other end of the air. "Lynley, you have to come home right away," she articulated with palpable self-control. This measured tone, reminiscent of a Boris Karloff character, was even more alarming than the panic.

I jumped up, sending Pumpkin scurrying out from behind my chair. She stopped when she realized how exposed she was, hissed, then walked sedately to the seat I had just vacated, hopped up and eyed us with catly defiance.

I was processing none of that. "Why? What's happened?"

"I'm at your house," Carol moaned.

"What's wrong? Is it the cats?"

"Yes. No. It's not the cats but you need to come home *right now*. I can't find them all, and they're going to get out and..." Her voice rose as she slipped back into panic-speak.

I gave Frannie and Denny a fearful look.

"What is it?" Frannie mouthed.

"I can't tell. It's Carol, something to do with the cats."

"No, no, Lynley," Carol cried. "It's your house! They're making a horrible mess! They're running back and forth and leaving the door open half the time. I'm doing what I can but I'm just afraid the kitties will get out anyway."

"Who's running back and forth making a mess? The cats?"

"No, I told you it wasn't the cats," she snapped.

"Then who?"

For a moment there was silence, then Carol whispered urgently, "The cops are here."

Chapter 18

In just seven years, one female cat and her offspring can produce 420,000 kittens. In just seven years one female cat and her offspring can produce 420,000 kittens. No, it's not a typo but a significant fact that's worth mentioning more than once.

"I'll be right there!" I slammed the phone shut and stuffed it back in my pocket. Adrenaline shot through me like an electric shock; I felt like a cat in water. Though I wanted desperately to move, I was frozen in place. Frannie and Denny were beside me in a heartbeat, and I think without them I might have crumpled into a worthless heap on the tile floor.

"It's the police," I spluttered. I shook my head with disbelief and rage. "Apparently they're searching my house."

A light bulb went on in both Frannie's and my minds: "Gathering evidence!" we said simultaneously.

Denny looked sheepish. "That's what I was about to say. Procedure would be to get a search warrant and see if they can find something incriminating among your personal items."

"Oh really!" I wailed. "It's not like on TV where they pour out the flour and dump all your underwear on the floor, is it?"

"Well, no. Not usually. They try to be as careful as they can. But search and seizure isn't a tidy process, and they're usually pressed for time. At least they think so."

I groaned.

"Look at it from their side. They're chasing a killer, trying to apprehend him before he has a chance to hurt someone else."

I rolled my eyes. "Right. And that's supposed to make me feel better?" I pulled myself together. "I've got to go make sure they don't let the cats get out. Frannie, would you mind...?"

"Putting Pumpkin back in her kennel? Absolutely not. You just do what you gotta do and call me later. Or do you want to wait a minute and I'll take you? You don't look in any condition to drive."

"I'll take her," Denny volunteered, then he looked at me. "If you want."

"You're not too busy?"

"I've got a presentation on the importance of spaying and neutering tonight at Lincoln High School, but I'm clear for now."

I nodded gratefully. "Well, then, yes, please. Thanks. I can pick my car up later. Right now, I just have to get home."

"If there's anything I can do..." said Frannie.

I gave her a quick hug. "Wish me luck."

* * *

Denny and I arrived into the pit of chaos. No matter what Denny may have thought, to me it looked worse that any cop show I'd seen on television: my front door gaped open; people, uniformed and plain clothes, were rushing in and out; black-and-whites, which in Portland are now only -whites, lined the street, and all my neighbors were out to catch a glimpse of the action.

My mother was standing on the front porch, looking

like an eighty-year-old stray. When she saw me, she tottered down the steps with her arms wide. I didn't know if she was going to hug me or attempt to fly. It turned out to be a gesture of pure frustration on her part, though I'm not sure how the flapping motion fit in with her exaggerated shrug.

"Lynley! Oh, for heaven's sake, dear! I don't know what's happening. I tried to stop them, to make them wait for you, but they didn't listen to a word I said!" She looked blackly at the invaders.

I paused long enough to blurt, "That's okay, Mum. I know you did," before I pushed past her and bolted for the door.

"What's it all about?" she asked as I burned by.

"I'll tell you in a minute," I called over my shoulder, not missing a stride.

I wasn't concerned with the mess, the turmoil, or even the intrusion; all I cared about was getting my cats corralled before they had a chance to bolt. Staring around my living room in desperation, I realized I was too late—there was not a whisker in sight.

Detective Croft was talking to an armed officer in the kitchen. I ran up to her and grabbed her arm, which got a rise out of the officer who in turn, grabbed mine.

Croft turned to me. "It is alright, Donovan."

He hesitated, but when I let go and held my hands up in submission, he reluctantly complied.

"You let my cats out!" was all I could think of to say, so I said it again: "*You let my cats out!!*"

"Calm down, Ms. Cannon. Please..."

"But they're indoor cats! Most of them have never even been outside! They'll run in front of cars! They'll get lost! They're probably scared to death..."

"Ms. Cannon!" the detective intervened sharply. "Hold on. Your cats are fine. We took the liberty." She led me into my office where six carriers were lined up in a row against the wall. Catly protests were coming from inside.

I was aghast. "You got them all?"

"I think so. Your mother said there were six, so unless we have an imposter, they are all accounted for."

"Even Solo?" I said incredulously.

"Solo?"

"The white one who lives under the couch. She usually won't let anyone near her. She's deaf."

"Actually we had a very proficient man from Animal Control come down to do the honors. They may not be happy, but they are all safe."

I slumped with relief, then looked at her. I couldn't believe she'd gone to all that trouble.

Croft read my mind and gave a very small, very quick smile. "I have cats too," was all she said.

"May I see them?" I asked cautiously. Mine, not hers.

"Yes, but I do not have to tell you that if you let any of them out, we cannot be responsible for their safety."

I nodded.

"Officer Donovan will stay with you while you check." She motioned the officer inside. "We have already cleared this room but please do not touch anything. And when you are finished, come and see me." Her tone had reverted back to the authoritative deadpan. I nodded again and bent down to the cages.

While I opened each in turn, giving the occupant a little pet and a few calm words of encouragement, my guard dog took up residence at the door. He had his eye on my every move. Maybe he expected me to use one of the cats as a deadly weapon. I've read about cats who jump on the villain and save the day, but I doubted my lazy bunch would be up for anything like that. Besides, as I kept reminding myself, the police were not the enemy.

Everyone was safe—even Solo! I was so thankful. Whoever had secured them had done a good job. Each carrier had been fitted with a soft bed and a water bowl; the small cats got the small carriers and the big ones got the large ones. Violet got the jumbo shuttle that was reserved for her. I'd had the empty crates stacked in the corner with the clean beds sitting on top, so once the MCAS guy caught the cats, it wouldn't have been that difficult to cage them; I was just amazed he'd taken the time.

"I'm finished," I said to Guard Dog. He stepped aside, and I went to join Croft. She was sitting at my kitchen table which she had appropriated as her command center. Special Agent Paris sat across from her and the two were deep in conversation. I figured that was a good thing; maybe he'd be able to translate all the cop jargon into English for me.

The two quit their dialogue and peered up as I came over. "I want to thank you for taking care of my cats," I said to Croft. "I really appreciate your consideration."

She gave a crisp and generic *You are welcome*.

"But," I added, staring helplessly around me, "what's going on? What are you doing here in the first place?"

Croft shuffled papers and came up with an official looking document. She held it out to me. "This is a search warrant. It authorizes us to conduct a search for evidence of a crime and to confiscate any evidence found."

I looked at the document in her hand but made no move to take it. "What sort of evidence?"

"Specifically we are concentrating on finding a firearm

or any indication of a firearm used in the past thirty days."

"You mean, like a gun?" I snorted. "Well then, search away. I told you at the station that I didn't own a gun, so you're wasting your time."

The detective eyed me with her coldest of cold stares. "Searching for the truth is never a waste of time, Ms. Cannon. Now you may either wait outside or sit down and be quiet until the officers have completed their work."

I glared at the younger woman. I didn't take well to commands, especially from a whippersnapper like Croft, and decided then and there to go for the third option: I called my lawyer.

* * *

Halle, looking snazzy in a puce Polo shirt, tan Marc Jacobs slacks and a pair of shiny chestnut Clark's boots—an outfit that probably cost as much as my monthly retirement check but was incredibly casual for her—joined Frannie, Denny, Carol, and me at the kitchen table, the only place we could find that wasn't in complete disarray. I couldn't face the cleanup yet, and I wasn't about to let anyone else do it for me though both Frannie and Mum had offered.

The cats were free again. Little, Violet, and Fluffs had inspected the new decor and let me know that the piles of books taken from shelves, sofa cushions strewn across the floor, and drawers hanging open, though mildly amusing, didn't meet their usual high standards. Red had reverted to his near-feral shyness and was hiding somewhere upstairs. Dirty Harry, outraged by the intrusion on his daily routine, noisily stalked back and forth, threatening to spray. Solo was back under the couch; who knew what she was thinking? I had fed everybody generous amounts of wet food, given treats and as much love as I could muster in my traumatized state. That would have to do them for now.

Carol, in a throwback to her Scottish heritage, had made some strong black tea, and I was holding on to my cup for dear life. It was the one I'd had made at the photo shop from a collage of my foster cats, and I must say that looking into the eyes of Addison, Rajah, Spot, Cruiser and the others, if only on porcelain, made me feel a little better. I was not a criminal—I was a good person. Not only was I a crazy-for-cats lady but also a mother, grandmother, daughter, friend, volunteer, and a Mackey to boot! I needed to remember that.

Everyone there was on my side and I knew it; I just wasn't sure how they could help. Halle was my only hope, and though she was doing her lawyer best to reassure me, she wasn't sounding quite as confident as I might have wished.

"First thing tomorrow," she was saying, "I'll get on the horn and find out exactly what's going on with your case." She shook her head. "I should have done it today, but I never thought things would get this far this fast."

"It's Sunday, for goodness' sake," Frannie put in. "Day of rest. Don't the cops know that?"

"I still don't understand what's going on." Carol pulled out a chair and sat down, only to jump up again for a carton of milk and the Fiesta sugar bowl. "Anyone need lemon? You have a lemon, dear?"

"There should be one in the fridge," I said without enthusiasm, "unless they took it as evidence." Centering on the small stuff rather than the big ugly picture was how my mother coped with catastrophe. It worked for her, and I had learned from birth just to go with her flow.

Carol retrieved the yellow citrus, inspected it

carefully—wouldn't want to serve an inferior lemon to guests at a pity party—found it satisfactory and began to slice it on a cutting board she magically pulled out of the clutter. "Well?" she urged. "Why are the police searching your house? Can you explain it to me?"

"I can't explain what I don't know, Mum. I've already told you that."

"Yes, you said they suspect you of killing those horrible men who beat you, abducted you, and then left you for dead."

"They didn't leave me for dead; they just left me."

"Whatever. Still, you are the victim here. I don't see how they can think otherwise."

"That's what I told her," Frannie said to Carol. "It just seems like some big mistake to me."

"Did they seize anything during their search?" asked Halle, ever the voice of reason.

I was thankful for a question I could actually answer. "They took the clothes and shoes I was wearing when I was kidnapped. I told them I'd washed the dress at least twice since then. They didn't seem to mind."

"Looking for blood splatter and gun powder residue," Denny muttered thoughtfully.

I shrugged. "They're not going to find any."

Halle smiled. "Then you should be off the hook in no time. This search may be to our advantage."

"Wonderful," I said flatly.

"No, really!" Halle's round eyes were wide. "They can't arrest you without evidence, which they obviously don't have or they would have done it yesterday—wow, was that just yesterday?" she reflected. "Seems like longer."

"To me it feels like yesterday never ended," I said.

"Isn't the perception of time an interesting thing?" Carol offered along with a small dish of lemon slices.

"Did they take anything else?" Halle pursued, treating mum's philosophical query as rhetorical, which it was.

"Not really. Just some work gloves they found in the back of the closet. And the garbage."

"Your garbage?" Carol snickered.

"Recycle, compost—the whole bit." I laughed, and so did most everyone else. The image of the well-dressed Detective Croft pawing through my food scraps, coffee grounds, and junk mail was absurd. Then again, she probably had flunkies to do that for her.

Denny was the only one who wasn't finding the garbage evidence humorous. His face was pensive, his eyes were staring a hole in a floral centerpiece that had somehow survived the sanctioned vandalism of the police search.

"Something on your mind, Special Agent Paris?" I asked.

He looked up in surprise as if he'd been caught napping. "Oh, nothing really. Just a hunch, a feeling, nothing conclusive."

"Well, you're the detective. I'd be happy to hear what you've got to say."

"A detective?" Carol broke in excitedly. "Really?"

"Yup," Frannie said proudly. "Denny's a Special Agent working out of the Northwest Humane Society. Just like Rockford for the animals."

"Maybe more like Magnum, P.I.," I put in.

Denny stared at us as if we'd lost our minds. "Before your time," I told him.

"I know who Magnum is," he said defensively. "My mom has all eight seasons on DVD."

Frannie and I exchanged knowing looks. "We're dating ourselves," I commented.

Carol rolled her eyes. "Peter Gunn would be dating yourselves—he was my hero back in the day." She turned to Denny, giving the young investigator a once over. "Is that true? You're really a detective?"

"I'm what they call a humane investigator. I look into cases of criminal animal abuse and neglect. I am a commissioned police officer," he added with modest pride.

"So what's your theory?"

"Well," he drawled. "I don't have anything even close to a theory. I'm just concerned. I know a little about cop mentality, and they really seem to want to pin this on Lynley. Probably for lack of another suspect. Sometimes if they have a likely suspect, they don't do that great a job of looking any farther. Sorry," he added when he saw the glares on the surrounding faces.

"Well, that's not very fair," Carol remarked. "How can they justify doing a poor job when people's lives are at stake?"

"It's just the way it is. Lots of reasons—from cutbacks and budgets to less than brilliant detecting to political pressure for a quick wrap-up of a case. Detective Croft seems like a good cop and I don't feel she thinks Lynley's guilty, but she isn't the only force at work here. Unless she finds another suspect or at least evidence that there might be another suspect, she's probably going to have to make an arrest."

I sat back in my chair, feeling like the breath had been knocked out of me. "Oh, boy..." I exhaled. "I guess I'd better start making arrangements for my cats while I'm in jail."

Denny looked mortified. "I don't mean to say that's

what will happen, Lynley. It's only one possibility." Realizing that didn't sound much better, he stuttered, "Just a slight, very small possibility. Oh, dang, I'm sorry. I didn't mean to upset you."

"That's okay, Denny. You're just putting into words what I've been thinking all along. This isn't going to go away anytime soon."

"But Halle said when the search comes up empty, that would be the end of it," Carol pointed out hopefully. "Right, Halle?"

Halle nodded. She was smiling but I could see an uneasiness in her eyes. "That's what we would hope. It's important to keep a positive attitude."

"But?" I articulated for her.

"Pardon?"

"I hear a *but* in there somewhere. Come on, spill."

She ran her hand through her crimson spikes, leaving a tuft of bangs sticking straight up like a tiny flame. "There's always a question when it comes to the law. Nothing's for sure until the case is dismissed or the suspect is acquitted."

"Or charged," I put in.

Halle gave me a stern look.

"Yeah, I know," I said. "I'm innocent and must act it at all times."

"That's right. Your deportment may be the thing that tips the balance to our side."

Then I'm in big trouble, I thought, but I mustered enough control to keep it to myself this time.

"Well, the solution is obvious. Does anyone need more tea?" Carol held up the pot. "Only take a moment to fix some hot."

I stared at my mother. "I like tea, too, but I hardly think it's the solution to my problem."

"Oh, no dear. That wasn't what I meant. Even the British know that tea isn't always the answer."

"Then what is? I'm all ears."

Carol stood up and moved around the table until she was standing behind Denny Paris. She put her wrinkled hands on the brawny shoulders.

"It's simple, dear. Special Agent Paris has got to find the real killer. So we can all go back to our normal lives."

Chapter 19

Lilies are highly poisonous to cats. Even pollen dusted onto the fur in passing can cause kidney failure and death. Luckily most lilies grow very tall and don't pose a threat if strategically placed in the garden.

"That's a great idea!" Frannie exclaimed. "If the cops aren't going to clear her, then we will! And finding the real killer is the best way of doing that, don't you think?"

"I'd do it myself," Carol put in, "but I'm afraid the old gray mare ain't what she used to be." She held out her arms to emphasize the betrayal age had wrought upon her elderly form. "But I can always consult. Rather like Nero Wolfe. He rarely left his house, you know, insisting the information come to him instead."

"I'll help," Frannie volunteered. "We all will." She looked enthusiastically at the group around the table. "Right?" she urged when no one replied in what she considered to be a timely manner.

"I don't know," I began. "What do you think, Halle?"

She gave a little shrug. "We could use an investigator. Attorneys often utilize their help to clear a client."

"See?" Carol beamed, proud to have come up with the idea.

"But Denny's an animal investigator. He looks for hoarders, not murderers," I argued.

"Denny deals with people who abuse animals," Frannie retorted. "It's a proven fact that animal abusers often hurt people too. He may have already dealt with murderers, even if that's not what he was going after them for."

"This person, assuming Denny can find him, might be... *is* dangerous. He's already killed two people."

"Some of the jerks Denny has to confront are dangerous too. Gangs who own fighting dogs, crazy people, desperate not to have their animals taken away even though they can't take care of them themselves. What about that guy last winter who shot at him when he was trying to rescue that starving horse? His job is more than just going to schools to educate the kids on how to treat their pets."

"I know, but..." I paused, turning to the man in the spotlight. "I'd never forgive myself if anything happened to you because of me."

Carol held up a hand, commanding silence. "Shouldn't we be asking Denny how he feels about the whole thing?"

All eyes turned to the special agent. Denny's gaze drifted to his hands, a shy smile playing on his lips. "I'm not a licensed detective. I'm sure you could find someone better. Someone with real experience."

"But you have real experience," Frannie contended. "And you know Lynley in person, which counts for something."

"It counts for a lot," Halle agreed. "It's an edge you have over the police detectives."

"You really think so?"

Halle gave the young agent her brightest smile. "Sure. You may be able to find a lead the police missed. Stranger things have happened."

Carol gave his shoulders a final persuading squeeze and moved back to her chair. "Just give it some thought, dear, will you?"

Denny looked around at all the encouraging faces, which included mine as I realized this was the first ray of hope I'd had since the whole thing began.

Denny blushed. "Okay, let's do it!" he declared. "But I'm going to need all your help. And I don't know how far this will go. I can't promise any results, let alone actually finding a criminal who has left no clues."

"No clues the police have picked up on," Frannie corrected.

"Right." Denny's eyes had taken on a gleam; he shifted in his chair as if he were antsy to get on with his new pursuit. The atmosphere in the room had gone from bleak to bright in a few momentous seconds.

I gasped a sigh of relief, realizing that I had been holding my breath. *For how long?* I mused. I knew Denny's investigation wouldn't resolve everything, or maybe anything at all, but at least I felt heartened. I finally had a little control over my fate.

"Okay, friends," I said with an optimism I hadn't imagined I could muster only moments ago. "Where do we start?"

* * *

The first thing Denny did in his official capacity as my unofficial gumshoe was to send everyone home. He exchanged numbers and email addresses with Halle so they could get hold of each other if there was any news. She wasn't sure how far she would get at the police station on a Sunday, but she was headed there anyway. She had friends in high places, and she wasn't above calling in favors.

I was instructed to go back about my normal business,

exuding that aura of innocence Halle had put forth so vehemently. Denny had to be at work at five, but he wanted to have a chat with my neighbors first to see if they'd seen, heard, or remembered anything strange. He promised he'd be by in the morning to talk about his findings.

I didn't know it but Mum had called Seleia who popped right over with a couple of her friends to help me put my house in order. This time I didn't refuse, and their bright faces and happy chatter were probably the best example of innocence I could have had. In no time, things were back where they were supposed to be; the police, unlike true vandals, hadn't done any actual damage— they'd just made a big mess. My granddaughter and crew went above and beyond; when they were finished, the place was cleaner than it had been in years.

I fixed lemonade with the leftover lemon from mum's tea party, a dash of bottled lime juice, a few shots of soda, and lots of ice, Mexican style. We sat on the back patio and watched the shadows lengthen and the twilight come on. Robins sang their evening song which always takes me back to a time before I was Seleia's age. The crickets began at dusk: one, then another, then a whole symphony of chirps. Stars twinkled into the velvet sky. The new moon shown out over the west hills like a cat claw.

I turned on a string of lantern-shaped fairy lights and we sat for a while longer, talking about nothing. I was more than content to listen to the girls chitchat about school, boys, movie stars—innocuous things that had nothing to do with murder or criminal investigations. I'm still amazed how they can talk and text at the same time; I takes me every bit of concentration I can muster just to text at all—those buttons are so little and I'm always punching past the letter I want.

"Lynley?"

I woke with a start. Seleia was shaking my shoulder. "Grandma, we're going to take off now. Unless you need anything else."

I straightened myself in my lawn chair, slightly embarrassed that I'd fallen asleep. "No, that's okay, love. You're my hero—you're all my heroes. Thanks for all your help."

"Let me know how things go," Seleia said. To her, the idea of her grandmother being a person of interest in a murder case was quite exciting.

"You don't have to tell the whole world, you know."

She gave me a shocked look. "I'd never..." She broke into a smile. "But it's not like you did it or anything."

"I know—someday we'll look back and laugh, right?"

The crew giggled and flounced their way back into the house to collect packs, purses, laptops, and other teen paraphernalia.

"Make sure the front door's locked when you go out. And set the alarm, would you?"

I heard a titter of assents, then the slam of the door and the sound of happy voices going off down the street to the bus stop. As the sound dwindled, I became aware of how quiet it was in the garden; the crickets and the city hum were the only constants. The rev of a big motor, the scream of a siren, the distant whistle of a train down by the waterfront—those were only passing.

I was wide awake now, hyper-aware. The saucer heads of white Oriental lilies glowed like fringed moons in the high border, their fragrance heady in the stillness; the stars hung in the sky, as bright as the lily blooms.

Suddenly a loud blast rang through the streets, echoing

up Mt. Tabor and back again. It was impossible to tell from which direction it had come. A firecracker? A backfire?

A gunshot?

I was up and out of my chair, my heart beating fast. As I ran into my house like a scared kitten, locking the sliding door behind me, I chided myself. Even if it were a gunshot, which was only marginally likely, they were not unheard of in the neighborhood. It was the price one paid for living in an urban community. There was absolutely no reason to think it had anything to do with me. And I really didn't think that. My nerves were fried; I was exhausted.

I checked the front door and set the remainder of the alarms. Staggering like a drunk, I made for the stairs and dragged myself up, one by one. I stumbled to my room and fell onto my bed, displacing Red who was curled up asleep on my fuzzy bathrobe. The windows were open, letting in a cool breeze through the screens. I listened with paranoid intensity, but the only sound was the soft, hypnotic drone of a city that never sleeps.

* * *

There is a moment between sleep and waking where all bad things are forgotten, where you're one with the morning and even the thought of coffee hasn't broken the spell of the past night's dreams. Then it all comes thundering back, as tangible as a headache.

I sat up as if I had been injected with amphetamines, rudely displacing Little who had been sleeping on my chest. "Sorry, Little," I said, giving her a pet on a velveteen sideburn. She was having none of it; now that I was so obviously awake, it was time for breakfast. In case I had forgotten how to get to the kitchen, she hopped down, ready to lead.

I glanced at the clock. Nine fifteen said the red robotic numbers—make that nine sixteen. Time was blinking by and I was still lazy in bed. I usually don't sleep so late, but I wasn't surprised and I didn't feel the least bit guilty.

Violet waddled into the room and trained her lovely liquid eyes on me. Disappointment shone in their ice-green gaze. She uttered a tiny mew and then headed back from whence she came.

I pulled myself out of bed—sometime last night I'd managed to get undressed and under the sheets though I didn't remember when—and shrugged on my bathrobe. I pulled on a pair of pajama pants and was good to go for the morning, at least until something inspired me to dress more formally.

In the kitchen, a clowder of cats had gathered near their feeding stations. Six pairs of eyes stared at me with rapt attention. (Even Solo ventured out of hiding for food.)

I rinsed the coffee pot and filled the machine with fresh water. "Mind if I make some coffee first?" I asked politely. I took their silence as a yes and went on with the job. Pulling a filter out of a tin, I scooped in a few tablespoons of French Roast. Flipping the green button to On, I listened for the satisfying gurgle.

The coffee was half-way dripped and the cat bowls filled though not yet presented when the phone rang. Though it felt as if it should be too early for phone calls, the time was actually nine-thirty on a Monday morning. Everybody else in my part of the country had been up for hours, working away at their various places of employment. Once again I gave a quick but heartfelt thanks that I was retired and had put that weekly grind behind me.

The bells were tinkling cheerfully away. I checked the

174

display: it was Carol. I thought about not answering, but I knew that she'd just call again and again until I picked up.

"Hi, dear. How are you this morning? Did you get a good night's rest?" she put forth in best motherly form.

"Actually I did. Thanks for asking the girls over to help clean. I'm sure Seleia wouldn't want it to get out, but she's a real vacuum dynamo."

"Wait until she gets her own place, then we'll see."

"It's always more fun to clean someone else's, don't you think?"

Carol hesitated. "You're asking the wrong person, dear. You know I really never cared for housekeeping. But think of it this way, I'm supporting the economy by employing a maid."

"Edith's a gem," I agreed.

Edith, mum's house cleaner, had to be nearly the same age as Carol and had been with her for literally decades. It was a symbiotic relationship: Edith would do light cleaning (lighter every year) while all the time updating Carol on the trials and tribulations of her children, grandchildren, and great-grandchildren; Carol would listen and coo or tsk, whatever was required of the situation. Edith would go home with sixty bucks in her pocket and her need to gossip appeased; Carol would get a clean house that she could mess up guilt-free over the next two weeks until they did it all over again.

"I can hear the cats," Carol said. "Whatever are you doing to them?"

"We're in the middle of breakfast. What did you call about, Mum?" I switched the phone to my left hand and began distributing the cat food.

"Just to see how you were. And, well, I did think of one thing. Something that might help with your case."

175

"Really?" I asked with a mix of hope and dread.

"Yes. You see, one of my dear friends is a mystic..." This didn't surprise me in the least. Carol had friends in all walks of life, and I mean *all*. "And maybe she could help us figure out who killed your kidnappers."

"A mystic, eh? Don't you think that's kind of a long shot?" I was extremely proud of my patience which had translated my true thoughts on psychic crime-solving into something I could say in polite company. Not that I have anything against *the calling*; we have a pet psychic at the shelter who is extremely good at divining some of the more esoteric kitty issues, such as why one doesn't like her litter box or what makes one bite when you try to pet him from a certain angle. She even gives classes, and I attend whenever I can, though to date, I've shown a dismal lack of proficiency.

"I just thought that because there wasn't much else to go on right now, she might be helpful."

"I'll keep her in mind," I assured. "But let's see what Special Agent Paris can come up with first, okay?"

"Maybe I should give him her number."

"Why don't you give it to me? I can tell him all about her and that way he can get in touch at his convenience."

"Oh, good idea, dear. It's... got a pencil?"

"Yes," I lied.

She gave me the phone number, cell number, email address and website, all of which I pretended to write down while in reality, I poured myself a much-needed cup of coffee. Strong, black, aromatic. If Denny decided he wanted help from the *other side*, I could easily ask for the information again.

"You got all that, Lynley?"

"Yes, Mum." And since one lie often begets another, I

added, "I'll tell him when I see him, first thing."

"Then I'll let you go. You must be busy. Remember to take care of yourself, dear. If you don't, no one else will."

"I know. Thanks for the reminder though. Talk to you soon."

I flipped the phone closed and noticed that the battery was running low. I couldn't remember the last time I'd charged it and was about to plug it into the wall cord when it rang for a second time.

"Hey, Lynley. It's Frannie. How's it going?"

"Hi, Frannie. Well, it's not going anywhere yet. I just got up."

"So late? Well, good for you. You must have been exhausted."

"Little bit." I went back to the table and sat down by my coffee. I never knew how long Frannie would talk. Usually I didn't mind, but this morning I might cut short the friendly camaraderie for once.

She caught me off guard by saying, "I'm not going to keep you. I just wanted to let you know I'm at the shelter. I saw Kerry a little while ago, and she told me she was thinking of calling you about a cat who needs fostering. I said you were, um, *involved* right now so she said she could probably find someone else. But then I got to thinking how much you love to foster and how a nice foster cat to care for might take your mind off things. You interested?"

I was about to decline—she was right, I had enough on my plate without taking on a two- to six-week feline obligation—when I found myself saying, "I'll do it!"

"Well, you better call her before she gives the patient to someone else. I know she'd rather have you. It's kind of a special deal."

"What's wrong with the kitty?"

"Dislocated hip. They're going to do a surgery, but he's got a cracked pelvis as well. They want that to heal up on its own a little before they go in."

I felt the customary rush of excitement when taking on a sick cat. I love caring for them, watching them improve: their coats going from dull to shiny, their eyes becoming clear and happy again. Fostering isn't for everyone, even the most devoted animal-lovers, because at the end, when they're all better and you've come to love them, you have to give them back. It's hard to place them in the hands of a total stranger, but the quick adoption rate for a foster cat is amazing, and that's what it's all about. Obviously I can't adopt them all myself, though I must admit, I've kept a few.

I looked at Little as she daintily slurped her food. She was a foster failure, as they're called at the shelter. No failure to me, though. She was part of my household now.

"I'll give Kerry a call," I said with a smile. "Thanks for letting me know."

"*De nada*," she said. "See you later?"

"Probably."

Even before I hung up, I was already anticipating the distraction a foster would afford me. In fact, I was clinging to it for dear life. I would have to get the kennel ready—a cat with a hip problem would need a nice soft bed in a confined space where he wouldn't have to walk or jump. I still had to recharge my phone, but I'd call Kerry first to make the arrangements.

Suddenly I remembered I'd left my car at the shelter yesterday. I could get there by bus, but it would take a little planning—mass transit in Portland could get you anywhere, but it often meant a transfer or two along the way. It had been a long time since I'd bused it to the shelter, and I'd have to look it up on the website trip-planner to make sure of meeting all my connections. Something else to add to my list; this day was becoming more complicated by the minute.

First things first, I reminded myself. I'd call the foster office and take it from there.

I was about punch the contacts button on my phone when it rang for a third time. I checked the caller. Halle.

"What's up?" I asked in lieu of a greeting.

"You dressed, hon?" she asked, her voice low and somber.

"Not really." I felt a shiver of apprehension.

"Then go put something on, not too nice. Jeans and a tee shirt maybe."

"Okay, but why?"

"Denny and I will be by to pick you up in about fifteen minutes. We're going on an evidence hunt. And you need to be ready for anything."

Chapter 20

Humane Societies, unlike government-funded animal control services, are generally private, non-profit organizations that depend on donations and volunteers. They are not related to each other or the HSUS.

Denny's Silverado sped down I-5 toward Longview. Since this wasn't a Northwest Humane Society investigation, he couldn't use the company vehicle, but the Chevy truck was just as versatile and probably smelled less like dog. I sat in the front seat and Halle and Connie Lee were in the back. Denny was driving.

Halle's trip to the cop shop had been fruitful. She'd established that the location of the Sinclairii brothers shooting was indeed my mountain, and the timeline, though indefinite, worked with the theory that it had happened soon after they'd left me. I hadn't heard the shots but that wasn't surprising; the wind could have been blowing the wrong way or maybe I was in too much of a fog to notice.

Halle had also been successful at uncovering the police evidence that implicated me in the murders. Apparently they had found blood inside the car, and as their forensics experts nit-picked through the samples, they verified mine along with the brothers'. Well, not exactly *along* with the brothers—actually my specimen was *on top* of a great splotch of George's blood.

From that, they extrapolated that I had been alive and

bleeding after George was already injured — or dead.

There were some flaws to that assumption, including the fact that I hadn't done it, but it left enough of a question to implicate me. I personally had no notion how it could have come about. I didn't remember bleeding in the car. Though the brothers had handled me with a certain amount of unnecessary roughness, they had never cut me or caused any wounds that could account for blood.

The whole thing sounded pretty iffy, but because the police had no other suspects, I guess it made sense to follow the only lead available. Me.

The two had been shot with a nine-millimeter handgun. The gun had not been recovered, no shell casings retrieved, and ballistics had come up empty on a match. The fact that in my nearly six decades I'd never learned to fire a pistol seemed to be superfluous; after all, I could be lying. I might be Annie Oakley in disguise.

At first I hadn't been too sure about the idea of visiting the scene of the crime or *re*-visiting the scene of my worst nightmare, but as I stared out at the tangle of trees that lined that section of the freeway, I began to appreciate the plan. It had been Denny's decision to bring Special Agent Lee on board; at this point I figured we could use all the help we could get.

After the initial hi-how-are-you chatter, everyone had gotten really quiet. Denny was concentrating on passing everything in sight without going more than the acceptable five miles over the speed limit; Halle had her iPod — whether she was listening to Hip Hop, bagpipes, or Shakespeare, one could never tell; Connie Lee was reading something Wiccan on a Kindle. I found myself tossed back and forth between anger at the stupidity of my plight and delight that I would be picking up my new foster cat when

I got back to town. The one made me furious, the other made me happy. Guess which I tried to center on? Guess how well that worked?

Denny pulled off the freeway at the Longview exit and headed for Highway Four which would take us down the Columbia and its various adjoining sloughs in search of the little dock where Larry and George had moored the boat. From there, I anticipated no problem in finding the logging road. I wondered if there would still be any sign of the crime scene, and if not, how we'd be able to tell where it was. From what Halle said, it sounded like the Badass boys had just paused somewhere along the way and got themselves shot. No scuffle, crash, or bleeding out on the dirt. The car would undoubtedly be gone. Unless the sheriff's forensics investigations team had made a mess or the killer left a note saying X-marks-the-spot, the exact site of their demise might be hard to pinpoint.

Anyone could have shot them: a mugger or psycho or Deliverance-type hillbilly who hadn't wanted trespassers on his land. Okay, now I was reaching, but I just didn't see why they had to blame me. Oh, yeah. The blood. That awful blood for which I couldn't begin to account.

Denny veered east onto the truck route that took us by the log yards, train yards, and industrial yards around the edge of town. We rolled past a green sign that read *Longview Humane Society*, and I wondered briefly what the LHS was like. Not as nice as FOF I figured, but then nothing was. Still you never knew. Some of the small country shelters were exceptional. Someday I'd have to check it out.

"Pit stop," Denny said as he swerved into a Chevron station and glided to a halt by the mini-mart. "Anybody want anything?"

"I need to use the facilities," Halle claimed.

"Might be a good idea. Last chance if you don't want to make like the bears."

"How about some food in case we get lost?" I joked.

"Okay," Connie agreed. From her size, I could tell she liked her donuts, though most of her bulk was muscle.

Five minutes later we were back on the road, relieved, revived, and ready to roll. We had a shopping bag full of Cheetos, sodas, juice boxes, candy bars, apples and—surprise of surprises—donuts.

"We could hold out for days," Halle remarked when she saw the haul.

I shuddered. The thought of being marooned up in that desolate forest again hit a little too close to home for me.

I must say the drive was more relaxing now that we were off the freeway. Denny didn't seem to be in Maserati-mode anymore, and the anticipatory hush morphed into quiet banal conversation. I surveyed the scenery with appreciation. We passed a series of black lakes, thick with iris and water lilies and alive with ducks and birds. Soon the sheer face of wildflower-strewn basalt loomed on our right and the gray-blue expanse of the country's fourth-largest river, the Columbia, spread out to the left. Boats sailed in holiday leisure; ships and barges chugged to or from the Port of Portland some forty miles upriver.

It didn't take nearly as long as I thought it would to find the little dock. "That's it!" I yelped as it zoomed up on the left.

Denny pulled into the gravel lot next to a Volkswagen and switched off the engine. I stared around the place, amazed at how fast my heart was racing. In the hot July sunshine, it looked nothing like the foggy nightmare of my memory. There were a few other cars besides the Volksie as well as several trucks with boat trailers. The little wooden dock was quaint and inviting; the river sparkled with gold coins of light. A family was having a picnic at a table by the water. Children's laughter and the sounds of happy boaters didn't jibe at all with my recollection of pain, dread, and uncertainty.

We piled out of the Silverado and began to explore. "What are we looking for?" I asked Denny.

"Not sure." He kicked at a cigarette butt in the gravel.

"You think it's a clue?" I asked.

"I think it's litter and whoever dropped it should be cited."

Denny pulled a Kleenex out of his utility vest, picked up the offending butt and tossed it in a green garbage can. Then he shoved his hands in his pockets and sauntered down to the end of the dock. I rarely saw him in plain clothes, and he looked younger, more vulnerable. Funny how the uniform creates a persona of its own. Connie Lee was the same—in uniform, her stocky build was intimidating, but here, wearing Levis and a layered tee, she was just one of the gang, a smiling friendly twenty-something kid you'd see at the grocery store buying melons or grapes—or donuts.

Denny was heading back toward me. "We done here?" he asked.

"It's up to you—this is your show, Special Agent Paris," I told him as we set out for the truck. "Did you find anything of interest?"

"Everything's of interest, Lynley."

"But I mean, interest to my case? What were you hoping for anyway?"

"Nothing really. Just trying to get a picture of the event. Visualization is an important part of detection."

"Oh." I wasn't sure what he meant but it sounded good.

Halle was already in the truck, checking a large Triple-A map.

"Can you see where we are?"

"Not exactly." She poked at a twist in the blue line of river. "I'd guess about there."

I studied the colorful intermix of lines and dots. "What's that little town up ahead?"

She squinted at the tiny type. "Stella. Never heard of it, but then it looks like one of those places that's easy to miss if you blink."

We were all seated and belted except for Connie who was still lingering by the dock. I saw her lean over and pick something up, examine it and put it in her pocket. She jogged to the truck and hopped in with a smile on her face.

"Find something good?" I asked.

She fished in her pocket, retrieving a small shiny object. With a broad grin, she showed it to me. "Lucky penny."

* * *

I had my doubts how lucky a lost penny was going to be to my case, but one thing I'd learned about Special Agent Lee was her penchant for the occult. What's more, she made it work for her. Where Denny set out on an investigation armed with facts and information, she ran in headfirst with heart, soul, and spirit—or *spirits.* Now, Connie would probably appreciate my mum's psychic friend.

The logging road wasn't as steep and treacherous as I'd remembered it. The Silverado had all-wheel drive and good suspension, and we bounced along relatively painlessly. At each cut-back, I expected to see something familiar, something that would confirm it as the road I'd traveled on that fateful night, but each time I was disappointed. We could have been anywhere in the Pacific Northwest for the lack of identifiable landmarks if you didn't count gnarled trees or bushes that looked like bunnies. A woodsman perhaps could read those things but not me. I wondered at times if I'd led us on a goose chase and we'd taken the wrong way, but there had been only one route leading up the hill from the dock and this was it.

Finally after what seemed like five miles but was probably more like one or less, we came to the fork where I had lost my way.

"Stop. Stop here!"

I jumped out as soon as the truck rolled to a standstill. "We must have passed it," I said, gazing back the way we had come. "If they'd been any farther up, I would have walked right by them."

Denny set the brake and turned off the engine. "Okay, we'll take it by foot from here. Look for any signs that could tell us where the shootings actually took place. The car's long gone but we should be able to find some sign of the police search. Watch for anything not native to the area." He rummaged behind his car seat and pulled out some little pink flags set on sturdy wire. Handing them out, a few to each of us, he said, "When you find something, don't move it or touch it—just stick one of these in the ground nearby. If we do find a pertinent item, we'll have to get the locals up here to process it. Don't drop anything, scuff foot or tire prints, or otherwise contaminate the scene. Connie and Halle, you go down the way we came; I'm going to head up for a little way, just in case." He turned to me. "Lynley, what do you want to do?"

"Run away?" I chirped: half jest, half cry for help.

He waited patiently, now in total professional mode.

I straightened up my act. "I think I'll check out the side road, the one I took by mistake when I came down the mountain. I can't see how they could have gone that way in that big car but we might as well cover all bases."

"Okay." He looked at his watch. "Let's meet back here in half an hour. "Don't leave the road by yourself, any of you. Cell phones aren't reliable out here and we don't want this to turn into a search and rescue."

Halle was changing from her lawyer pumps to a pair of white Reeboks that looked like they had just come out of the box. When she was finished, she took one side of the road and Connie took the other. Connie had her flags stuffed into the back pocket of her pants like a rooster tail that bobbed up and down as she moved along.

Denny looked at me. "You okay with this?"

"Sure," I answered too quickly, then added, "I guess so."

"Well, don't feel pressured to do anything that makes you uncomfortable. Just come back to the truck. I'll leave it unlocked."

"But this is all my fault," I cried in a sudden fit of melancholy. "I'm the reason we're here."

"It's not your fault. And nobody made us come, remember that." He grabbed a handful of flags, gave a little wave, and began up the hill. He took the right-hand side, peering into the grass and brush, over to the forest, then back again in long, systematic sweeps.

I watched until he disappeared around a bend. Halle and Connie had moved out of sight as well though I could still hear them talking in the distance. Then that too was gone and I was alone in the silent wood.

* * *

Growing up in Oregon, I was never frightened by being out of doors. As a child—back in the dark ages—I spent summers at a rustic little cabin that boasted neither water nor heat nor indoor plumbing. Everything we had, we brought from town; if we ran out of something, we did without. At night, I slept soundly, the rush of the river as my lullaby; during the day, I had the run of the fields, forest, and mossy banks. I saw deer, raccoons, chipmunks, even the occasional beaver. I picked huckleberries and fiddleheads. Never once was I afraid of the wilderness.

And it wasn't wilderness that I was afraid of now. But I was afraid. Fear welled up from deep inside me like a hairball. I was choking on it. I couldn't breathe! I bent double, clutching my stomach. This was not good, not good at all.

Stoically I took myself in hand. I straightened, closed my eyes and recited every calming incantation I could think of. My chest eased and I managed a deep breath which made me feel a little better. I hadn't even started my search; I couldn't give up yet.

I opened my eyes and took in the leafy ambiance, tracing the patterns of the trees. I breathed the cool peat and honeysuckle scents; nothing scary here, nothing dangerous. The past was the past, and though being taken against my will had opened a doorway to hell that I doubted would ever completely close, I had to find a way to live with it.

Starting down the steep incline, careful not to skid on bits of gravel that had pried themselves loose from the narrow roadbed, I began to hum to myself. It was a wordless nameless tune that just popped into my head, maybe a medley of Debussy and Pink Floyd: Dark Side of the Moon. I glanced left and right, then decided to emulate Denny's measured search, beginning on one side, planning to come back the other. That should cover all ground.

My hunt revealed daisies, bright hot perennial peas, cowbane, and lots of heady grasses, waving in the quiet breeze. I found an ancient non-biodegradable McDonald's cup which, without intervention, would last longer than the earth itself. I put a pink flag beside it, planning to come back and collect it when I was done.

Though drier and dustier than it had been the month before, I remembered every inch of the terrain. It was as if the images had been branded into my brain: the big rock in the middle of the road that should have clued me in to the fact that the Ford had never driven up that way; the dry runoff gulch that wove from side to side; the break in the trees where there was a grassy micro-meadow. The grass had turned from green to gold since I'd seen it last, and the summer heat burned down upon it. I paused; the afternoon was waning, and the sunlight blazed in my eyes. I squinted, wishing I'd worn a hat. It was very like that day...

For a moment, I was back there: broken leg, throbbing head, panic-stricken, lost and alone. The memory was so vivid, I swear I could feel the pain. Stumbling, I slipped and sat down hard on the clay.

"Dang," I said out loud, looking around to make sure no one saw me fall on my ass. Oh, sweet vanity!

But someone had seen me, seen the whole embarrassing tumble. I could hear them in the bushes a little farther down the way. "Okay so I'm a klutz, I admit it," I said as bravely as possible.

No answer.

"Hello?" I ventured. The rustle had ceased and

suddenly I was unsure whether I'd heard it at all.

I peered into the undergrowth, but with the sun in my face, I saw only deep black shadow. Maybe it was the cat, the one who had led me to her house, though it had sounded much larger. Or had it?

"Kitty? Kitty, kitty?" I racked my brain but couldn't remember her name.

The rustling started up again, much closer this time. There was the snap of branches—big branches! This was no cat!

"Denny? Is that you?" My voice rasped into a whisper. Again no reply.

Instinct seized me. I vaulted to my feet and scuffled as fast as I could back toward the truck. It wasn't far, only a few hundred feet or so, but that was the longest sixty-yard dash I could have ever imagined. Not daring to look behind me, I heaved myself into the cab. Hands trembling, I reached over to the driver's door and punched the lock button.

From my glass and steel fortress, I stared around and around like an owl on hawk alert. Nothing moved. I cracked the window and listened, but the only sounds were the sigh of the wind in the tops of the Doug firs and the faint drone of trucks on the highway far below.

Then I heard it. This time the noise was almost on top of me! In the grass, right next to the truck. I stared out, frozen with fear.

Relief replaced adrenaline when I saw the little cat. It had been her after all! I felt silly at my absurdly disproportionate reactions. I guess it would take some time—a lot of time—to put my mistrust of the universe behind me.

Tammy—the name came back in a flood of affection.

Tammy, my little heroine. This forest was her back yard. I frowned, thinking about coyotes and other woodland dangers. Maybe I should speak to her people about keeping her in the house.

Still, risk aside, there was a bit of the feral in all cats, a symbiosis with nature where they can hunt and chase as their ancestors did for a thousand generations before them. The wiry tabby was beautiful as she stalked and pounced. She was definitely after something—a mouse? a grasshopper? a dryad?

There was a flash of light as a small, curved object sailed into the air and spun back down again. As much as I tried, I couldn't make the shape and size into anything definable, and since crazy cat ladies fall heir to their idols' curiosity, I was compelled to check it out.

Slowly I opened the cab door. I didn't want to scare Tammy into running away, but I needn't have worried; one glimpse of me and she came bouncing out of the grass and over to the truck. I stepped down to pet her and she nestled into my hand. For a moment, her green-gold eyes locked on mine, then she gave her little prmph and returned to her quarry.

"What have you got there?" I asked, moving closer. It took her a few seconds to relocate the object in the fringe of roadside brush. She sprung and launched it once more. When it landed, I stooped to have a look.

A roundish patch of shimmer nestled in the spiky shadows. I reached down and picked it up. It was firm to the touch, smooth and polished.

I swore and dropped it like a hot potato.

I had done the exact thing Denny had told us not to.

I had handled the evidence!

Because that's what it was, I was certain of it. How else

could you describe a loose glasses lens spattered with tiny brown splotches? This could be the thing we were looking for, and now I'd gone and contaminated it with my fingerprints—the very fingerprints I didn't want showing up on anything having to do with the Sinclairii murders.

The gravel crunched behind me. I swung around to see Denny heading my way.

"What you got?" he called out.

I just stared guiltily. Tammy disappeared into the forest, on her way back home I hoped.

Denny came up beside me, his cat-green eyes following my gaze. "Wow! Great, Lynley! This could really be something."

He pulled out a little camera and took a few close-ups. Producing a measuring tape from his vest, he peered around. When he saw what he wanted—a large rock embedded firmly in the dirt at the edge of the road—he took a measurement. He jotted the results in a small notebook, then looked again. This time it was a young hemlock tree opposite the rock. He repeated this activity once more, citing a fallen log a few feet back in the bush.

"Triangulation," he explained, though I hadn't asked. "You see, by logging the distance from three stationary objects to the object in question, I can get its exact position." He made a few more notes, then flipped the notebook shut and put it away. "May not mean anything, but it's always better to have more information than not enough."

He stuck a pink flag beside the lens, thought for a moment and put down another. "We want to make sure no one touches this. Those red spots look like blood, though I suppose they could be mud. It's a long shot, but if it pans out, it could put someone else at the scene, and lenses can be traced if they were prescribed by an optometrist. Then again, it might just be from a cheap drug store set, but I doubt it. I can see a bifocal line, and the cheap ones are usually set in permanent rims—the whole thing would come apart before the lenses themselves would fall out."

I hadn't moved throughout his commentary. He stared at me with sudden concern. "Lynley, what's wrong? This could be the break we were looking for. Here's a clue that definitely can't be tracked back to you."

He seemed so excited, so motivated. How was I supposed to tell him I'd ruined the only lead we had?

Chapter 21

Introduce a new cat slowly into your household. Start him in a small area, away from any others, then expand his horizons over the next several days. Exchange blankets or towels that each cat has slept on to get them used to each other's scent.

One thing that must be said for Special Agent Paris—he had the patience of a saint and the optimism of a cat who, upon hearing a can opener, assumes without question that it's going to mean something good. When I blurted out my blunder, he took it like a man. There was no yelling or reprimands which I knew I badly deserved. He called it an honest mistake and got on with matters.

He had alerted the Cowlitz County Sheriff's Office by way of the CB radio in his truck, and upon their arrival, he told them matter-of-factly just what had occurred. When the small, mousy detective began to give me grief about it, Denny didn't actually disagree, but he gallantly diverted the attention away from me and toward the other things we'd found. Halle and Connie had done their job well, producing a broken comb, a wad of spent chewing gum, several twist-top bottle caps, which bespoke a beer party more than a shooting, and a few other sundries. Nothing as promising as the lens, but good stuff just the same. Even though the likelihood of these things being missed in the original crime scene search was low, the detective had bagged and tagged everything, including my McDonald's cup. He was very thorough; so much so that I wondered if it might have been a comment on our amateur sleuthing.

The ride home was quiet. As the sun set, headlights appeared like pairs of luminescent cat eyes heralding the oncoming night. Denny assured me that all was not lost with the lens; even if there was an extraneous fingerprint or two, forensics might still find something underneath. I had to assume he was being straight with me and not just saying it to make me feel better. It was his case, but my life was on the line, and I had the most to lose.

By the time we made it to FOF where Denny dropped me so I could pick up both my car and my foster cat, it was nearing ten o'clock. The shelter was only open to the public until nine, but I had called Kerry to let her know I'd be a little late. She said that was fine; she had paperwork to do.

"The downside of the job," she commented as I walked in. She tamped a great pile of pages and put them in a basket. Placing a glass paperweight on top with a little flourish, she added. "It's never done, but I am." Straightening a few things on her desk and shutting down her computer for the night, she looked up at me.

"Ready for Mike?"

Managing a wan smile, I nodded.

Kerry scrutinized my face. "You don't have to take him if you don't want to. He's fine right here; we just thought it would be nice for him to be somewhere quiet before his surgery."

"No, I'm sorry. Of course I want him," I said. "It's been a really tiring day, but I've been looking forward to this. Mike...?"

"Yeah. We've been calling him Mikey, as in 'Mikey likes it!' from the old cereal commercial. He seems to like everything that can be classified as food."

I smiled again, this time the real thing. "Well, Mikey and I are going to go home and get a good night's rest."

"Sounds perfect. He's all ready for you. Hold on and I'll go get him."

I watched Kerry push through the heavy door to the back area where they kept the cats coming in and out of foster. She was so cute, tall and lithe, in her late twenties as were many of the shelter staff. Her short black hair was always as shiny as a panther; her brown eyes sparkled with possibilities, no matter how overworked she was. *Oh, to be young again!* I thought to myself. Except that when I was her age, I was squandering my life on the pursuit of higher highs, better sex, and ideals that were never going to pan out. This girl, on the other hand, seemed to know where she was going and what she wanted, and was on the fast track to making it happen. Good for her!

The door swung open again and Kerry hauled in a hefty carrier. Tiny mewling objections wafted from inside.

She put the carrier down with a grunt. "Don't let his cute little meow fool you—he must weigh a good twelve pounds. That's one of the reasons we have to keep him off his feet for the next few weeks. Just walking on the leg could injure it further."

"I'll put him in my kennel. It comes complete with all the amenities including a window that looks out into the trees. He can watch the birds right from his own bed."

"Sounds lovely. I made up a bag of goodies—some food and treats. His paperwork is in there too so you can check out his history. There isn't very much because he was brought in as a stray."

"Frannie said the vets thought he'd been hit by a car." I peered into the carrier and saw a sweet, furry face with big yellow eyes staring back at me.

"That's the assumption, but there are no exterior wounds, just the dislocated hip and cracked pelvis. Otherwise he's *purrfect*," she cooed into the carrier. She looked back at me. "No meds, just keep him quiet and bring him back in two weeks for the surgery."

I picked up the pink plastic box—Kerry was right, he was no lightweight! "What happens after that?"

"He'll go back into foster until he heals up a bit and can get around on his own. You can take him again if you like."

"Sure," I said with a smile—I loved him already.

"Here," Kerry said, grabbing the bag of stuff, "I'll help you out to your car."

We walked into the summer night in silence. She hadn't asked me any of the obvious questions—why I was so exhausted; why I looked like crap—and I was thankful.

I unlocked the trunk and she slung in the heavy sack. "Let me know if you have any questions or concerns."

"I will." I knew the drill.

The foster team was great. They fielded all sorts of queries from the urgent to the absurd with a smile and a straight answer. To foster moms and dads, the kitties they cared for were as precious as children, and when one spurned his kibbles, drank an inordinate amount of water, or tossed too many hairballs, they immediately sought medical advice. Better safe than sorry.

I put Mikey in the passenger side and scooted up the seat until the carrier was securely wedged between it and the dashboard. I got in the driver's side and waved goodbye to Kerry. Gazing at the box, I said, "Here we go, Mike. Don't be scared. We'll be home in a few minutes."

As I pulled out of the parking lot onto the deserted avenue, I rolled down my window. Air conditioning was great, but I needed the hot, smoggy summer wind on my face. I crooked an elbow outside, leaned back, and drove one-handed, remembering with nostalgia a simpler time: Hot rods, cold malts, poodle skirts, and sock hops—Ah! Those were the days! (In reality, I had been too young to partake of the fifties coolness, but I figured any generation that came before the advent of LSD must have gotten off easy.)

Mikey and I cruised toward home, enjoying the night. Mikey was quiet and so was I until I turned onto my street. Then without warning, a wave of anxiety hit me: What would I find when I got to the house? Burglars? Cops? Kidnappers? I knew the Badass boys were dead, but that fact didn't seem to diminish my paranoia.

For the first time since we left the shelter, Mike meowed. It was almost as if her were telling me not to worry. I looked at the carrier, feeling the strength of personality within.

"You're right, Mikey. We can handle anything that life throws at us—be it dislocated hip or murder charge."

That night, after putting him in his plush and well-appointed kennel, I sat down in the rocking chair and watched him settle. We had the jazz station on—I'd learned with my very first foster that cats liked jazz—and they were playing something sweet by Louie Armstrong. Mikey took a few bites of kibbles and a few laps of water; he sniffed his litter box, then went around to every corner of the grid-wire cage. He batted the toys, kneaded the carpet, smoothed against the cardboard scratcher mounted on the side, then climbed into his bed, curled up and closed his eyes. I closed my eyes as well, and that's the last thing I remember until morning.

* * *

I sat at the computer with Mikey on my lap, working on the Mackey family tree. I hadn't looked at it for weeks and the stacks of files, lists of websites, and albums of brittle sepia-toned photos called to me. Sometimes I caught myself assuming I had forever to work my project, but that wasn't true. If I passed before it was finished, how would my decedents know about Grandma Mackey who, during the Great Depression, saved the town of Ridgefield, Washington, by organizing a community garden on the unused cemetery grounds; or Harmon Hall, who was present with Howard Carter during the excavation of King Tut's tomb? How would they know where Uncle Frank and Aunt Julia were buried, orr how little Jacob drowned in the river when he was only three years old? I find the whole thing fascinating, though as I mentioned, my daughter couldn't care less. I'm hoping Seleia will pick up the baton. So far so good; she's actually asked me about some of the more engaging family members, and she even helped me transpose the diary of Fabian Mackey who came west with his family in the late eighteen-hundreds. His tiny, faded scrawl was almost impossible to decipher, but she got into it and we had the whole thing done in less than week. Most of the narrative was boring and factual, but there were a few treats among the kibble.

Currently I was trying to verify on the internet a tale about a pitstop Fabian and his family had made in the Shenandoah Valley, carefully searching for clues without hitting a porn site or a lethal virus by mistake. You could never tell by the search words anymore. I was staring at a perfect example: though thankfully nothing offensive or threatening, the keywords *Shenandoah Mackey* had taken me, not to early American history as I had expected, but to the site of an international gem wholesaler where close-up scans of loose-cut stones mingled with flashing Viagra ads.

I was just about to return to the search page when something caught my eye, a small photo of an irregular dusky brown stone with an insert of a lovely marquis-cut brown diamond at the top right corner. A long string of blue letters and numbers ran across the bottom, beckoning me.

Chocolate diamonds, the latest diamond fad. I had held two of the most unique specimens on earth in my hot little hands, yet I had never known their worth. How much did an egg-sized chocolate diamond go for? With a little thrill, I clicked the link.

Curiosity and a computer own a symbiotic relationship: if you have a question, you look it up on the internet. Maybe you find your answer, maybe not, but it's a cinch you'll come up with another question and probably two. The link gave me an enlarged version of the photo, a list of details, and an email for more information. No prices. But now that I had asked the question, I wasn't about to give up.

Next I tried *chocolate+diamond+price* and then *chocolate+diamond+cost* and then *brown+diamond+cost*, brown diamond being what the previous site had told me was the old name for the newly popular stone. *Buy Chocolate Diamond on eBay* had pulled up a few unimpressive examples of pre-set stones that ranged from ninety-nine cents to forty-seven thousand dollars, depending on the settings, makers, quality, and the whim of the buyers who happened to be watching when the auction ended, but that wasn't much help.

Back on the search page, I scrolled down in hopes of something more promising, but all I found was junk. I was about ready to get back to my ancestry when a caption at the bottom of the page caught my eye. It had nothing to do with the value of the diamond market and everything to do with another question altogether, a question I hadn't asked myself until that very moment.

* * *

Two valuable diamonds turn up on my property, one in the house and the other in my garden pool mixed in with twenty years' worth of Pacific Ocean beach agates. Where had they come from? How had they gotten there? Why?

I suppose I'd wondered about it at some point, but something more pressing always got in the way: my house was ravaged; I was grabbed and hurt; I got nabbed by the police for the murders of the men who turned out to be the thieves. I knew from the start that the stones were the center of the whole deal. Two peerless brown diamonds, so valuable that they had their own names. Worth millions, Badass had said. Stolen from a rich eccentric with brown-eyed cats, according to the brief synopsis Detective Marsha had given me in the hospital. That was all I knew and suddenly I realized it wasn't enough.

Somewhere along the line I'd given up on the whys and wherefores, but that was silly. There had to be some record of a heist that big out there on the worldwide web. The answers were right at my fingertips and had been all the time, if I'd just bothered to look.

With a whole new fervor and a fearlessness I hadn't felt for a long time, I peered at the link. Decisively, I clicked.

I surveyed the caption: *Cats' Eyes Theft Leaves Police and Owner Baffled.* It was a web news article dated four months previous. I peered closer, my mind full of wonder and expectation at finally solving the mystery.

I had just begun to sift through the page of tiny print when my phone rang. Mikey launched from my lap but with cat's paw swiftness, I caught him mid-air, saving his bum leg from a nasty surprise. It was hard to explain to a cat that he must take it easy; he just stares at you with a look that clearly says *you're not the boss of me*.

I gently conveyed Mikey to the floor and picked up the phone.

"Lyn? It's Halle," came the familiar voice of my friend, attorney, and clan-mate.

I tensed. Which hat was she wearing tonight? I hadn't heard from her for a week which I took as a sign that things were going smoothly with my case. "I hope it's not bad news. Because I'm not sure I could deal with another setback," I said, my previous self-assurance beginning to scatter like catnip in the wind.

"It's not. In fact it's all good. You've been cleared of any suspicion in the Sinclairii murders case."

"Wow!" I stammered, then I paused waiting for her to give me the punch line.

"Well, you don't sound very happy for someone who just got her life back."

"Oh, I am. Very happy." I sank back into my chair, leaned over and hugged my knees like you're supposed to do when you're dizzy. Call it a preemptive strike. "That's great news. So what happened? What made them change their minds?"

"I'll tell you when I get there, I mean if it's okay to drop by. I'm just down the street."

"Sure, come on over. I think I've got some interesting news for you as well."

* * *

202

I put Mikey in the kennel, filled his food bowl and promised I'd be back later. Leaving John Coltrane bluesing away on the radio, I got to the front door just about the same time as Halle. I could tell she was excited: her face was flushed to a color that rivaled her hair and she was smiling. Not that generic grin she used in her practice, but the real, genuine thing.

She came in and dropped onto the couch in a move befitting a trucker. I sat down at the other end and tucked my legs underneath me. Little was up in no time, balancing on my thigh; she didn't need a whole lap, any body part would do, Zen cat that she was.

"So what's up?" we both said simultaneously, then we both laughed.

"You first," we said to each other, again in perfect harmony.

Again we laughed. We laughed and laughed. It wasn't that funny but who cares? I was letting go of that two-ton weight that had been hanging over my head. Relief can be more passionate than sex.

"You're off the hook, hon," she beamed, unbuttoning her dark business jacket and loosening her tie. "Of course, you can't be one hundred percent sure with these things until someone's actually tried and convicted, but all the evidence—good evidence this time, not that circumstantial crap they tried to pull on you—points to a brand-new suspect."

"Did they get something from the stuff we gave them?"

"They did indeed. It was that darned lens. After they stripped off your fingerprints—I have no idea how they do that, some very complex chemical process I suppose—they found another set underneath. The spatter was blood—

Sinclairii blood, no doubt about it. It was both over and under the prints which pretty much puts the note in the milk bottle."

"Do they know whose they are?

"Not yet. The prints aren't on record."

"Denny said they might be able to find him through his optometrist."

Halle shrugged. "Not our problem, hon. Tentatively speaking, we can put this whole thing behind us and get on with our lives."

Get on with our lives, I mused. It sounded so simple. And maybe it was. The brothers were dead; I was free; any further interest I took in chocolate diamonds or million-dollar heists was of my own choosing.

Suddenly the information that had seemed so important to me an hour ago meant absolutely nothing. I didn't care a hoot how much those flipping rocks were worth or where they had come from. Or where they were now, for that matter—well, maybe that, just as a point of curiosity.

"Do you know if the police ever recovered the diamonds?" I asked.

"They didn't. Not a sign."

"Hum."

"Hum, what?"

"Hum nothing at all." I scooped Little off my leg which was beginning to fall asleep and placed her gently on the couch. I rose. "I don't give a flying you-know-what about you-know-what. I'm done with drama. I'm done with intrigue. I'm just plain done!"

"Good for you! Now I think we deserve a well-earned drink. You want to walk up to the Pub and Pony? I'll buy."

"Why not?" I replied. Halle was well aware that for

me, a drink meant ginger ale. She liked her beer with Jack back, and we often did cocktails together. We were just like anyone else, except I could drive home afterwards.

I got my purse, Halle grabbed her man-bag, and we headed for the door.

"You wanted to tell me something."

"Huh?" I mumbled as I searched for my keys to lock up.

"You said you had something to tell me. Some 'interesting news'."

"Oh, that." I paused, then said quietly. "Never mind, it's not important anymore."

"Then let's get on with it!" she giggled.

Walking out that door, I felt free as a wild cat and just as smart. I'd made it through what may have been the most difficult time of my life and come out relatively unscathed. What a relief knowing odds were I'd never have to go through anything like that for the rest of my days.

The alarm set, I pulled the door shut and locked it blithely as if I had not a care in the world. I gazed around me, drinking it all in. I saw the azure blue of the sky; I saw the verdant green of the trees; I saw the blazing orange-yellow of the setting sun and it was beautiful.

What I didn't see was Fraulein Fluffs sitting on the bookshelf watching me go. Maybe if I'd caught her worried look and the sense of foreboding she projected toward me, I wouldn't have been quite so quick to let down my guard. As it turned out, my serenity was only illusion; the eye of the hurricane with thunderclouds still gathering and more storms to come.

Chapter 22

Chronic Kidney Disease, the progressive, irreversible loss of kidney function over time, is one of the most common conditions affecting older cats. Advancement of the disease may be slowed by diet and care, and symptoms may be relieved so the cat is comfortable, but CKD has only one outcome which must, for the sake of both cat and companion, be faced with courage, love, and grace.

At first I watched the news for mention of an arrest in the Sinclairii case, but as days turned to weeks and weeks to a month, my interest waned. No surprise: the human attention span is comparable to that of a flea. Besides, I was busy. I'd got back into my yoga for really the first time since my broken leg; the senior ladies had upped the stakes by registering for the Liver Walk in early September and were trekking their little hearts out; my garden, what there was of it this year, was beginning to produce so I was out at dawn pulling weeds from the carrots and kohlrabi.

The cats were all fine—someone was drinking more water than usual which would have to be watched since excessive thirst can be a sign of kidney disease, and the fleas were rampant this summer so I had to stay vigilant with the topical flea treatment (Thank you, God, for small miracles!)—but otherwise fine. Mike was still with me though he'd had his surgery and was springing about like a bunny on his newly improved hip. He liked my home and he got along with the other cats. Little had made him her project and groomed his luxurious fur whenever he sat still long enough for her to nab him.

Mikey was now well enough to be adopted so his picture was up on the website as an outreach cat; if someone were interested in him, they would contact me through the shelter, and we would make arrangements to meet. Granted it was a bit more difficult to adopt out that way since there wasn't that spontaneous 'love at first sight' factor the shelter offered, but it was worth a try. He still needed supervised exercise on that leg which would be hard to manage in the small shelter kennel. Besides, I liked his company.

August was a busy month for FOF. There was the A-*cat*-emy Awards where our most generous benefactors were duly honored; the kids' camp that ran in consecutive weekly sessions from August to Labor Day; and the booth at the Clark County Fair. Frannie and I always did the fair, passing out flyers and information on the shelter and showing off an elite group of cats and kittens deemed stoic enough to weather the hot, dusty, busy macrocosm of the festival.

Actually, though hectic as ever, the event was no longer hot or dusty. A huge expo center had been built and now instead of the colony of barns and lodges, we had one big, air-conditioned room the size of a football field. The farm animals—cows, sheep, pigs, chickens, and rabbits—had their own structure; our building held crafts, quilts, art, photography and the mandatory strange vegetable exhibits as well as the commercial booths of which we were one.

For those of you too young to remember the fun of a good old county fair, take it from me, it's a great way to spend a hot summer day. Perusing the fruits of our county's gifted citizens' labors; getting sticky on unnaturally-hued cotton candy; reveling in the panorama of colored lights on the midway. Viewing the stars from atop a Ferris wheel can't be described to someone who hasn't been there in person.

As you may have guessed, I was looking forward to the fair. For me, there was always an air of anticipation that took me back to days long gone. Our wonderful cattery manager, Kate, had picked out three cats and a late litter of four-month-old kittens for us to take; Robert, young, strong, and willing, would be driving us there in the shelter van. He would help us load in and set up, then do the same in reverse order when the day was done. The fair ran for five days but the cats were only there on the weekend; the rest of the time, another pair of volunteers would represent the shelter sans the feline complement.

I had done this event for years, but my fascination never wavered. As I set out my clothes for the morning—Robert would be by at seven to collect me—I thought about how lucky I was. Not lucky, I amended, as much as blessed. Things were good; all was in order. There was a serenity to my life I had never thought possible when I was younger. I guess it was God's little compensation for the Great Unknown that lay inevitably ahead.

Suddenly I shivered in spite of the August heat. If the trials I had been through had taught me anything, it was that the Great Unknown could be just a heartbeat away. I dropped the maroon Humane Society tee shirt onto the bed, all interest in my wardrobe gone by the wayside.

I *was* blessed.

Life *was* good,

But...

I looked at the clock. It was nearly midnight. I pulled

back the covers and crawled into bed, clothes and all. Fluffs was in my spot and I moved her gently. Red jumped up and settled at my feet, blinking smiles at me with his mandarin eyes. Violet was sleeping on the carpet, softly snoring. Even Dirty Harry had graced me with his presence in a rare upstairs visitation. They were all congregating, I thought to myself. Was it a sign?

With a sigh, I switched off the bedside lamp. Staring into the darkened room, I wondered what tomorrow might bring.

Chapter 23

Feline Immunodeficiency Virus is a misunderstood disease. It is species-specific and poses no threat to humans. Most FIV-positive cats live long, healthy lives. My neighbor had an FIV-positive kitty who lived, vivacious and vet-free, to the age of nineteen. Can't ask much more than that.

The new day blazed into being on beams of golden sunshine. I could almost imagine Apollo up there in his chariot of fire. I had woken early, which was good since in my sulk of the night before, I had forgotten to set the alarm. There were things I had to do before Robert arrived, feeding the cats not the least of them.

I was a miracle of efficiency: by the time Robert pulled up in front of the house, I had not only fed cats, changed their water, filled the fountain, and cleaned the litter boxes—I'd started laundry, watered the geraniums, paid some pesky bills, looked over my Facebook page, and packed a lunch. In the light of day, my premonition of evil or whatever it had been faded into obscurity, and now I couldn't even remember what had got me so down. I wrote it off as fatigue and staying up too late—not enough rest and I turn into a cranky tiger.

Robert had picked Frannie up first, so I hopped in the back next to a tower of cat carriers strapped securely onto the van's special tie-down hooks. I peered at the grid fronts but couldn't see a whisker in the murky shadows.

"Who did we get?" I asked Frannie.

She turned in her seat. "Hum, let me see. It's Pete the Geek on the bottom there, Eudora in the middle, and Russell on top. The kittens are in the back," she added unnecessarily since I could hardly miss the mew-fest coming from behind me.

"Good choice." I wiggled my fingers in through the grill of the middle carrier and was rewarded with Eudora's soft gray face rubbing against them.

Eudora was the perfect cat, lovely in both body and temperament. She was young and strong and the only reason she hadn't been adopted yet was because she had FIV.

People are afraid of the immune-inhibiting virus, likening it to the horrors of its human equivalent, HIV, but though both viruses attack the immune system, they're not related. With good care, an FIV-positive cat can be as healthy as any other. Part of our job as FOF representatives is to educate, so bringing Eudora to the fair was a perfect opportunity to do that.

The Clark County Fairgrounds was a good half-hour drive north from Portland on a nondescript section of I-5. "How about some music?" Frannie asked Robert as we pulled onto the freeway.

"Sure." He punched the buttons. "What do you like? Oldies? Classical?"

"Put it on one-oh-seven-point-five," suggested Frannie. She looked at me and winked.

"But that's hip-hop. You're kidding, right?"

"It's a guilty pleasure," I chuckled. "Us old folks gotta keep up with the times."

"What about the language? The sex and drugs and stuff? That doesn't bother you?"

Frannie patted the young man on the shoulder. "They

211

said four letter words when we were young too, believe it or not."

"And we won't even start about the sex and drugs," I put in. "Let's just say that in 1968, we were the 'new generation of party people'."

"But the rap...?"

"Frank Sinatra did rap back in the forties. I hate to tell you, but there's really nothing new under the sun."

Robert looked flustered; I wasn't surprised. Frannie and I had surprised members of the younger set before with our atypical taste in car radio music. "Some songs are better than others," I conceded. "But the content's the same as it's always been: love, lust, anger."

"Frustration with the establishment," Frannie took up, "and making a better life for our kids."

"And grandkids," I added.

Robert shrugged and punched in the station, though the look on his face declared his adamant refusal to admit any correlation between his generation and ours.

The music blasted with passionate vocals and a blood-stirring base line, a song about hardships, hostilities, and hope for a new day. Frannie and I sat back and listened happily as we cruised up the road.

* * *

The day at the fair was busy, busy, busy! We gave out stacks of brochures and boxes of lapel ribbons with cat faces that had been glued onto the crisscross by a band of dedicated volunteers. The donation jar was full of dimes, dollars, and checks. All the kittens had been adopted out, papers signed, and arrangements made to pick them up at the shelter. There's always one or two folk who don't understand why they can't take the cat right away and carry it around the fair for the next several hours in their pocket or purse, but most get the drill.

We were thrilled when Eudora was adopted by a woman who wanted a companion for her own FIV-positive cat. It seemed like the perfect match. She was knowledgeable about the virus and how to avoid the pitfalls that might hinder the cats from living happy, ordinary lives.

A man had put a twenty-four hour hold on Russell so his wife who was at work could meet him before a decision was made. I didn't think it would be much of a contest; his two little daughters whom he was escorting around the fair were already in love with the big tabby. The meet-and-greet with mom would be only a formality.

That left Pete the Geek. Pete was shy, and shy cats are routinely passed over because they don't have that *in your face with a big meow and purr* attitude. He was also quite plain as cats go: black and a little scrawny with greasy fur and dandruff on his nether regions from the stress of shelter life. It had been a long shot to bring him to such a loud and boisterous place, but in the end it was decided that the odds of his getting noticed in the small collective were worth the try. All he needed was someone who could see past his deficiencies to the great cat he would be once he had a loving home. With love, the shyness would diminish and the stress would ease; his coat would become soft and glossy and his gauntness would fill out. We'd seen it before many times.

It was getting near closing when the miracle occurred. Many of the booths had already packed up for the night and the crowd was thinning out, gravitating toward the corn dogs, deep-fried Mars bars, and neon-bedecked thrill rides. Frannie had gone to get us a veggie-burger and I had

Pete out on my lap. It was against the rules, but he'd been stuck in the big wire 'dog' kennel all day and I felt sorry for him. He had his walking harness on just in case he got spooked, and I was brushing his back end when I heard a little *ahem*.

Looking up, I saw a small, slightly scrawny, slightly scruffy young man. His brown hair hadn't been anywhere near a pair of scissors for a while and his green and yellow Oregon Ducks shirt had seen better days, but his twinkling eyes were clear and his smile was genuine.

"Excuse me," he said shyly, "Uh, would it be alright for me to see the kitty?"

At first I was a little reluctant—a lot of people think a shelter is a petting zoo—but there was something in this fellow's bright gaze that told me to take a chance.

"Sure. His name is Pete the Geek. He's kind of shy."

The man reached out a tentative hand, let Pete sniff it, then gently rubbed his head. Pete rubbed back and before I knew it, Pete was in his arms instead of mine.

"I think he likes you," I said, an understatement of the love-in I was witnessing.

"Uh, I like him too," said the man. "Is he adoptable? Because if he is, you know, I'd like to have him. I've been looking for a cat just like this one."

"Of course!" I tried not to be too excited though my heart was leaping. "Would you like to see his paperwork?"

"Okay," the man said as Pete snuggled and purred.

I pulled out a thin sheaf. "We don't have too much information on him because he was a stray, but everyone at the shelter has fallen in love with him."

The man studied the front page. "He's been there since February?" he gasped. "That's six months!"

I was waiting for the inevitable 'What's wrong with

214

him?' that we often get when a cat's been with us a long time.

Instead he said, "Well, that cinches it!" To Pete, he crooned, "You're coming home with me."

"Really?" I gasped.

"Really!" he exclaimed.

I was elated. The match seemed made in Kitty Heaven for the two lost souls who from this day forward would have each other to lean on. Maybe I was projecting—I really had no reason besides a gut instinct to think this young man a lost soul, but even had he been the Prince of Wales, the rapport between man and cat was as apparent as the sun in the sky.

I handed him a blue form. "Just fill this out and we'll get things started. Want me to hold him so you can write?"

"No, he's fine," said the man as he shifted Pete to his other arm and took up a pen. He paused and looked at me with a glimmer of amusement in his eye. "My name's Pete, too, you know."

* * *

We sat like happy zombies in our metal folding chairs while Robert took the cats back to the van. It had been a good day, but I was ready for it to end. There was still some foot traffic checking out the few die-hard booths that remained open, but the huge room, so busy a few hours before, now echoed with abandonment. Frannie and I spoke in hushed whispers, as if in a cathedral rather than a commercial building. Voices carried: a shrill laugh, the clack of a hard-soled boot.

Suddenly I stiffened.

Frannie frowned. "What is it, Lynley?"

I sat, listening, looking, but it was gone, whatever it

was that had grabbed my subconscious attention.

I shook my head. "It's nothing. I guess," I added.

Frannie looked around anxiously. "You sure? You seemed upset."

"I don't know. For a moment, I had a feeling..." I paused. It sounded so silly, so dramatic. "I had the feeling I was being watched."

"Oh, is that all?" she snickered in visible relief. "I hate to tell you, Lynley, but we're in a very public place surrounded by people—chances that someone's looking at you are pretty high."

"Yeah, I know. But it wasn't like that," I sulked, not appreciating her humor at the moment.

Frannie reached over and patted my hand. "I'm sorry. I didn't mean to be flippant. I'm just tired, and so are you. Our minds play tricks with us sometimes, that's all."

"I know," I conceded. My mind played tricks with me all the time.

"Ready to roll?" Robert called from the big doorway.

I stood, folded up my chair, and leaned it against the table for the morning. Frannie did the same. She put her arm around me as we headed for the van. "Let's go listen to some nice hip-hop and be proud of a job well done."

"Amen!" I agreed as all thought of the unknown watcher slipped out of my head.

Chapter 24

Cats have many reasons for inappropriate litter box use. If your cat suddenly starts peeing outside the box, have him checked for an infection or inflammation of the lower urinary tract before moving on to a psychological cause.

Things at the fair played out just about the same the next day with a new group of cats and a restock of ribbon pins. It was Sunday so the building opened an hour later which had given me some much-appreciated time to relax with my coffee and the paper before Robert arrived.

The Sunday morning crowd was different from the high-energy Saturday bunch: quieter, better dressed, and noticeably sparser. The population would increase as the day went on, but I had to say I liked this more sedate pace where people stopped to talk, look at the cats, and listen to our spiel about all the great things Friends of Felines did for our community.

In between customers, Frannie and I chatted and drank thermos coffee out of mugs from home—no three-dollar five-hundred-calorie coffee in a purportedly biodegradable paper cup for us, no matter what it says—or doesn't say— on the logo.

"You feeling better this morning?" Frannie asked me out of the blue.

I wiped brown liquid from my mouth. "Better? Was I feeling bad?"

"Oh, I don't know." She paused. "You were feeling a

little insecure last night, sort of thought you were being observed, remember?"

I tensed. "Oh, that," I said as nonchalantly as I could with chills running down my spine. "I'm sure you were right, just nerves after a long day. I mean, what else could it be?"

"Well, Lynley, that's just it. What else *could* it have been?" She turned in her chair to face me. "I know you've been through a lot in the last few months, and you had good reason to be scared, but it's over now. You need to let it go. Whatever it takes."

I frowned. "What are you getting at, Frannie? I'm not following."

She looked with sudden interest at the passersby. A man was taking a ribbon pin and putting a bill in the jar.

"Thank you," Frannie told him with a gracious smile.

I smiled too, but when he had moved on, I sobered again. "Come on, Frannie, spit it out. What are you trying to say?"

"We've been friends for a long time and don't take this the wrong way, but don't you see? This seems to be happening a lot lately. This... paranoia."

Paranoia? The accusation hit me from left field. I admitted to having a few unpleasant feelings from time to time, but that was to be expected, wasn't it? And some of them had turned out to be somewhat prescient, hadn't they? Paranoia? I mean, really!

"Look, I know it's not what you want to hear," Frannie rushed on, "but have you thought about seeing someone? A counselor or something? Where you could talk it out, you know. And what about attending a PTSD support group? After all, I think being assaulted and kidnapped qualifies as traumatic stress."

To say nothing of being accused of murder, I thought to myself.

Everything in my being rallied against her assessment but my logical mind recognized a little kernel of truth. If it had been anyone but Frannie, I might have let my embarrassment, pride, and hurt feelings dictate my reply, but I knew she had my best interests at heart.

I found myself saying, "I guess you have a point. They suggested trauma counseling the first time I went to the hospital, after Badass broke my leg. I just never got around to it."

"Did they give you a name?"

"As a matter of fact they did. If I can find it again." I visualized my big, cluttered house and thought the odds were slim.

"You could call them again, or ask your PCP," Frannie suggested. She was not about to let this go until she got the response she wanted.

So I gave it to her. "I'll look into it. I promise."

The building was beginning to fill up and I was rescued from the uncomfortable conversation by a pack of girl scouts. I must say, I was relieved to focus on shelter cats and away from my delirium. Frannie had made a good case. I would think about it. Later.

As the crowd grew bigger and the booth got busier, Frannie and I concentrated on our job. No more was said about my state of mind or what others thought I should do about it, for which I think we were both relieved. No one likes to tell a friend she's crazy. Cat-crazy? Yes. Real crazy? Not so much.

The kittens were all adopted out by noon and we sent Robert to get another batch. We had a three-ring binder with eight-by-ten color glossies of all the cats available from the shelter, but most adopters preferred to touch and hold before they chose a pet, even a cute kitten in a little yellow bow posing before a nice sky-blue background.

The album was popular though; people who weren't quite ready to make that commitment liked to check it out, take a business card or a brochure, and plan to visit the shelter at a later date. Some of them actually did. A few placed holds so they could be assured their choice was still there when they came. If they changed their minds or didn't show up within the twenty-four-hour period, they would lose their fifteen dollars, but since, as we explained to them with a smile, it served as a contribution to Friends of Felines, their loss was FOF's gain as well as a tax deduction.

Some folks can make up their minds about a pet right then and there; others have to think about it, discuss it with loved ones, consult the stars. Whatever it takes is alright with us since making a good match is the primary aim of adoption. One woman had come back to look at the album at least three times. I'd noticed her lingering over the enticing pictures but had been busy helping other clients. When she rolled around for the fourth pass, I was free.

"Find anyone you like?" I asked, giving her my best shelter smile.

She looked up as if I'd startled her. Or maybe it was just her roundish, styleless glasses and the way her lanky dark brown hair fell around her long, waif-like face. She was about my height—five-four—but younger and slimmer. In jeans and a plain black tee shirt, she gave no indication as to what she did when she wasn't hanging around the county fair.

You may think my assessment intrusive, but it's part of

what we do as adoption consultants. For example, there's probably no point in showing a shaggy yellow longhair stray to a sophisticated lady in a black couture dress, or a feisty tortie senior to a family with small children. This woman was inscrutable, however: she could have been a mom (a couple of cutesy kittens would do nicely); a college grad student (an independent mid-age tabby might be the one there) or even a nurse (a special needs case: diabetic, renal failure, or hyperthyroid with whom she could sympathize.)

"I was just looking," she said. He voice was dry and I felt as if I wanted to give her a drink of water.

"Do you have animals in your home now?" Another interview question.

"Uh, no. But I've been thinking about getting a cat," she added.

"Well, you've come to the right place. You have anything in mind?" I glanced at the page she had selected and with a rush of excitement, saw it was Mike, my foster.

"Not really, This one's nice." She, too, looked at the head shot of the gorgeous longhair.

Nice? I thought to myself. I personally considered Mike, with his luxurious sable and white coat, his sweetheart face and his melting golden eyes to be one of the most beautiful cats I'd even seen, but maybe she just wasn't good at expressing herself.

"That's Mike," I told her proudly. "Would you like to see his paperwork, get to know a little more about him?"

"Oh, I don't know," she hedged.

"Actually I know Mikey really well. He happens to be staying with me while he recovers from hip surgery. He's all healed up now but needs supervised exercise, which is easier to do at home than in the shelter. He still can't jump up very well. He climbs like a pro, though." I thought fondly of the first time I saw Mike scramble up into his kennel. The kennel sits on a table at window height; I'd had him out for some exercise, but I guess he was done because next thing I knew, he was standing on his back legs stretching his long body up to the kennel door. He grabbed the lip with his front paws, and in a move something like a fast chin-up, was inside looking out the window at the birds.

"Really?" said the woman, a spark of interest in her eyes. "You have him at your house?"

"Yes."

"Can I come see him? Or... where do you live?"

I hesitated. "Inner southeast, the Hawthorne District, but usually we do the meetings at the shelter."

"Where's that?"

"It's in the Sunderland Neighborhood. That's a ways out but really not that far if you take Martin Luther King. Or you can come down by the airport as well."

She looked downcast. "My car's in the shop. It won't be out until next week. By then, someone else might have got him."

"You can put a hold on him, if you like. It's only twenty-four hours, but you can extend it another twenty-four. Maybe by then you could get a friend to take you."

"What if I adopt him right now? Then could I come get him from you?"

"I... I suppose so. Don't you want to check out his paperwork?" I shuffled through the pile until I found the stapled sheaf. I handed it to the woman who began to leaf through the pages. "He was a stray so there isn't a lot of information, but there are the vet notes from his surgery, and I can vouch for how sweet and well-behaved he is."

"Great," she said with a sigh and a smile. "What next? I suppose I have to fill something out."

With mixed emotions, I handed her the blue form.

* * *

As quiet as the morning had been, the afternoon was just the reverse. For everyone who had planned to go to the county fair and hadn't made it yet, the countdown of hours had begun. Tonight was the grand farewell, with fireworks over the midway and special family rates for rides. I think there had been a two-for-one coupon in the paper as well, so everybody and their mother-in-law was there. Of course not all the thousands of fair-goers were interested in shelter cats, but by my calculation, it seemed as if we talked to at least half of them.

Not everyone who stops to chat is looking for an adoption, of course. People tend to think of us as feline experts and come up with a vast array of cat questions: Why is Muffin hiding all the time? Why has Miss Kitty suddenly stopped using her litter box? Why does Tiger fight with Princess? The tendency is to give specific advice based on our vast experience with *Felis catus*, but we've learned that a general overview and a flyer for our veterinary behaviorist is usually the wisest counsel.

The constant flow of traffic kept me busy and my mind off what had happened with Tina, the young woman who was about to take my Mikey, but when it was all over and Frannie and I were having a good-bye drink in the little cocktail lounge on the observation deck overlooking the bright lights of the fairgrounds, the magnitude of the adoption came down on me full force.

"I don't know," I told Frannie. "What if she's not right for Mike? She didn't sound very cat-savvy—what if she doesn't appreciate him? Maybe I should have gone ahead and adopted him myself. I was thinking about it, you know."

"Oh, Lynley, you always feel this way when one of your fosters gets adopted. No one's ever good enough. But it seems to work out, doesn't it?"

"Yeah, but this is different. Mike still limps like crazy. What if she doesn't take care of him? What if she lets him outside?"

Frannie took a sip of her gin and tonic; I took a gulp of my ginger ale. "She signed the contract, didn't she? She promised to keep him as an indoor cat."

"Yeah, but what if she lied?"

"Lynley, stop," Frannie charged. "Listen to yourself. It's going to be okay. She'll probably be a great mom. And besides, Mike's a good strong cat. He may limp a little but that sure doesn't slow him down. I've seen him play with Little, run up and down the stairs and through the house with the best of them. He'll be fine, even if she turns out to be less than the pinnacle of perfection that you'd like her to be."

"I know," I conceded. "But fostering's hard. You get this poor, sick cat, nurse it back to health, care for it, make it feel wanted and come to love it; then when it's all healthy, happy and adjusted, when its coat is glossy and its eyes are clear and its wounds are healed, you send it out into the big wide world for some stranger."

"And you adore doing it," Frannie reminded me. "There's another one out there right now who needs you. And besides, you can't adopt them all. With your six, you've already got your crazy cat lady status. Any more and they'll have Denny cite you for hoarding."

The instant she said it, she was mortified. "Oh, Lynley,

I'm sorry. I wasn't thinking. I'd forgotten all about that bogus charge of abuse."

"That's okay, Frannie. I know what you meant. I'll tell you one thing, though: I could still rip an animal abuser to shreds with my bare hands, or worse, but since that night Denny came with the warrant to confiscate my cats, I've had a little more sympathy for the hoarders. Most of them start out like you or me—well, more like me, I guess—but they don't know where to draw the line. At some point, it just gets out of hand for them. That doesn't mean they love those cats any less for not being able to care for them properly."

"I know. And you're nowhere near that point. I was just making a joke. And not a very good one either."

I laughed. "It doesn't hurt to remind me that I am not a one-woman cat shelter." I raised my glass with a sigh. "Here's to Mike's new home."

Frannie clinked my tumbler with hers. "To a successful weekend. We did good."

"We did, didn't we?"

I don't know if it was coincidence or synchronicity but at that very moment the first triumphant report of fireworks burst through the air. Outside the sky lit up like a constellation of birthday candles with red, white, blue, and purple florets so bright they dimmed the lights of the midway. The silhouette of the Ferris wheel stood out black against the neon heavens. I knew it was silly and egotistical, but somehow I felt the display was just for me.

Chapter 25

The definition of an animal hoarder is someone who keeps higher than usual numbers of pets without being able to properly care for them, while at the same time denying the problem.

Mikey's bags were packed and ready to go—his bed, his catnip pillow, and the little red and gray afghan I had crocheted for him were set beside his carrier. I'd faxed Tina's application to the FOF counselor and was still waiting on the final okay but that was only a formality. FOF did background checks on all potential adopters but rarely did they find a problem that would impact the adoption.

Tina was set to come by in the afternoon. I still had second thoughts but I quashed them. This was why I fostered, I kept reminding myself.

Mike was lounging in his kennel, blissfully ignorant of the upcoming upheaval. The kennel door was open, and I had installed a set of pet steps after the chin-up incident so he could get in and out anytime he wanted, but he liked the small, safe niche with its window onto the world. I smiled—everybody loved the kennel.

I heard church bells in the kitchen and went to answer my phone. It was Denny.

"Special Agent Paris, what can I do for you?"

"Lynley, we have a situation," he began. His voice was strained and formal.

I immediately sobered. "What is it?"

"Early this morning we were called in to investigate a case of suspected animal neglect, a hoarding situation. Because of an eye-witness account, we were able to obtain a search warrant, and Connie, Frank, and I went to the site." He sighed so heavily it was almost a moan. "Lynley, it's one of the worst we've ever seen. Fifty-four adult cats and we haven't even established how many kittens but at least two dozen—over eighty total, all living in one big, absolutely disgusting room. The funny thing is the owner—or I should say *former* owner because she did finally relinquish the cats to Northwest Humane—she isn't poor by any means. In fact you'd never guess by looking at the home what was inside. The house is up on Portland Heights where the rich people live, but some of those cats were starving and all are severely undernourished. It's a nightmare. Mercifully we got there in time."

I listened with a mix of disgust, rage, and sympathy. Hoarding was a sickness, almost an addiction in some cases. When people think of cat hoarders, they envision an uneducated, sloppy old lady in a trailer, but that's only one scenario. Hoarding transcends the boundaries of class, sex, and wealth. I thought back to my conversation with Frannie in the bar the night before. *There but for the Grace of God*, and all.

"What can I do?" I asked.

"We need trained volunteers to help with the rescue effort. We have three STAR members but we're going to need everyone we can get. I warn you though, it's going to redefine your idea of filth. You can decline and no one will think any less of you. I just thought since you've been through all the rescue training and have worked with us before, how you'd be a real asset."

STAR, the Shelter Technical Animal Rescue team,

didn't usually participate in hoarding cases. They were the ones who rappelled down a cliff to save a fallen dog or climbed under a bridge after a stranded cat. For them to aid investigations meant this was a really big thing.

"Of course I'll help, but when are you going? I've got an adopter coming by my house to get her cat at two-thirty."

"It took a while to get the paperwork in order, but we're heading there right now. It'll probably take most of the day. Once the cats are seized, we move them to the Veterinary Learning Center to get checked out. The VLC is standing by with all the medical students, assistants, and volunteers they can muster. Any cats who are basically healthy and have already been altered will be bathed and groomed, treated for fleas, worms, ear mites, and lice, and given their shots, then transferred to several shelters around the area for personality assessments and if all goes well, adoption. The sick ones will stay at the hospital and so will the ones needing spay and neuter. We could sure use another pair of hands, but if you have prior obligations..."

I looked at the clock. It was nearing noon. I'd been on these ventures before and knew they could last long into the night. With resolve, I made a snap decision. "Denny, I can get someone else to handle the adoption. Frannie can probably come get Mike and take him to the shelter, and the girl can pick him up there. Let me make a few calls and then where should I meet you?"

He recited an address that raised my eyebrows. In that part of town, they weren't called houses; they were estates. With hoarders, you just never knew!

"Wear something that covers your entire body, coveralls, long-sleeved shirt, etcetera. We'll have paper booties, gloves, goggles, and face masks at the site."

"Will do. See you soon." Booties? Face masks? This wasn't going to be pretty.

* * *

Frannie and another FOF friend, Carla, came to my rescue so I could come to the rescue of the eighty starving cats. I car-pooled with Rick Schwartz, a STAR member, and found out a little more about the case.

An anonymous tip had come in to the investigations department the day before, he told me, stating that someone had three hundred cats locked up in their attic. The operator took the address and passed it to the on-call investigator, Special Agent Frank Dawson, per protocol. Frank began the warrant process but knew it wasn't going to come through until morning at the very earliest. If it was an abuse charge, he might have been able to push it faster, but hoarding, though contemptible, wasn't usually an immediate threat to the animals. Besides, from experience he knew that an anonymous accusation of three hundred cats would most likely turn out to be an exaggeration. He anticipated a far lesser number if it was a real situation at all. Like nine-one-one, people called in with all sorts of tales—true, partially true, and sometimes downright lies. Unlike nine-one-one, unless they gave a name and number, they were basically untraceable. It wasn't against the law to screw with the Humane Investigators—it was just exceedingly bad form.

"Then we got a second call," Rick said as he maneuvered his way through Monday downtown traffic toward the West Hills. "I don't know if it was the same person—I doubt it because this one was way more forthcoming. They had no qualms about giving their name; they were the neighbors of the suspect and reported hearing some serious yowling coming from an upstairs window. They also described a horrendous smell."

"Why hadn't they reported it before?"

"Frank asked them that, and they said this was the first time the small dormer window had been open all summer. Well, that really got us going, as you can imagine. Unless the place has air conditioning, which I seriously doubt in that age of house, the temperature in an attic with the windows shut in the August heat can get up into the triple digits. If there were cats locked up there, they could die of dehydration in a very short time."

"But there aren't really three hundred cats, are there?"

Rick shook his head. "No, of course not."

"Denny said maybe fifty-some and a raft of kittens?"

"Yeah, the unofficial count is up to eighty-two."

"Oh, well, that's not so bad," I said sarcastically.

Rick's eyes shot over at me. "You ever see eighty neglected cats in one room?" He shuddered. Obviously he had.

"Sorry, bad joke. It's a heck of a big number. That's about twice the population of FOF on a good day."

"Yeah."

For the rest of the journey, we were quiet. I couldn't guess what he was thinking, but I was beginning to wonder what I'd gotten myself into.

We pulled up in front of an absolutely gorgeous vintage Victorian mini-mansion, joining the Northwest Humane investigations van and several other official and unofficial vehicles. The lawn was lush green and impeccably trimmed, the kind you see in the Turf Builder commercials; the garden was pristine with a flawless array of colorful flowers, plants, and trees. The house itself looked to be freshly painted and meticulously kept.

We walked through the open door, and I saw that the interior was even more impressive: dark polished wood shone like smoky glass, silk-covered walls must have cost a fortune, high ceilings were hung with enough crystal to stock a high-end lighting store. Everything was immaculate and ordered, which was why the overpowering smell of feces, urine, and other bad things I refused to name was so impossibly incongruous.

"Woah!" I said as I got a whiff.

"No kidding," Denny agreed as he met me in the hallway. He was wearing his mask and sweat was dripping from where it fit against his nose and cheeks. With mask and goggles, he was barely recognizable: only the bronze star-shaped badge on his official Northwest Humane investigations hat proclaimed his identity since below the neck, every inch of him was protected by a blue canvas jumpsuit. I knew he must be sweltering in all that heavy clothing, but in spite of the heat factor, I suddenly wished I'd worn another layer myself.

Denny handed me a mask, a set of paper booties, and a paper shower cap. "This is the weirdest thing I've ever seen," he proclaimed, shaking his alien-looking head. "The place is top class all the way until you get to the third floor. Then it's like you stepped through a portal into another world and not a good one either. Cats everywhere. We haven't been able to get any kind of accurate count. Some are in really bad shape. A few of them are dead."

"We found three carcasses in the freezer," Connie Lee announced as she joined the briefing. Pulling down her mask and wiped her face with a bandana. "Now who does that, I ask you? This woman's a real nut-case."

I began donning the protective attire. "Where is she?"

Denny nodded toward the adjoining room—a living room or maybe it was the parlor? I wasn't really up on the anatomy of a mansion. "In there. Frank's gathering evidence to bring neglect charges against her."

"Or it may end up being classified as abuse, depending on how bad off the cats really are," Connie added. Her fury was clear in spite of her restrained tone of voice.

I stared at the woman in the living room. She didn't look like an animal abuser; in a pink lamb's wool suit and ruffled blouse, she seemed more like someone's matronly grandmother. She was wringing her hands and tears were cascading down her doughy face. I couldn't keep but feel sorry for her. Then again, I hadn't been upstairs yet.

"She's probably a little bit crazy. She inherited the house from an elderly maiden aunt and lives here by herself," said Denny.

"With eighty cats," Connie broke in.

"She calls them her babies. Seems to know them all by name. She has moments of lucidity where she understands what's going on—what she's done—but most of the time, she thinks everything's fine. Thinks the attic's some kind of cross between Heaven and a penthouse flat."

"How sad," I said and truly meant it.

"Yeah. It really is," Connie grudgingly conceded. "She's voluntarily relinquished the cats. Now they can get the care they need."

"They're the lucky ones," Denny said gravely. "It looks horrible, but these guys are safe now. Or will be, once we get moving and get 'em out of here."

* * *

I won't describe the details of the rescue but suffice it to say the vision of those poor kitties all squished together in that filthy, stifling attic isn't something I'll forget any time soon. Nor is the smell, which seemed to scorch my nostrils and stay with me for days. I was surprised that people didn't stop me on the street and say, *You reek of cat pee!* but I guess it was psychosomatic.

We were actually very lucky. When we got the cats to the hospital, they checked out with nothing worse than upper respiratory infection, malnourishment, and parasites; all things that would resolve with proper care in a matter of days. Then the behaviorists would come in and assess the psychological damage. Who knew how many of them had grown up in that squalor? Second-generation hoardies tended to be almost feral, having been starved for human affection from birth, and they always required special attention. Before I left the hospital that evening, I had committed to fostering three and possibly four two-year-old siblings once they were out of detox. With a pang of nostalgia, I admitted that Mike's adoption had been perfectly timed, leaving me free to deal with these very needful beings.

It was about nine o'clock when we finally finished up. The hospital staff was still at it and would be for hours more, but the rescue effort was successfully over: all cats had been removed and every aspect of the filthy conditions documented with both photographs and video reports. In spite of the damage only affecting a small portion of the house, the Housing Authority had declared the place unfit for human habitation until the attic was cleaned and sanitized. I was beyond exhausted, but the cats were safe and my work was done.

Denny Paris had offered to take me home. When I got out to the parking lot he was already waiting.

"Sorry about that," I said. "One of the medical

assistants needed help with a feisty male. I showed her how to gently scruff him so he couldn't move his head and then get him into a football hold. Funny thing is, once he was in the hold, he settled down instantly. Just scared, I guess. And who can blame him? He'll probably be a sweetheart once he feels more secure."

I started to open the car door, but Denny caught my arm. "Lynley, can we talk for a minute?"

I'd stripped off all the paper coverings along with my scrubs coat and changed pants and shoes, but I still felt odious. "Sure, Denny, but I'm pretty gross. I can't wait till I get home and into a hot bath. Or two."

"You and me both!" He took a drag off his cigarette. "I just want to finish this."

"I didn't know you smoked," I said, watching the ghostly vapor waft away in the evening breeze. The sky was that dusky violet which could signify either sunset or sunrise. If I hadn't known, I could have gone either way.

"Only in times of great stress."

"Ah." That was comment enough; I'd probably be smoking too after the day he'd had. "What did you want to talk to me about?"

"You been following the Sinclairii murder case?" he asked out of the blue.

"I watched the news for a while after our excursion, but I haven't seen a word. Why? Did something happen?"

He took a slow drag on his cigarette, then crushed it out and put the butt in his pocket. "You could say that. They found out whose lens it was."

Chapter 26

Why buy a pet from a breeder when so many "accidental" animals need loving homes? And if you must have that special breed, try a Breed Rescue. Shelters also offer purebred animals as well as mutts. Adopt, don't shop.

As I gazed at the first star in the sky, which as everyone knows was really a planet, I tried to take in what Denny had told me. That whole business seemed so long ago, and I wasn't sure I really cared who the suspect was as long as it wasn't me. But since Denny had gone to the trouble to eke out this bit of news, I supposed I should at least listen to what he had to say.

"Oh?" was about all I could manage. And then, with great effort, "Did they make an arrest?"

"No. The blood spatter on the lens establishes probable cause, but they have no idea where she is at present. They've got some good detectives out looking for her though."

"Her?" I asked with surprise. "Somehow I'd always assumed the murderer was a man."

"Yup. It's the victims' sister. That's family ties for you, eh?"

Denny ducked in the driver's side of the Silverado. I got in the passenger side, threw my bag of dirty clothes in the back seat, and buzzed down the window—air conditioning was great for keeping cool, but I needed more than coolth to dispel the smell of the day's hard work.

We pulled out of the parking lot across the vacant avenue onto a little side street that led over the railroad tracks. Now that Denny had dropped the bombshell, he seemed totally content to drive along in silence. That wasn't going to work for me, however. It's amazing how quickly a few words can bring back a whole raft of rot.

"Are they sure she did it?"

Denny pulled to a stop at a red light. "Did what?"

"Denny!" I said with exasperation, "The sister—are the authorities sure she's the killer?"

"Innocent until proven guilty," Denny reminded me with a chuckle. "But it sounds pretty much a done deal." The light turned green, and he accelerated to a lawful thirty-five miles per hour. "Apparently the three of them had pulled off the Cats' Eyes heist together. Theft's sort of a family business, I guess. It must have gone bad somewhere along the line and she turned on the other two. That could be why they didn't find the diamonds on the brothers' bodies."

I thought about it for a minute. "You didn't get this from any newspaper," I charged. "I've read enough to know that none of what you're telling me was ever published in the *Oregonian*."

Denny looked over at me with a supercilious grin on his face but remained annoyingly silent.

"Okay, spill, as Mike Hammer would say."

"Who?" Denny asked.

"Never mind. Just tell me how you found out."

"Oh, it's really no great feat or anything. I've still got a few friends on the force. Hugh Burgdorf and I went to cop school together; now he's working the case. He's been passing on information to me all along—only the non-classified stuff, of course."

"Of course."

"They're ready to make an arrest, once they find her."

"What's her name?" I asked, my feline-esque curiosity finally piqued.

"Crystal or Christie—she's known to use aliases—Sinclairii. Last sighting was years ago, back when she was in her twenties. No one's seen her since."

"Wow! A real mystery woman."

"They'll find her. Hugh's got some leads—of course I don't know what they are." In the twilight, I thought I saw him wink.

Denny pulled neatly to the curb in front of my house. "Well, here you go." He put on the parking brake and took my hand. "Thanks, Lynley, for everything you did today. I know it wasn't easy, but you really made a difference in the lives of eighty cats, and that's no small thing."

I gave his hand a squeeze. "Back at you, Special Agent Paris. Without you, those cats wouldn't have had a chance."

We beamed at each other for a moment, then I broke away and opened the car door. "Enough of the mutual admiration society. Go get a shower."

"I already had one at the hospital," he said with a mock pout.

"Then get another one. And this time use soap."

Like a gentleman, he watched until I had got inside the house and closed the door with a wave. Little was waiting for me in the entrance hall, but she took one whiff, bristled her back like a Halloween cat and leapt away with a hiss. Reaction from the others was all in the same vein: Fluffs hid; Red ran away; Violet growled—an intimidating sound coming from so large an animal. Yes, a bath (since my old house has no shower) was in order, before my cats fell on me in a combined effort to eradicate the beast that stank of eighty strays.

I tossed my dirty clothes down the basement stairs where the cats were not allowed—even the best-behaved kitty may be inclined to pee inappropriately on items that smell of alien cats—and began to draw a bath. While the hot water steamed into the old claw-foot tub, I stripped down to my bra and panties and sent the jeans and shirt down with the others even though they'd been worn for less than an hour.

The red light of my answering machine was blinking, and enjoying the cool evening breeze from the open window on my overheated body, I pushed the play button. The first call was from Frannie. After the beep, she said: "Hi Lynley. I left a message on your cell phone, but I wanted to make sure I got you. I got hold of your adopter, but she didn't want to come out to the shelter and she said she'll give you a call about Mike tomorrow. The inconvenient thing is, I brought him out here before I knew she wasn't going to be coming. But I can get him back to you in the morning, so it should be alright. Poor Mike, all that traveling but he seems not to mind..." With another beep, Frannie's voice was cut off; she never remembers my machine is a dinosaur and only gives the caller sixty seconds to say their piece. Oh, well, I got the picture.

The second message was from the shelter itself: "Hi, Lynley. This is Ann Ryan, counselor for Friends of Felines. We looked into your adopter, Tina Thomas, and there seems to be a problem. Can you give me a call before you do the adoption? I'm sure it's just a misunderstanding, but don't go ahead with the adoption until you talk to me. If she has any questions, field them off to us. We don't want you to have to deal with anything unpleasant."

Ann gave her direct number, nice and slow so I could actually write it down without having to go through the whole thing again. It was too late to call now; another bit of business for the morning. With a little shiver that had nothing to do with standing in the middle of the kitchen nearly naked, I wondered what the problem could be? In my many years at FOF, I'd rarely seen them refuse an adoption. Sometimes people failed to mention they lived in a no-pets apartment and didn't get that we call the landlords to check for that exact thing. Once in a great while, there was someone who'd been charged with animal neglect—usually hoarding—and was no longer allowed to have a pet. FOF was actually pretty lenient when it came to lifestyle, concentrating only on potential dangers to the animal. They did both follow-up calls and home visits, which turned off most people who had something to hide.

There was still a third call. I paused the tape and went to turn off my bath. Little was sitting on the bathroom vanity meowing, which meant she thought it was full. Little was the unofficial bath monitor, making sure we were conservative with the water. When the tub was empty and dry, she liked to get in and bat around a sparkly ball, but that's another story.

I was tempted to jump into the warm, steaming water and slip down until only my nose stuck out, but that third message tugged at my interest. Most of my friends call my cell phone, so a message on my land line was rare, let alone three. Probably just my bank calling to try to sell me insurance or the firemen pressing for a donation, but then again, it could be an old school chum trying to find me after forty-some years. Wouldn't want to miss that.

239

I restarted the tape. There was a click and then silence, then another click but not the kind it makes when the other party hangs up. I listened closer and could hear something in the background, very faint, like voices and cars.

A pay phone? I wondered. Do they still have them anymore, now that even small children and old grannies like me carry cells?

There was another click, and this time whoever it was did ring off. I shrugged to show my nonexistent audience that hang-up calls didn't worry me in the least. "Wrong number," I told them, choosing not to acknowledge their understandable if imaginary skepticism.

Assertively I punched the erase button. The machine proudly announced that my messages had been deleted.

I think my brain had been deleted as well, because any concern I might have had about the muddle with Mike, the counselor's warning and the crank call disappeared as I shed my undies and stepped into the bath. I couldn't believe how tired I was. Twenty years ago, I thought to myself with a mixture of incredulity and fear, I would have done today's labors and gone out dancing afterward. But that wasn't exactly true: twenty years ago, I would probably have been sitting in a barroom, not been out rescuing cats.

The water was as lovely as I'd anticipated. I'd added some Japanese bath salts that smelled mildly of wisteria, a perfect scent when your olfactory senses have been barraged with cat pee. For a moment, I wished I'd lit some candles, put on some music, done the whole spa treatment, but it really wouldn't have mattered much since basically I was too tired to care. My eyes slipped shut, envisioning the candlelight flickering on the high gloss of the bathroom walls; I could hear Debussy playing in my head.

Wasn't the imagination a wonderful thing? I mused, my last coherent thought before I drifted off to a warm and watery slumber.

* * *

I knew something was wrong the moment I woke. I was freezing: my wonderful hot bath had gone cold and slimy, but that wasn't it. My soggy nap hadn't refreshed me at all; in fact if anything, the tease of a few minutes' sleep had made things worse. My head ached; my neck was stiff from straining at a right angle to my body, but in spite of my distress, I had the overwhelming feeling that I shouldn't move.

I opened my eyes just a slit and realized with dismay that the bathroom light was out. That shouldn't have bothered me since the pesky bulbs were always blowing in that particular fixture, but it did. Resisting the inclination to leap from the water, I listened. Sure enough, there was a sound I couldn't account for. I tried to make it into one of the miscellaneous scuffles and bumps created by a household of cats, but this time it just didn't fit.

The sound was barely audible, and much to my frustration, every other little noise obscured it. In between cars passing on the street, the ice maker plunking in my freezer, and the sporadic notes of loud music coming from a barbeque next door, I strained my ears to catch the phantom whisper. With a shot of adrenaline that literally made my frigid body ache, I realized what it was.

Breathing.

The unmistakable in-and-out soughs of living breath.

Now, if it had been coming from the floor or even the counter, I could have passed it off as a cat; Harry's quite a wheezer when he sleeps, and Red's so big that everything he does makes a racket. Fluffs' petite purr might be mistaken for breaths, but unless the fraulein had climbed a five-foot ladder, that was out of the question. Which left the very possibility I had been trying so hard to circumnavigate: the culprit was human.

I could see the intruder now, a shadow looming in the doorway. I couldn't make out any features, and for a moment, I convinced myself my eyes were deceiving me. Then the shadow moved, and it was all over.

Quietly as possible, I rose from the bath, slipping and sliding on the wet tile floor as I reached for a towel. The shadow was gone now, and a light came on in the living room. I heard someone rooting around and knew immediately what I had to do.

I tucked the towel ineffectively around my naked torso and silently slithered in search of a weapon. When I could come up with nothing better than a stainless steel sauce pot or the blender pitcher (I keep my cast-iron frying pans in the pantry), I suddenly, for probably the first time in my life, wished I owned a gun.

Choosing the pot, I crept toward the phone, then stopped. The land phone made a great clamor, with an amplified dial tone and a loud atonal beep for each number pressed so that just in case you were hard of hearing, you'd still know you were making a call. That would never do. I thought about my cell phone but in my fear-blanked brain could not for the life of me remember where I'd left it when I came in.

The invader seemed to be busy amusing himself with ravaging the living room. It sounded like he was having a great time tossing my things around. Not again! I flashed briefly on the Sinclairii brothers and wondered suddenly if they were back for a second round. But they couldn't be—

they were dead. That left one logical suspect, the murderous sister. To me, a woman who had ruthlessly killed her own siblings was scarier than the biggest, nastiest man.

Cell phone in purse, my brain suddenly announced. Sure thing! But now where was the purse? Think back...

Oh, right. I'd dropped it by the front door when I got home. The front door... right across the living room where Ms. Badass was doing her business.

Naked or not, it was time to get out of there. I'm not sure why I hadn't considered the option before. That's how ingrained our inhibitions go—I'd rather expose myself to danger than expose myself.

But that was the old me; the new me didn't give a rat's patootie who saw my aging bod. Without another thought, I set the pan on the counter and ran for the back door.

My foot hit against something soft and furry. There was a yowl of indignation from one of the cats—I think it was Dirty Harry. I shuffled in a move we cat-people practice to protect our feline friends who lounge so guilelessly beneath our feet—a stop-twist-slide maneuver. Kitty got away with only a gentle nudge, but in my haste, I tripped and went down with a crash.

Now, everyone knows that it's dangerous for older people to take a fall. Osteoporosis, cracked pelvises, and hip replacement surgery spring to mind. But this time, a broken bone was the least of my worries. The kitchen light blazed on with an unsympathetic glare. As I sprawled on the floor, the wind knocked out of me, I saw Harry—it was indeed himself over whom I had stumbled. He was crouching, muscles taut, ready to spring. His lips were pulled back in a grimace as he tested the air; his ears were flat against his head and his pupils were widely dilated which meant he didn't like the taste. I had a feeling I wasn't going to like it either.

Cautiously I turned my gaze toward the light switch at the other end of the room and found myself staring into the hard, cold eyes of Tina Thomas.

Chapter 27

A domestic cat can sprint at about thirty-one miles per hour.

Harry was gone, leaving me in his dust. In that split second of inertia, my first thought was *Thank goodness she didn't adopt Mike!* Then with a *duh!* revelation, I realized Tina—if that was her real name—had never been the least bit interested in Mike or any other cat. For some unknown reason, she wanted me.

Suddenly her insistence on coming to my home clicked in place. I kicked myself for being so naïve—there was a reason adoptions were supposed to be okayed by a counselor before giving out any personal information. Ann Ryan's message suddenly made deadly sense. When she said there was a problem, I'd assumed they had come up with an obsolete address or a disconnected phone number—things that can slip by in our fast-moving society—but now I knew the truth: the issue hadn't been clerical at all, it had been downright extremely real.

What did Tina want? Money? Jewelry? It must have been obvious by looking around that I had no abundance of either.

Tina reached around behind her waist and pulled out a gun. Keeping me in her sights—literally—she moved to the window and drew the blinds. She'd lost that waifish look she'd had at the fair; as she paced around the room in her tight black clothes, she exuded power, and something else. I couldn't quite put my finger on it until I looked her in the face and saw the insanity there.

"What do you want?" I asked. My feeble voice echoed like a mew in the wilderness. I cleared my throat; just because I was lying naked on the floor while a madwoman threatened me with a deadly weapon, I needn't give the impression I was scared.

She had foregone her drab glasses, but her gaze was keen as an eagle's. She stared for a moment, then was on me in three long strides. She grabbed my arm and yanked. "Get up! Get on the chair!"

I did as she said, fumbling for the towel which had come loose in the fall.

She kicked it away. "You don't need that. Just sit!"

She stuck the gun in her belt while she rummaged in a slim pack strapped across her back and came up with a roll of duct tape.

Uh-oh! I thought with appropriate consternation.

"Put your hands behind the chair." As she ran off a piece of tape and whipped it around my wrists in an expert motion, I wondered if she had done this before. How many times?

The tacky tape tugged at my skin as she wound it tight. Instinctively I raised my feet to kick her away, but she used the move against me and before I knew it, my ankles were bound as well. She added an extra strip securing them to the chair legs and then stood back to examine her work.

I'd watched my share of gritty cop shows where the victim meets with all types of demoralization in the name of entertainment. Now I was the victim and it wasn't the least bit amusing. Never had I felt so helpless.

As a finale, she ripped off a short piece. With the strip hanging from her finger, she scrutinized the kitchen until she found what she wanted, a terry washcloth to serve as a gag. Shoving it in between my teeth—thank goodness for small favors she picked a clean one—she strapped it in with the tape. *This is going to hurt when it comes off*, I thought to myself. *If I live that long*, my brain added unnecessarily.

"Now, I'm going to ask you some questions. All you need to do is nod for yes and shake your head for no. Got it?"

I nodded.

"You know what I'm looking for."

It seemed like a statement, but as the silence drew out and she roughly prodded my bare foot with the toe of her boot, I realized it required a reply.

Quickly I shook my head no.

Her boot came down on the bridge of my foot, and I screamed into my gag, then inhaled a deep breath of terry lint and began to heave and cough.

"Wrong answer! I know you have it. I saw you pick it up in the forest."

I stared at her blankly.

"On the mountain! You can't deny it. Did you give it to the man?"

Give what to the man? What man? She wasn't making sense unless...

The words *forest* and *mountain* suddenly leapt out at me like a pouncing tiger. Things began to click into place.

The *forest* was where the Badass Boys had taken me when I was kidnapped—the forest on the *mountain*. In the forest on the mountain, Tina had seen me pick something up. Something I gave to *the man*.

I recalled it all: Tammy, the lens, my stupid move when I contaminated the evidence. I had given it to Denny.

Was that what she was talking about?

I nodded ambivalently.

Tina cursed. "Then this is pointless." She ripped away the gag—and yes, it did hurt, but I was so glad to get it off my face I didn't care. "You give me his address, tell me where I can find him."

"Why?" I spat out bits of washcloth filament. "What's so important about a glasses lens?"

"Lens?" she ejaculated. "I'm talking about the diamond, the Babylon, twin to the Burma. I saw you with it, there in the woods."

"Diamond? I never..."

"I spent days looking for those Eyes." Her voice was thick as grease. "I found the one, but before I could find the other, you and your group turned up and spoiled everything."

A light bulb came on in my head. "So that was you I heard rustling around up there." The bulb went out again. "But how did the diamond get lost...?"

I stopped short; she had that gun out again and its one black, deadly, vacant eye seemed even larger than before.

"If you don't have the stone, then you're no use to me." I heard the safety click off.

"Wait! Wait, I'll tell you! I'll tell you everything."

She paused, wondering whether to believe me. I guess she thought it worth a try because she reset the safety and lowered the weapon. After all, she could always kill me later if I didn't give her what she wanted to know.

Which was the quandary, because I knew absolutely nothing about the stone's whereabouts. I hadn't seen it since the Badass Brothers took it from me over a month ago.

"Okay," she said carefully. "But this better be the truth.

You think after killing my own dear brothers that I'd give a second thought about shooting you?"

"No, I suppose not," I murmured. Then in a Jessica Fletcher moment, I added, "That must have been very hard for you. George and Larry must have really hurt you to make you do something like that."

I thought I saw a bit of softness cross her black, beady eyes, so I pressed on. "After all the hard work you did, all the chances you took. It must have been awful."

"You don't know what you're talking about," she lashed.

"No, Tina. How could I? But I know you loved them and helped them the best you could."

"You bet I did! Curse them for making me do it."

Tina sunk into a chair opposite me. *Wow! This murder-she-wrote stuff was actually working!* I thought in amazement, until the pistol came back up, trained on my heart. But her hold was different this time: not as aggressive, not as assured. I figured another effort couldn't do any harm.

"I bet you're the older sister, always helping those guys, pulling them through the hard times, getting them out of trouble."

"What do you care?"

I shrugged, then winced. My right shoulder hurt from the fall and shrugging with my arms wrenched unnaturally behind my back felt akin to ripping the joint out of its socket, but I ignored the pain; this tactic, if it were to work, was about her agony, not mine. "Not everybody you meet is hardhearted and callous, Tina," I said in my most sympathetic voice. "I care about lots of things—it's who I am."

"Like, you're a cat volunteer? Helping the poor

pussycats?" she said with overt sarcasm.

I tried not to be defensive. "Yeah. Like that."

She sighed and the gun went a little to the right, no longer aimed at my chest; now it would most likely blow off my arm instead, but it was an improvement. "I respect that," she admitted. "Believe it or not, I'm a compassionate person myself. It's only circumstance and bad luck that put me where I am."

I shifted my position, an aborted move that made little difference to my comfort level but brought my hand in contact with something sharp on the back of the chair. It was a gash in the antique slat that I'd meant to fix years ago. Now I was glad of my procrastination because it felt like if I rubbed the tape just right, maybe in a day or two it might work through.

I looked at Tina, sure my discovery was written all over my face, but she wasn't watching. Quickly I took up the conversation again. "I understand. Bad stuff happens to good people. Life's unfair, you see it all the time."

"Yeah, all the time." Tina lapsed into a thoughtful silence. The gun was all the way down now and she began absentmindedly scraping the muzzle across the surface of my mission oak table. I cringed as I saw honey-colored gouges appear in the patina, but I held my tongue. Better the table than me.

"Same old story, since you asked. Drunk dad, dead mom. I raised the boys from when they were toddlers. Pop finally died of liver disease—surprise surprise—but only after he'd run the family into debt so deep a backhoe couldn't have dug us out. I was eighteen then so I managed to pull off a post-death bankruptcy thing which fixed the legal problems, but that wasn't pop's only legacy. He had creditors up the wazoo, the not-so-legal type, and they weren't about to write us off just because he wasn't around anymore. They wanted payment, if not money, then something… else."

She paused.

"Go on," I urged, rubbing as subtly as I could against the splinter. So far I hadn't made a lick of progress, but any minute now, I promised myself.

Tina looked around the room, at the phone, at the door.

"No one's going to interrupt us, if that's what you're worried about. When I was young like you, sure. Friends dropped by at all hours, day and night. But no one ever comes or calls." I tried to sound as desolate as possible. "I'm in bed each night by nine. If I died in my sleep, no one would even know I was gone."

The girl looked at me skeptically but accepted my exaggerations. Why not? Wasn't that how people her age viewed anyone over fifty? Forlorn and lonely and waiting to die?

"I can just imagine what those creditors wanted from a lovely young girl like you," I continued.

She looked surprised, then her eyes narrowed. "You know a lot for an old lady. Yeah, this one guy thought I could pay him off in skin. But there was no way. I'd seen other girls go that route and it always turned out bad. So I came up with an alternate plan."

"You became a cat burglar, pulled a heist?"

She chuckled at my dated terminology. "That's right. The first job I did by myself; the boys were twelve and fourteen and I didn't want them getting involved with anything illegal. But by the second and third time, there was no stopping them; they were right in there with me. What teens lack in experience, they make up for in pure instinctive deception. We made a good team, got out from under those asshats and began to live the life we deserved."

"So what went wrong?"

"Boys grew up into men, that's what went wrong! Big sister didn't seem so smart anymore. They got greedy and arrogant. I put up with their attitude for a long time—I mean, I didn't need flattery, only a safe and successful job. But finally even that got sticky. They began taking stupid risks. Because we'd got clean away every time before, they thought they were untouchable."

"The Cats' Eyes diamonds? There was a screw-up?"

"You got it. It was a perfect plan. *My* plan." She allowed herself a ghost of a grin. "And I did the tricky stuff; all they had to do was impersonation—a security guard and a gemologist's assistant to sign for the delivery. I'd taken care of the real guys. The boys knew how to play a part, but they were careless and got made. No one ever guessed about me, but they were chased, and they had the rocks."

Tina's face was turning an unhealthy crimson and I knew I was touching on unstable ground if I pushed her now, but again, what choice did I have? Once she finished the story, I'd have to tell her where the stone was stashed and that was something I couldn't do. Better draw this out as long as possible. In spite of my speech, maybe a friend would drop by. Maybe one of my cats would jump on her head. Maybe a comet would fall or the world would blow up or she'd have a heart attack. There might still be a chance, given time.

"Then what happened?"

Tina looked at me, her eyes blazing. "They betrayed me! Those little twerps! My own dear brothers betrayed me..."

A tear rolled down her cheek. She dropped the gun on the table and rose quickly, kicking the chair as she ran into the bathroom. I could hear her vomiting. I guess I'd touched a nerve.

"Are you okay, dear?" I called after the retching had ceased. "There are some towels in the basket."

I braced myself for an outburst, but instead I heard the water run, and Tina came back out, wiping her face with a mauve face cloth.

Her complexion had gone from red to greenish-white and I knew she was suffering. Not that I could muster up much sympathy for the person who was holding me captive in such a painful and embarrassing way.

This time she remained standing. Steeling herself, she reached for the gun, and I knew I had to act fast.

"Tell me about it, Tina."

"My name isn't Tina!" she charged. "It's Cristine. Cristine Montrose Sinclairii! For what it's worth," she added gloomily.

"Okay, Cristine then. But it's obvious you could use a good vent. It'll make you feel better, and I don't suppose you have many people you can be completely honest with. You may as well take advantage of the situation. Tell me how your brothers betrayed you."

Chapter 28

Cats hunt more than 1,000 species for food.

Leaving the weapon where it lay, her hand crept to the chair back and her fingers closed hard around the smooth old wood as if she were grasping a lifeline.

"When the delivery guy started getting suspicious, George panicked and ran. As you can imagine, we were pursued. We separated. They had the Cats' Eyes. They figured they should stash them in case they got caught."

"In my pond," I prompted.

She gave me a strange look. "I suppose it sounds simple to you. What would you know? You've probably never done an illegal thing in your life."

That's what you think, I reflected but held my tongue and blinked at her innocently, a move I learned from my cats, though in this case, it was not intended as anything resembling a smile.

Cristine began stalking around the big kitchen, picking up objects and putting them down again. She took up a Japanese teacup with a cat face on it and fingered it indifferently. "Crazy twits thought your little water feature would make a good cache, in with all the other rocks. Actually it was pretty smart in a pinch." The cup came down hard on the counter, shattering into a million tiny porcelain pieces. "But that's not how they told it to me. When we finally regrouped, they gave me a completely different story."

"You mean they lied to you?"

She shot me an incredulous look. "Don't believe that 'honor among thieves' crap for a minute! There's nothing that ruins relationships faster than wealth, or the ruthless pursuit of it."

Her flash of insight surprised me, and for a moment I had the feeling she'd take it all back if she could.

"Yes, they lied!" she blasted. "Obviously it was Larry. He was the smarter of the two, and George just went along with whatever he said. They spun this tale about splitting up, each taking one of the Eyes. Larry said he'd found an unlocked house, slipped inside to wait for the police to clear out, and then hid the Burma on a shelf in case he got picked up later. George's story was the same, but different rock, different house."

"I never leave my house unlocked. I don't think anyone in the neighborhood does." Not that it's a bad neighborhood, I wanted to add, but this was Cristine's show, not mine.

"They said..." the woman cooed sarcastically, "they couldn't remember which houses, that all the houses on the block looked the same. Larry blamed George, and I just went right along with it. I should have seen from the start that the whole thing was ridiculous. Misplacing million-dollar chocolate diamonds was too stupid a move, even for George, but I was busy being mad because now I'd have to go in and clean up the mess. Again.

"They had me looking up and down the street, tossing all the houses. They were laughing at me while I was out there risking everything."

"So you were the one..." I hesitated, but she was sharp enough to get my drift.

"The one who battered your neighbor?"

"Mr. Johnson. He left a wife, two kids, and three grandkids you know," I said before I could stop myself.

"Yeah, that was me," she said, instantly defensive. "The boys had nothing to do with it. It was all me. I never meant for him to die."

Cristine ran her fingers along the wall, then in a fit of anger, punched hard. I heard a crunch that had to have been her knuckles because unlike sheetrock, the lath and plaster in an old house like mine is hard as granite. She sucked in a breath and turned a greener shade of pale but didn't miss a beat.

"All the time they knew exactly where they'd put the freaking Eyes. They were planning to go back later, without me...

"Without me!"

For a moment I thought she was going to go for another round with the plaster, but she must have thought better of it. A pity. It would have been a great help to me if she incapacitated herself, especially the hand that wielded the weapon. But instead, she began to laugh. It was a shrill sound and not the least bit mirthful.

"Boy, they were amazed when I came up with the Burma! They just couldn't believe it. I thought they were just happy I'd found the thing. It almost felt like old times again, back when the boys used to look up to me." She paused as a bittersweet smile hovered on her thin lips. "But of course I had totally misinterpreted their reaction. It was only because they couldn't figure out how it had got from the pond into the house for me to find at all." She suddenly eyed me. "Why didn't you call the police?"

The turn of the inquiry took me by surprise. "Pardon?"

"Obviously you found the Eye—it was right here in a basket on the counter. Why didn't you call the cops?" Her eyes narrowed. "Did you think you could keep it for yourself?"

I shook my head. "I have no idea how it got here. The only explanation I can come up with is that my cat must have come across it. He likes sparkly things. I didn't even know what it was."

"One of the most famous stones in modern civilization," she scoffed, "and you didn't recognize it?"

"Not everybody has your fascination with precious gems, Cristine. Or your expertise," I placated.

"And why ever did you separate them?" she went on. "I never understood that. Was it to throw me off?"

"As I said, my cat brought it in. He's a pretty smart cat, but I don't think he realized there was a pair."

"You and your cats!" Cristine grabbed up a vegetable cleaver off the wooden cutting block. I cringed, ineffectively pushing back in my chair. The gun was bad enough, but was she crazy enough to start in with a knife? If so, Oh, cripes, was I scared!

She slammed the point into the cutting board and continued her perusal of my kitchen. I nearly peed my pants with relief, except I wasn't wearing any.

When she was nicely away from the deadly utensil, I decided to go for the gusto. "Just two things, Cristine."

She paused to look at me. "What's that?"

"I want to know why you killed your brothers."

"And?"

"I want my clothes, or at least my towel. I don't want to die like this. What will they think when they discover my body? I don't..." My little sob surprised me as much as it did her. "What if my granddaughter's the one who finds me? It would scar her for life. I can't stand the thought of it."

"Oh, stop!" Cristine exclaimed. She picked up the towel I had dropped when I fell and draped it across my shoulder. It didn't do much for the backside but at least it made a toga-like sweep down the front. "Better?"

"Thank you," I said in all sincerity.

"I killed my brothers because they were just like our pop. Greedy, selfish, and incorrigible, except without the drinking. And that probably would have come in time. I couldn't let them go on like that. Better to put an end to it right there and then."

"But why up on the mountain? Were you following us?"

"Certainly," she said smartly. "They'd taken the Burma. You don't think I'd let those guys out of my sight as long as they had the diamond, do you?"

She turned her back, which I took as a sign she thought me no threat, which of course I wasn't. No matter how hard I rubbed the duct tape against the rough gash on the chair, nothing happened. She must have sprung for the good stuff, that's for sure.

"Actually I didn't catch on right away. If I hadn't called to see if they'd be home for dinner, I might never have known the treachery they had planned." Cristine pulled the blind away from the window sash just enough to peer out into the night. Whether she was checking for intruders or meditating on the moon, I couldn't guess. "The second George picked up, I felt something was wrong. His voice had that whine it got when he was lying; I can tell every time. When I asked him where they were, he said on a boat. He began to say Stella—he got out the *Stel*—before Larry pulled the phone out of his hand. Larry was quick with a cover—said they were at the *boat ramp* by Oak Bottoms over in Sellwood and he wanted steak for dinner like everything was okay."

She let the blind fall back in place—obviously the FBI wasn't outside getting ready to save me.

"After the call, I couldn't stop thinking about it. Larry was nervous; George was lying. George said they were on a boat near Stella, Washington and Larry said they were down at the ramp right here in Portland. If George's slip had been truth then I knew where they were going. They had a friend, Harmonie, who was an exotic dancer at the Stellar Inn. She owed them a few favors; maybe it was time to pay up. I acted on the hunch, jumped in my car and drove like a demon.

"All the way up there I tried to think of a reasonable explanation for the discrepancy, but I could only come up with one: they were planning to run off with our retirement fund.

"And I'm worrying about what to feed them for dinner!" she exhaled. "That's a hoot!"

"Your retirement fund? You were going to quit?"

"My life of crime?" she took up. "That's right. The Cats' Eyes job was supposed to be our last. With the money our buyer offered, we'd have settled down for life. No more risk or running. We could have been just like any old millionaire on the block." She barked out a strangled laugh. "I couldn't wait. You may not be able to tell, but my nerves are shot. I'm not getting any younger, you know. But I guess Larry and George weren't quite so ready to change their lifestyle. I don't know why not. Greed? Excitement? Stupidity?

"Well, there you have it," she sighed. "I'm to blame for everything. After all, I'd brought them up into the life. What else did they know?"

She picked up a vintage saltshaker shaped like a black

cat with an orange parasol, studied the tiny detail and then put it back down, gently this time. "You really are the crazy cat lady, aren't you?" She chuckled as if she had made the most innovative joke.

"I'm not crazy yet," I muttered, my standard reply to the analogy, which, in spite of Cristine's glee, I'd heard a time or two before. Suddenly I wondered if it were still true.

"Huh?"

"Nothing. Go on. Please."

"I caught them coming down off the mountain. When I confronted them and found out they had both Burma and Babylon, and were planning to split with them, I..." She faltered. "I guess I went a little nuts. Sometimes I have anger management issues," she said solemnly, as if she were sharing her deepest secret. "They laughed at me."

She turned away. "Things got a crazy. I told them to hand over the stones and get back home pronto. Larry said he wasn't going to take orders from a nag like me anymore, that he'd rather no one had the Eyes than give them to me. Those were his own words! He threw them in the bushes and got in behind the wheel.

"They were going to leave me!" she choked. "Even without the Eyes, Larry said they were going away and never coming back.

"You can imagine that kind of set me off. That's when I... well, you know... sort of shot at them, at kind of close range... and they died."

Cristine swiveled around and I saw tears streaming down her face. "Now you know. Now I've told you everything. So why don't I feel any better?"

"You will, I promise," I said quickly. "Maybe there's something you still need to do."

"Yeah, there is." She grabbed up the gun and brought it sharply front and center. "I still need to get the Babylon, and now it's time for you to give it over."

Hot adrenaline blasted through me, and I realized that in spite of the warmth of the summer night, I had been chilled.

"Cristine, I have a confession to make."

Chapter 29

Notable ailurophobes include Dwight D. Eisenhower, Napoleon Bonaparte, and Hitler.

With a jarring jangle that made us both jump, the land line rang. No church bells or catchy melodies; just the plain old ring-ring that's brought people running for decades past.

Cristine swung around as if slapped. "You said no one calls you," she hissed. "Now you're lying to me too?"

"No..."

"Shhh! Shut up! Don't answer!" she said, a moot point since I was bound to a chair.

She fell silent and we both listened as the ringing cut off and the machine clicked on.

"Hi, Lynley," said a woman's voice. "This is Patty from next door. If you're there, pick up."

There was a space of crackly quiet, then she came back on. "Oh well, I know it's late. Maybe you're asleep. I just wanted to let you know I have your cat."

I sucked in a breath as a new kind of fear swept through me.

"I know you have more than one." Through the phone, I heard the clink of metal identification tags. "Ah, this is Dirty Harry. He was meowing on our porch, and since I know you usually keep your cats indoors, I thought you'd want him back and safe. Anyway I'll just keep him here for now. He's fine; Jim and I like him—Don't we, Harry?" she added in a sing-song voice I knew was meant for the cat.

"You just call when you get this message. Don't worry. Goodnight."

She rang off with a click; the machine beeped then settled into a rhythmic ruby blink to show it had something to say.

Horror-stricken, I realized I hadn't seen or heard a single cat since Tina's—Cristine's home invasion. I'd attributed their absence to shyness and smarts—who knew what she might have done to a passing cat? But now I wasn't so sure.

For the first time since my capture, I struggled—really struggled—in my chair.

"How did you get in?" I squeaked. "Did you leave something open?"

Cristine looked at me as if I'd gone mad—I guess I qualified, yelling at a woman with a gun trained on me. Maybe I was the crazy cat lady after all, because the thought of my kitties out there in a jungle of dogs and cars and places to get lost scared me more than the weapon.

She shrugged. "I don't know. Who cares?"

"I do, you fool!" I threw back at her as I battled my bonds.

"Stop that!" she hissed. Her gun hand came across my face. I saw electric glitter and then the pain set in, but I barely noticed.

"Let me go!" I screamed. "You left the window open and now my cats have got out and who knows what will happen to them out there!"

Cristine stared at me. I guess I'd shocked her. I think I shocked myself. I was crying and my nose was running, which it always did when I cried, which why I couldn't be an actor because, while tears are emotion-evoking, having snot dripping out of your nose isn't. I

263

wiped the offender on the towel as best I could. A runny nose was the least of my problems at the moment.

"Fluffs!" I called pathetically. "Little! Red! Solo! Violet! Kitty-kitty!" It was an empty gesture because the chance of those astute felines sauntering into the kitchen with their tails held high was next to nil and I knew it; even if they hadn't opted for the freedom of the wild, they would have smelled the danger that permeated the room like a raging tomcat.

"For pity's sake!" Cristine shouted. "Will you shut up about your stupid cats?" With a move like an attacking Weimaraner, she stepped in and grabbed me by the shoulders. "Where is that stone? No more stalling! Tell me now or I'll track down those cats and kill them one by one!"

Railing against my restraints, I bawled, "I don't have your stupid diamond! I never did. Last I knew, your brothers had them both and were heading for the hills. If they threw them in the bushes, I don't know anything about it. The only thing I found up on the mountain was your glasses lens which is why the police are on to you!"

Cristine paused. "You found my lens? Was that what you were babbling about? And now the cops know too?"

I sniffed and nodded.

"And you don't have the Eye after all?"

I shook my head.

"And you never did? You were just playing me this whole time?"

"Cristine," I started.

She cut me off. Cold as dry ice she said. "Then you're no use to me."

The gun came up.

I closed my eyes.

In my mind, I could hear the meows of all my cats who had Crossed the Rainbow Bridge before me. They were calling though I couldn't quite hear what they said.

Then I understood. *Not yet!* they chimed. *We will be waiting for you when it comes time, but not yet.*

There was a tiny prrumph and a plop on the table beside me. My eyes flew open and to my horror, there was Fluffs in all her gaunt, gray glory.

The gun swung from me to her; I saw Cristine's finger closing on the trigger.

"I hate cats," she muttered under her breath.

With all my strength and then some, I lunged. The duct tape I'd been trying so desperately to shred and all but given up on suddenly gave way with a miracle snap, and I grabbed at her gun arm. My legs were still taped to the heavy oak chair; the move catapulted me forward and the sheer force knocked her sideways. I heard a blast as we both went down; Fluffs was nowhere to be seen.

My shoulder was on fire. I couldn't move it. Blood was trickling down onto Cristine's black jacket and I knew it was mine. She shoved me off her; my body twisted away from my bound legs and I heard a gruesome snap. Cristine scrambled to her feet and leveled the gun at me once more. I heard a second blast.

* * *

Cristine stiffened, then scuffled out of my limited sideways vision. For some reason I couldn't move, so I lay there in a puddle of pain, waiting for the axe to fall.

I could hear noises throughout the house. Heavy footsteps merged with the percussion pounding in my ears. Voices; shouting; a bullhorn's robot tones: *This is the police. Come out with your hands up. We have you surrounded.*

What? Had she turned on the TV? I was fading. My eyes slipped shut and the sounds dulled. There seemed to be something going on but I couldn't place it; I didn't care. Cristine was gone, and now maybe I could get some rest.

Soft fur stroked across my cheek and my eyes blinked open. All I could see was a blur of copper-gray and then a huge green cat's eye—not the diamond type but the real, beautiful thing. Fluffs gave a little mummmph and smoothed her silky sideburn against my chin. I tried to smile but it was beyond my ability.

Fraulein Fluffs was replaced in my field of vision by the handsome face of Denny Paris. I felt the feather-light touch of a sheet fall across my body.

"Hi, beautiful," he said softly. "You're safe now. We'll have you out of here in no time. Ah, here they are."

A gaggle of tactical boots clomped into range and Denny moved aside to make room for the EMTs. A strong hand took my pulse; the cool head of a stethoscope was pressed to my chest. Someone was carefully snipping the tape around my legs. I heard the soft buzz of conversation but couldn't make out the words.

"...cats," I choked.

"Don't try to talk," a male paramedic said as they prepared me for yet another trip to the hospital. I realized he didn't understand the importance of my statement so I reiterated as forcefully as possible. "...CATS! My cats! Denny?"

"I'm here," the humane investigator answered.

"I think," I gasped, "Window... open... Outside?"

"Don't worry, Lynley," his voice soothed from somewhere down a very long tunnel. "We'll take care of the cats. I promise."

There was a scream from another room, then yelling

and some of the most innovative curses I'd ever heard. Once they got me strapped onto the stretcher, I could see my house was teaming with police—wonderful police!

As they wheeled me out, I saw Cristine. She was quiet now, in handcuffs, the forlorn little waif again. I almost felt sorry for her. Almost. Her story was tragic, and I knew she was mentally ill, but she had threatened my cats and that was something I could never forgive.

My neighbor, Patty, was waiting on the sidewalk as they rolled me up to the ambulance, her pixie features lined with worry.

"Lynley? Oh, what happened to you? No, don't talk. I just wanted you to know we have Dirty Harry. Little too. They're both fine."

"Little?" I croaked.

"Yeah, she was out too. That's how we knew there was a problem. If it'd just been Harry, I'd have passed it off as a slip up. Stuff happens, I know. But when Little showed up, we knew something was wrong. Didn't we, Jim?"

Jim stepped over with a look of concern. "That's right. Her tag said to call you if she was outside. Patty'd already tried your number."

"So we called your friend," Patty took up. "The special agent. He'd given us his card when he was doing his inquiries awhile back. Whatever came of that anyway?"

"We can talk about that later, darling," Jim said quietly. "Lynley's on her way to the hospital now."

"Oh, for sure. I'm sorry. You go—we'll just keep the two cats with us, if you want. They're asleep in the clothes basket by the fire. Don't worry about a thing."

"Thank you," I managed before I was shoved into the emergency truck, stretcher and all.

The paramedic got in with me and secured me in place.

He stuck an IV in my hand and then began all sorts of medical things that I couldn't and frankly didn't want to comprehend.

Then there was Denny.

"Frannie's here and she'll make sure all the cats are accounted for and the house is closed up when the police leave. She's planning on spending the night, what's left of it, to calm the kitties."

I breathed a sigh of relief. "Ride with me?" I whispered.

"You got it." He settled himself on the bench beside the paramedic and took my hand.

"Cat lady," he said fondly.

"Not crazy?" I asked.

He smiled his Colgate grin. "No, Lynley, not yet."

Chapter 30

Notable ailurophiles include Albert Einstein, Florence Nightingale, H.G. Wells, Sir Winston Churchill, Pope Benedict XVI, George Burns, John Lennon, Mark Twain, Edgar Allan Poe, Queen Victoria, Nostradamus, and Vanna White. Freddie Mercury of the band, Queen, phoned home to his cats when he was on tour.

A red leaf fell from the vine maple and landed light as a whisker in the pond.

"I can't believe it's fall already," I told Frannie as she handed me a glass of sparkling lemonade.

"Time goes faster when you get to our age," she replied, taking a sip of her own cold drink. "Besides, you missed a lot of the summer being sick in the hospital."

Being sick was a polite euphemism for: hospital trip one, broken leg and bashed head; hospital trip two, drugged, kidnapped and left to die on a mountain; and hospital trip three, gunshot wound grazing the left shoulder, dislocated kneecap, and various batterings and bruisings. I had to agree it had kept me pretty busy for those three short months.

The last event had been by far the worst. I was still recovering, both physically and mentally, from Cristine Sinclairii's raving assault. The shoulder wound had been superficial, but that didn't mean it didn't hurt like the dickens. The knee was uncomfortable and unpredictable. Even with the brace that I nearly lived in, it would decide out of the blue that it didn't want to work right, and then I'd be down for the count until it said otherwise.

I didn't care; I was alive, and so were my cats. Some people might have crawled into a hole after what I'd been through, but then they'd be missing a great party.

"What's the occasion?" asked Patty, my neighbor and new cat-sitting best friend. "The invitation was a little vague."

"Does there have to be an occasion?"

"Well, no, but..."

"Life!" I broke in. "Life, love, and the pursuit of happiness. I figure I owe a lot of people a big thank you for their help and consideration during my bad times. And what better way?" I gestured around the garden, where friends and family gathered to eat, drink, and be merry. "Besides, after the medical bills, a party was all I could afford, though each and every one of these people deserves a whole lot more."

"Oh, come on," Frannie said with a slight blush illuminating her perfect makeup. "We're your friends. We just did what anybody would do."

"You know that's not true. Not everyone would come over at the drop of a hat to spend the night with a bunch of traumatized cats because their mom's in the hospital." I turned to Patty and Jim. "And not everybody would think twice about a cat meowing at their door in the middle of the night, let alone construe it as a sign of danger and call in the police."

"Your friend called the police," Patty deferred.

"But you called Denny, right?"

She nodded.

I looked around for Special Agent Paris and found him talking shop with Connie and Frank. "And Denny, of course, is watchdog to all his four-legged friends, but this time he went the extra mile for this two-legged one."

"What about me, Grandmother?" Seleia piped up as she floated by with a tray of bruschetta. "I stayed the night when you broke your leg. And my friends and I cleaned up that horrible mess the cops made when they thought you'd killed those guys."

I raised an eyebrow—subtlety wasn't one of Seleia's strong points—then I grabbed her and gave her a hug. "You bet, girl. I couldn't have made it without you."

A young man with the face of Adonis and thick brown shoulder-length hair came over and put his arm around Seleia's other side. Seleia giggled and melted into his protective grasp. The two would have made a great toothpaste advertisement.

"Isn't she the best?" Vinnie said proudly.

"She is that."

The young couple wandered off to pass out some more bruschetta and joy. My gaze followed them; I tried to remember the last time I had felt like that and failed.

I caught my mother looking at me from across the garden. Was she thinking the same thoughts? At eighty-three, does fifty-nine seem young? I supposed it did. I gave a little wave; she waved back. There are no words that could express how thankful I was that my mother is still in my life. I watched her for a little while. She had gone back to a deep discussion with her roommate, Candy. Probably trying to solve some great television crime mystery, I conjectured. I couldn't balk though; without her quick wit, I would never have thought about enlisting Denny's help to get me off the murder rap.

Denny again. It always came back to Denny.

"Denny!" I called out. "Can you come over here for a

minute? You too, Connie, Frank."

The investigators looked up from their conversation, then sauntered over. Denny was in uniform because he was on his lunch hour; soon he would have to put on his hero hat and go back to work. Frank and Connie were off duty and dressed comfortably in jeans and tee shirts.

"We were talking about friends and thanks and how much everyone's helped me these last few months. Especially you."

Denny started to get his *aw, shucks* look, but I wasn't going to let him bow out this time. He had saved my life—more than once—and deserved to be acknowledged for it.

"Friends!" I said loudly.

Frannie clinked a big citrine ring against her glass for attention. The chatter wound down and smiling faces turned toward me.

"Friends, thanks so much for coming today. I just wanted to say..." I paused. *What did I want to say? Thank you? I love you? All of the above?* I took a deep breath and it all poured out.

"I just wanted to tell everyone... to remind everyone that life is a gift. That you never know what might happen next. That even the worst situation can suddenly turn around and become something amazing. That we can do things together we can't do alone. That every moment is precious.

"I sound like a walking platitude," I said aside to Frannie.

"No, you don't. You sound very..."

"Serene," put in Halle who had just come through the garden gate looking cool and crisp in an ecru linen suit, "and very wise."

I grinned at my clan-mate-slash-attorney, another

friend without whose help I would have shriveled up and died. "I don't know about the wise part, but there is a certain serenity that's come into my life."

"To life," said Carol, holding up her lemonade.

"To Lynley," Seleia furthered.

There was the clink of glasses and smiles and *hear-hears* from the older faction who still knew what it meant.

The pledges over, people began to drift back into their little circles. I had to sit down; my knee was not in a party mood. Halle, Frannie, Denny, Carol, and Patty joined me around the glass-topped table.

"Well, here we are again," Carol noted.

I gave her a questioning look, then understood her reference; with the exception of Patty, it was the same group that had sat around another table at another time, plotting and planning how to get me off the hook for the murder of the Badass Brothers.

Halle put her hand over mine. "Well, it's been a long haul, hasn't it, hon?"

"It sure has," I agreed. "Crazy!"

"So what happened?" Patty asked. "I can't quite put it all together."

I'd told the story so many times to so many people I couldn't keep track of who knew what, but the diva in me didn't mind going through it once more for the benefit of a new audience. I gave my neighbor the short version: the theft of the Cats' Eyes diamonds; the antipathy between sister and brothers; the mistaken belief that I had the stones; the final conflict that resulted in double fratricide. I skipped the attack of the lunatic Cristine; Patty had been there, front and center, for that part.

"So you had two priceless diamonds in your possession and you didn't even know it?" Patty asked, her pixie face alight with intrigue.

"Well, I can't really say they were in my possession since I didn't know they were here, but yes, literally I suppose I did."

"Amazing those little rocks could create so much turmoil," Halle mused.

"They weren't so little," I remarked. "Some sixty carats each."

"Were they very beautiful?" Patty asked, that *diamonds are a girl's best friend* glint in her eye.

I shrugged. "I guess. They were rough so I never had an inkling they were anything but pretty rocks. I'm sure they'll be spectacular when they're cut, though."

"Did they ever find the one that was lost? The one the sister thought you had taken?" asked Carol.

"Yes, I hear they did. The guy who owned them had a trained search team out walking the woods until they turned it up."

"Which one was it? The Burma or the Babylon?"

"No idea. I never could keep them straight."

"So they were finally returned to the owner," said Halle, running her fingers through her spikes, which were more of a wine color today. "Do you think he went ahead with the Portland gem cutter or sent them off somewhere else with better security?" She snickered.

I propped my leg on a vacant chair and made a little sigh-groan. "Who knows? The local man is supposed to be the best."

"I wish I could see them when they're done," Patty said longingly.

I envisioned the Cats' Eyes with all those glittery facets and the dark, pupil-like inclusions. "They're trying to match the eyes of his own prize cats. Hence the appellation, *Cats' Eyes*."

I turned to my shelter buddy and feline authority. "Frannie, what breed of cat has copper eyes? I couldn't think of one."

"Bombay cat," she said without hesitation. "They're a hybrid of the black American shorthair and the sable Burmese. Cat Fancy says the bright copper-penny eyes are its signature feature, along with its deep midnight coat."

"Oh yes! I forgot all about the Bombay cat. I bet that's the one."

Carol frowned thoughtfully. "What I don't understand is why the Sinclairii brothers would leave the diamonds in your pond for so long. It doesn't seem prudent. I can see them stashing the goods when they were being chased by the cops, but you'd think they'd want to come back and get them asap."

"I don't know. They were hiding them from their sister as well as from the police. Maybe they needed to make some arrangements before they could pick up and go. That car they had waiting for them at the boat dock for example—it didn't appear out of nowhere. Besides, they weren't the smartest cats in the kennel; especially George."

"So how come the sister thought you had one of the stones?" Frannie asked.

"After Brother Larry tossed them out the window up on the mountain, she'd been out searching. She managed to find one but not the other. When I picked up the glasses lens..."

"*Her* glasses lens," Halle interjected.

I nodded. "...she happened to be hiding in the bushes watching me. Maybe it caught the light, and she mistook it for the diamond."

"Could happen. She had diamonds on the brain."

"But didn't she realize you'd handed the thing over to the police?" Patty asked.

"I know she saw me talking with Denny. She asked me if I'd given *it* to *the man*. But I doubt she stuck around when the Cowlitz County Sheriff showed up, for obvious reasons."

"She probably assumed you'd pocketed it, because that's what she would have done," Denny put in. "But until she saw you at the county fair, she had no way of knowing who you were or how to find you."

"Then her seeing me at the FOF booth was a total coincidence?"

"That would be my guess."

"Just my luck!" I swore.

"I wonder what she was doing there, at the county fair?" Patty reflected. "I mean, it hardly seems in character for a killer."

Halle shrugged. "Psychotics are people too. Deep down, she was probably just a lost little girl. Her warped sense of devotion convinced her that the things she was doing were right."

In spite of the warmth of the night, I was suddenly chilled. Even though I'd finally taken Frannie's—and my doctor's—advice and begun PTSD counseling, I still had a hard time not falling into the Pit of Evil whenever I recalled that night.

Those nights.

Those days and nights.

Carol saw it right away. "Come on now, everybody," she said in a lively tone that belied her age in so many ways. "Let's not dwell on the past. The murderer is caught; the thieves are defunct; the diamonds are back where they belong; and Lynley's safe. Nothing else matters, does it?"

There was a round of sympathetic consent and a quick switch to other, safer subjects with which I was thankfully distracted. For about a minute.

"You know," I said thoughtfully. "There's still one question that was never resolved—the forensic evidence that pointed the finger at me in the first place. How did my blood get spilled on top of George's in the old station wagon?"

Silence.

I looked at Halle.

She shrugged. "Nobody would tell me, though you have to know I asked."

"Well, maybe they'll be more forthcoming now," I declared impetuously.

I pulled my cell phone out of my pocket and punched the number for Detective Marcia Croft, which for some prescient reason I hadn't deleted.

She picked up after the first ring. "Detective Croft. What can I do for you, Lynley?"

"Yes. Hi," I stammered, always caught off balance when people know who I am before I've said hello. "Well, I'm sure you're busy so I'll get to the point. I have a question about the Sinclairii case, about my involvement."

"You have been completely cleared," she assured me.

"I know. Thanks and all. But when you first thought I might have been your killer, it was because of some evidence you'd found?"

"The blood."

"Yeah, that. Well, I still don't understand how it could have happened. The brothers weren't very nice to me but I don't remember them doing anything that would have drawn blood."

There was a stretch of silence on her end. "I am going

277

to have to check my files. I cannot remember offhand."

"I understand," I said, beginning to feel a brush-off. "But will you call me back when you find out?"

I was surprised when she said, "No need. I have it up on the computer now... Just checking... Ah-ha, here it is."

Another break. "Alright, Lynley. I have the forensics report in front of me."

I waited while she translated the doctor-ese into English.

"It looks as if they found trace amounts of blood on a sleeping bag that was in the back seat of the vehicle."

"Trace amounts? Like microscopic?"

"As from a pinpoint wound. Possibly the injection they gave you."

"Oh, right. I hadn't thought of that." I considered what she was telling me. "But what about George? Where did his blood come from? Was it old? I mean the sleeping bag wasn't the cleanest."

"That possibility was ruled out. Apparently both specimens were intermingled in such a way that they had to have been concurrent."

"Well, as much as I might have liked to, I certainly didn't do anything to him. My hands were tied. And I don't remember Larry being violent. So what happened?"

"There is no way of knowing for certain. Speculation?" she asked.

"Sure."

"George Sinclairii had no medical knowledge that we are aware of. Maybe in the course of injecting you with the drug, he gave himself a needle stick by accident."

"You're kidding?"

"No, actually I am not, Lynley. It is very common with the untrained. One sees them in the hospital all the time for follow-up testing. To make sure they did not inadvertently contract a blood-borne disease," she elaborated.

"Well, I guess George won't have to worry about that."

"Now, you must understand," she appended, "this is only extrapolation—an educated guess."

"Yes, but a good one. Thanks so much for your time."

"Is there anything else I can do for you?" she offered politely.

"No, that's it. Thanks again for all you did."

"Goodbye," she said and rang off.

I closed my phone and looked at the people around me, all eyes and rapt attention. I took a deep breath, just beginning to understand how tentative a hold the authorities had on me in the first place. "Detective Croft thinks it might have been from a needle stick when George was shooting me up with the knockout drugs. Only a guess though—there's no way to know for sure."

"Serves him right," said Carol.

"But that would only account for the smallest droplet," said Frannie.

"That's all it takes," Denny assured her. "Forensic science can do amazing things."

"Yeah, but in this case, it steered the investigation in the wrong direction," said Carol. "If they hadn't wasted all that time trying to charge Lynley, maybe they would have caught the sister before she'd had time to do any more harm."

"What kind of sister shoots her brothers in cold blood?" Patty said with a little shiver. "I can't imagine."

"That's a good thing," I replied. "If we start thinking like the criminals, we'll all be in trouble."

Denny pushed back his wrought-iron chair and rose.

"All good things, Lynley. Sorry to leave you but I have to go to work." He came around and kissed me on the cheek. I noted that he smelled like chestnuts, which was a surprisingly sexy scent on a young man. "Don't get up, I can see myself out."

I took his hand. "Thanks for coming. And everything else you've done," I told him.

He did his *aw, shucks* thing, which I enjoyed with relish, then donned his official Northwest Humane baseball cap and strode away to his animal-rescuing destiny. As I watched him walk off into the sunset like a present-day John Wayne, I realized I truly loved that man.

"I should probably be going too," said Patty, staring around the garden. "I've lost Jim. I think he must have slipped back next door. I know he had a few things he wanted to finish up before work tomorrow."

"Don't forget," she said with an elfin smile, "I'm always available to cat-sit. Since our silly landlord won't let us have one of our own, I can at least get my kitty-fix vicariously through yours." She gave a little laugh. "Thanks for the party. From both Jim and me." She glided out the gate toward the apartments next door.

I gazed around the garden, treasuring the last blooms of summer: a rainbow of fat-headed roses and even fatter-headed dahlias; a flurry of chrysanthemum blossoms in fall yellows, browns, and purples. Soon it would be autumn and then winter but I didn't want to think about that right now. The sun was sinking into twilight, earlier every day. The strings of fairy lights in the trees were beginning to stand out against the dusk like—well—like fairies.

Suddenly I was exhausted. Completely drained. That happened these days; without warning, I would power down like a robot.

"I'm going inside for a minute," I said, trying to sound as nonchalant as my wearied voice would allow. "Carol, Halle, would you make sure the party keeps going? I'll only be a sec. Or two."

"Fine," soothed Carol. "Halle and I will take care of everything, won't we, dear?"

Halle nodded assertively. "You go get some rest."

"If anyone asks, we'll tell them you needed a time out," said Carol.

I laughed. "You make me sound like a willful child."

"Okay, we'll tell them the truth then: that you've been to the end of the world and back and..."

"I just need five minutes. You don't have to tell anyone anything." I wrangled my leg off the chair and stood up. "Five minutes," I reiterated.

Once inside the house, I fumbled my way to my office. I'd never got around to moving the bed back upstairs after my broken leg, and I sort of liked it that way. The cats certainly approved. Red, Little, Dirty Harry, and Fraulein Fluffs were curled up on the comforter in various states of repose. Solo was underneath the bedside table—I could see the green reflection of her eyes—and Violet lay on her back on the braided rug like a velvet goofball. I had relegated them to this room for the party. With so many people and open doors, it was easier to put them somewhere safe and forget about it, though I knew Harry was miffed about losing his outdoor privileges.

"Soon, Harry," I said to the old black and white. He bunted my hand, not seeming too upset at the moment.

Without thought, I collapsed onto the dusty gold bed spread in between Fluffs and Little. In a micro-second, Fluffs had climbed up on top of me.

There was a soft knock at the door. "Lynley, it's just me."

"Come on in, Frannie," I answered, not bothering to get up. "Watch the cats; they're all here."

She zipped through the door with the little shuffle that discourages darters with its inherent movement and sound. She needn't have bothered; all feline constituents were perfectly happy right where they were.

Frannie grinned. "You look so cute curled up with your kitties," she said. "Where's my camera?"

I petted two or three. "The kitties are cute; I'm not so sure about me."

Frannie came over and perched on the bed. "You look great considering everything you've been through."

"Thanks, I think."

She leaned down and scratched Violet's vast silken belly and was rewarded with a rumble that could have passed for volcanic activity or the beginnings of a thunderstorm. I stroked Fluffs' long gray locks. For that moment in time, we were the only beings in the whole wide universe.

The comfortable silence stretched between us, a warm and fuzzy empathy between friends.

"How are your hoarder fosters coming?" Frannie asked languidly.

"Only one left, and she goes back on Tuesday."

"Then what?"

"Kerry's picked out another for me. Tinkerbelle, a ten-year-old stray with a kitty cold. It'll be a swap."

Pause. Scratch. Purr.

"You doing the early shift at the shelter tomorrow?" I inquired.

"Yeah, seven till noon. Kennel cleaning, litter pan

washing and laundry until ten, then customer service. I hope Misty gets adopted soon. You know, the diabetic kitty?"

"Sure. She's very sweet. Aside from her medical condition, she's perfect."

Pause. Pet. Cuddle.

"I'm sorry you had to go through all this," Frannie said solemnly.

I sighed. "Yeah, me too."

Pause. Stroke.

"Do you believe things happen for a reason?" she added.

I shifted Little who had also climbed onto my lap and was grooming Fluff's fur. "Yes, but I don't think we're always privy to what those reasons might be."

Pause. Purr. Snuggle.

"I guess we should be getting back to the party," I said with a certain amount of reluctance.

"I suppose," Frannie agreed with matching ennui.

Neither of us moved.

Suddenly the strangest thing happened. Solo, soundless as a white ghost, poked her head out from under the table. Frannie and I watched in disbelief. It was rare for her to make an appearance when she and I were alone, and to show herself with someone else in the room was a tiny miracle.

Solo prumphed once, then hopped onto the bed. She nosed her way in between Fluffs and Little, circled my lap and curled up, lovingly blinking her green and blue eyes at me. Little sprung down, miffed at being displaced; Fluffs headed over and claimed Frannie's lap.

Frannie and I looked at each other in amazement.

"Guess we can't go now," she observed, scanning the

gray bundle reposing on her pink floral skirt.

"A few more minutes couldn't hurt," I agreed.

Frannie leaned back and got comfortable. "This might take a while."

I gazed down at Solo; her eyes were closed now and she didn't look like she was going anywhere soon. Turning to the window, I found I was quite content to watch the crimson leaves of the maple tree catch the breeze and drift to their eternity. The herald of change.

Strangely enough I was looking forward to the winter. Face it—I was looking forward to anything that put time, space, and seasons between myself and my disastrous summer. Besides, I had some great things planned. Nice reasonable things, blessedly bordering on the boring.

At the end of September was Cat-toberfest at the shelter. (Does anyone know why Oktoberfests are always held the month before October?) FOF had rented a hall and was expecting a huge turnout so we needed to make a good showing.

Over Thanksgiving, my affluent daughter and her husband had arranged a cruise for the extended family: Carol, Candy, Seleia, myself, and the two of them. In some ways I dreaded it: Lisa and I haven't always had the best rapport. Still, it might be a good opportunity for us to reacquaint ourselves. I didn't want to go to my grave with our discord hanging over my head, and if I didn't make inroads soon, who was going to push my wheelchair?

In January, I'm signed up for an intensive seminar in animal communication which I'm really looking forward to. The instructor is world-renowned for her psychic communion with animals of all sorts though she specializes in dogs and cats. She's written books on the subject which I bought and fully intend to read before the class begins. She only does a few sessions a year, and they're usually in places like San Francisco or New York, not podunk little Portland, so everyone in the animal world agreed it was a once-in-a-lifetime opportunity and well worth the hundred-dollar registration fee.

I didn't hold out a lot of hope that I would actually achieve any telepathic rapport with my kitties beyond the vibes I already understood—*I'm hungry; pet me; leave me alone*—but it sounded like fun. Besides, it was harmless. I mean, what kind of trouble could I possibly get into talking to cats? It's not like they're going to tell me some deep dark secret...

Are they?

About the Author

Native Oregonian Mollie Hunt has always had an affinity for cats, so it was a short step for her to become a cat writer. Mollie is the author of the award-winning Crazy Cat Lady Cozy Mystery Series, featuring Lynley Cannon, a sixty-something cat shelter volunteer who finds more trouble than a cat in catnip. Cat's Paw was a finalist for the 2016 Mystery & Mayhem Book Award, and Cat Café won the World's Best Cat Litter-ary Award in 2019. Cosmic Cat won the Cat Writers Association Muse Medallion for Best Mystery 2019.

Of her Cat Seasons Sci-fantasy Tetralogy where cats save the world, two have been published at this time. Cat Summer won the 2019 Muse Medallion for Best Sci-fi Fantasy. Cat Winter came out at the end of 2020.

Mollie's stand-alone mystery, Placid River Runs Deep, delves into murder, obsession, and the challenge of chronic illness in bucolic southwest Washington. She has penned a little book of Cat Poems as well.

Mollie is a member of the Oregon Writers' Colony, Sisters in Crime, the Northwest Independent Writers Association (NIWA), and the Cat Writers' Association. She lives in Portland with her husband and a varying number of cats. Like Lynley, she is a grateful shelter volunteer.

A NOTE FROM THE AUTHOR

Thanks so much for reading my cozy cat mystery, **Cat's Eyes**. I hope you enjoyed it. If you did, please consider leaving a review on your favorite book and social media sites. Reviews help indie authors such as myself to gain recognition in the literary jungle. Thank you in advance for your consideration.

Cat's Eyes is book one of the Crazy Cat Lady series. I'm now working on book eight, **Adventure Cat**, so be assured that Lynley has not cleaned her final litter box or solved her ultimate mystery.

Want more Crazy Cat Lady escapades? Find the rest of the series for Kindle or in print on my Amazon Page: *http://www.amazon.com/author/molliehunt*

For those of you who enjoy sci-fantasy, **Cat Summer**, book one of the Cat Seasons Tetralogy and winner of the Cat Writers Association Muse Medallion Award for best sci-fi/fantasy has been released through Fire Star Press. The second in the tetralogy, **Cat Winter**, was published in 2020.

"Mollie weaves a story that blurs the lines of mythology, spiritualism, mysticism, science and reality that took me into another world. With her use of vivid imagery, I wasn't reading about Lise, the human-cum-feline protagonist and the cats fighting evil, I was in the trenches with them. The continuous struggle of good fighting evil, well, it's frightening--not in the least because so many of the things she's written are real." — Ramona D. Marek MS Ed, CWA Author

*"A genre-bending fantasy, **Cat Summer** carries the flavor of Warriors and the author's own contemporary Cat Mysteries, together with Arthur Clark's 2001..., Tolkien and other dark fantasy. For cat-lovers and earth-lovers, a cool and fascinating tale."* —Sheila Deeth, author

Poetry lovers, check out **Cat Poems: For the Love of Cats.**

"This collection of cat poems touches on the joy of becoming acquainted with a newly adopted friend, the heartbreak of saying goodbye to an old one, viewing life through a cat's eyes, and celebrating those who foster and advocate for cats... Every one will touch your heart." —Mochas, Mysteries, and Meows

Not cat-centric? I've published a stand-alone mystery thriller, **Placid River Runs Deep.**

From the back cover:

When Ember Mackay learns she has a life-threatening illness, she runs away to her secluded river cabin, but instead of solace, she finds mystery, murder, and a revenge plot that has taken a generation to unfold.

"...A thrilling combination of menace and pastoral beauty. After reading this book you may want to rethink your summer holiday." —Lily Gardner, author of Betting Blind